Capture

SEASIDE PICTURES

1

by

RACHEL VAN DYKEN

Capture
by Rachel Van Dyken

This is a work of fiction. Names, places, characters, and events
are fictitious in every regard. Any similarities to actual events
and persons, living or dead, are purely coincidental. Any
trademarks, service marks, product names, or named features
are assumed to be the property of their respective owners, and
are used only for reference. There is no implied endorsement if
any of these terms are used. Except for review purposes, the
reproduction of this book in whole or part, electronically or
mechanically, constitutes a copyright violation.

CHAPTER ONE

Dani

THE ELEVATOR JOLTED TO A STOP. With sweaty fingers, I pounded the button to the penthouse floor.

A groaning noise filtered in from somewhere outside the elevator. I gripped the side railing, then slowly sunk down until I was on my haunches, breathing in and out and telling myself it wasn't a big deal. Elevators stall all the time, right? In a few seconds, everything would be fine, and I'd be telling the story to my sister Pris and her movie star husband.

They'd laugh.

I'd pretend to laugh.

And we'd forget about it.

Or they'd forget about it, and I'd have nightmares later that night about being stuck in an elevator while it plummeted twelve stories.

Two minutes went by, maybe three, and the elevator still wasn't moving. I'd never gone to Disneyland, never ridden on any of their rides, but I imagined that the Tower of Terror felt exactly like this moment... pure horror and then suddenly weightlessness.

Please let there be no weightlessness.

Logically, I knew I was fine. Knew I would be fine.

But logic had taken a long vacation from my brain — and had yet to return ever since my parents' death a year ago.

Because logic was that thing that kept me sane, the voice in the back of my head that said, *"Hey, it's fine. What are the odds that out of all the elevators in the world, yours is the one to crap out and plummet you to your untimely death at seventeen?"*

Logic would have asked about the odds that I got in a car accident? Furthermore, what were the odds that I'd be the only survivor? Apparently, my odds were pretty damn high. In a weak moment, I'd once typed the question into a search engine.

Just like I'd done with every other paranoia I had.

Anaphylactic shock via bee sting? Forty percent.

Getting trampled by a hippo? Higher than getting eaten by a shark. Yeah, let's just say I'm not going to be going on an African safari anytime soon, no matter what my sister's husband thought.

And that was another thing. What were the odds, out of all the people for my straight-laced sister to marry, she'd fall for action hero Jamie Jaymeson? One of People Magazine's sexiest men alive, who also happened to be best friends with rock duo, AD2?

Yeah, you couldn't Google that crap.

Not that it would matter.

The odds of that were next to one in a billion.

So it made sense that my parents were dead, right?

I mean logically?

I hated logic.

I shivered as the elevator made another weird warning alarm. The lights were still on, so at least we hadn't lost power — yet.

Another jolt, like the elevator was caught on something, and then it moved fast, too fast for my comfort, nearly sending me toppling forward into the doors.

It made a dinging noise, then stopped at the top floor.

With a strangled cry, I leapt mindlessly from the elevator.

And made contact with warm, muscled flesh.

The doors closed swiftly behind me, the air tickling the back of my bare legs.

Embarrassed that I was still clinging to some poor individual, who probably wasn't planning on getting accosted by a seventeen-year-old paranoid freak whose idea of fun was looking up a symptom checker at two in the morning, I jerked back, ready to apologize.

But, of course, the words died on my lips.

Because in a world full of odds, mathematics, calculations, and logic, I'd just managed to accost Hollywood's newest heartthrob.

Lincoln Greene.

Smoldering gray eyes, wild reddish-brown hair that reminded me of that Outlander guy, and a body that you could sharpen knives with, all matched together making the perfect male specimen.

And… I was *still* clinging.

With jerky movements, I released my hands and tucked my long blonde hair behind my ears.

He towered over me.

I took another cautious step back. At this rate, I was going to end up back on the elevator from hell.

His smile was wide, friendly, totally unaffected by my clammy fingers and trembling body. "Dani, right? Your sister's been looking for you."

Ha, so she sent a movie god after me?

Thanks, Pris. Really. It's not like I've been having trouble having complete conversations with a shrink or even our mailman. You had to send him?

My tongue felt thick in my mouth as I managed a weak whimper and a nod. His attractiveness had nothing to do with my inability to speak. It was me. I was at fault. Speaking meant attention, attention meant people would ask me about my feelings, ask why I didn't smile, or why I looked tired all the time. Speaking had officially turned into one of those things that terrified me.

Pris had sent me to so many shrinks I was starting to feel like nobody could help. It wasn't normal for a girl at seventeen to suddenly stop talking.

But I had.

A woman walked up behind him and wrapped a possessive arm around his chest. "Oh good, baby, you found her!"

My eyes honed in on a perfectly sculpted, model-thin Barbie doll with bright blonde hair and hypnotic green eyes. Red nails tapped against her chin as she tilted her head in mock amusement. I might not talk, but I wasn't stupid. She was staking her claim.

If I did talk, I would have told her not to waste her energy or whatever tiny brain power she had left.

I wasn't a threat.

Maybe a year ago I would have been.

Then again, a year ago, I was the most popular girl in school, cheerleading captain, dating the quarterback, and my biggest complaint was that my best friend spilled chocolate milk all over my new, white Coach purse.

"Does it speak?" She giggled.

Lincoln continued to stare at me. "Why don't you give us a minute, Jo-Jo?"

What the heck kind of name was Jo-Jo? And why did I suddenly want potatoes?

With ranch.

Jo-Jo huffed out a breath that made her hair scatter around her face before she pounded the elevator button, sashayed in, blew him a kiss, and disappeared.

Maybe we'd all get lucky and that would be the time the

elevator really would plummet.

I inwardly winced. When had I become such a bitch?

"So..." Lincoln's voice jarred my attention away from the elevator doors.

Slowly, I met his gaze, my eyes blinking slow enough to take in his gorgeous smile. It was one of those smiles that showed both rows of teeth — a smile that by all intents and purposes should have actually looked frightening but was endearing instead, like his whole face lit up with that one simple gesture. His eyes crinkled.

He was happy.

And immediately I was stabbed in the chest with jealousy because he had what I had somehow lost.

And had never been able to get back. No matter how hard I tried.

I didn't speak. He probably thought I was a freak. But embarrassment had gone out the window long ago when it came to my speech. The words formed; I could feel them rolling around my tongue, but it was impossible to blurt them out. An invisible wall kept me from saying hi. Shame was my constant companion along with hurt... regret.

I blinked twice.

"Why don't I walk you back into the suite? Since this involves me too?"

Curiosity piqued, I frowned and walked with him to the door. He didn't knock, simply let himself in.

I followed.

We'd been in Portland for the weekend while Pris and Jaymeson did publicity over the second movie in his latest blockbuster series — one that also starred my sister.

You can imagine how happy the press was to discover that not only had the Casanova settled down and gotten married to a pastor's daughter, but she was a debut actress, amazing really, and they were expecting their first child.

It was as if Christmas had thrown up on them and

missed me completely. Jaymeson had helped Pris get over our parents' death.

And he'd tried to help me.

Along with Demetri and Alec, the rock duo of AD2. Honestly, if there was any hope of me coming out of this, my money was on Demetri saying something ridiculously out of line and me responding.

They were also in Portland shooting the music video that went along with the theme song for the movie.

"Dannae Garcia!" Pris charged toward me, her hands on her hips. She looked like my mom so much it hurt.

Pain washed over me brand new as I braced myself against the granite counter and hung my head.

"I was worried sick about you! You said you were going to go for a walk four hours ago!"

I winced then offered a shrug.

"Dani…" She licked her lips and touched her softly rounded stomach. "… you have a phone. Use it."

Guilty, I reached for my phone and quickly typed in a message.

Dani: *Sorry? I'll buy you ice cream and try really hard to find a real live unicorn for my new niece.*

I added a smiley with a halo for good measure.

With a laugh, she lifted her head. "Yeah? Well you better."

Jaymeson sauntered out of one of the back rooms, his cell pressed against his ear as he made sweeping gestures with his hands. "Just get it done!"

Dani: *What's that about?*

Pris eyed Lincoln, who I'd conveniently ignored but hadn't forgotten about. "Directing your own movie is harder than he originally thought."

Lincoln snorted.

Pris smirked as Jaymeson made his way over to me slowly, then picked up speed.

I backed up, holding my hands in surrender and shaking my head violently as a *no* built up in my chest.

He said he'd charge me like a bull until I was man enough to yell stop.

And since I still wasn't speaking…

"Ahhh."

I laughed as he lifted me into the air and twirled me around. At least I still had that, my laugh. Not that it could convey much, but the sound was comforting, like another reminder that maybe one day this wouldn't be my reality.

"How's my favorite sister-in-law?" Jay set me back onto my feet.

I licked my lips and shrugged, then held up my finger and typed out a message to him.

He was already reaching for his phone before anything had been sent.

Dani: *Getting in trouble. Pris is going to be a great mom, has that mom look down scary good.*

The emoji that followed was a picture of Pris doing the exact face I'd been talking about.

Jaymeson burst out laughing. I'd always loved his sense of humor, and his slight British accent paired with his newly shaved hair just made him look too attractive for his own good.

"She gives it to me all the time." He winked then nodded once toward Lincoln. "You tell her yet?"

My skin started tingling.

"No chance," Lincoln said smoothly as he crossed his large arms and leaned against the wall. "Not with Pris scolding and you attacking."

Jaymeson rubbed his hands together. "Oh good, because I want to see her face."

I itched to ask what they were talking about. I was just about to send a text to one of them when Jaymeson wrapped an arm around me, causing me to emit a groan since he'd bulked up so much and had yet to adapt to his own strength.

"Dani, meet your new job."

I felt my eyes go wide as Lincoln took a step forward. "I don't think we've been properly introduced. I'm Lincoln Greene, and Jaymeson offered me your services during filming."

I shook my head a few times. Services?

"Words," Jaymeson challenged.

Jerking away from him, I typed vigorously on my phone, making sure that the smiley I sent also had a middle-finger salute.

Dani: *WTH?*

"See, that's just it." Jaymeson shrugged. "You can't hole up in the house forever, especially since Pris and I are going to be on set so much. It's not healthy. You finished your GED, and you refuse to do anything but work out, watch Bravo, cook, and stare at the ocean like it's going to eat you. Therefore, I got you a job."

I threw my hands into the air and typed.

Dani: *I don't need a damn job!*

"Oooo." Jaymeson showed his phone to Lincoln, "You're going to love her colorful language. She also has an affinity for every emoji on the planet, though none of them make sense with whatever she types. She just likes sending them. Her number should already be in your phone. I'll send her to your trailer tomorrow morning at six."

I stomped my foot to gain Jaymeson's attention.

He didn't look.

I stomped again.

Then texted.

Dani: *Six a.m.? Are you out of your freaking mind?*

"Never drops the F-bomb though." Jaymeson showed Lincoln my next text. "Pastor's daughter and all that." He hesitated, then seemed compelled to add, "You'll know when she wants to say it though. Trust me."

I groaned.

"So, I think this is going to go really well." Jaymeson let out a breath and eyed Pris. "Don't you, love?"

She grinned. "If they don't kill each other first."

I raised my hand.

Jaymeson's eyebrows rose as I quickly fired off another text.

Dani: *Do I not get a vote?*

"Nope." He was smiling, but it was one of those smiles that was laced with concern... pity.

I hated them.

"But if it makes you feel better, neither does Lincoln. His last assistant was caught trying to sell autographed shit on eBay, and for someone who claims he's really independent, he still can't do laundry."

Dani: *I can't do laundry!*

"She can do laundry, right?" Lincoln asked.

"Could have operated her own dry cleaners in another life." Jaymeson nodded encouragingly.

"Great." Lincoln looked relieved. "And she can keep her cool on set?"

Dani: *Dude. Last time you were talking to NFL star Wes Michels I passed out, into the pool — needed to be revived.*

I added a doctor sign.

"Ah…" Jaymeson waved in my direction. "She's used to being around celebrities. Hell, she puts up with me. She'll be fine on set."

Lincoln rubbed his hands together. "Well, great!"

No. Not great! Not great at all!

"I'll just text you later then."

I stared down at the counter, trying to figure out how to actually maneuver time, space, and matter so that I could jump into the small crevices and make myself one with the granite.

"Dani?" Jaymeson repeated.

My head jerked up.

"Lincoln was talking to you, not me."

My mouth dropped open. I managed a tight nod in Lincoln's direction, then held up my phone as if to say, *"Yeah, text me. I'll answer and try not to run into you, stare too hard, sweat too profusely, or stumble over my legs in your presence."*

I must have looked convincing because that devastating smile was back, and then he was gone.

"This will be good for you," Pris whispered in my ear, giving my body a tight squeeze. "Promise."

That's what she had said about cheerleading.

And look how that had ended?

Our parents' death — all because I'd wanted to compete.

CHAPTER TWO

Lincoln

SHE HAD TO BE THE MOST awkward person I'd ever encountered in my entire life. Granted, I was only twenty-two, had hardly lived, but I was Hollywood through and through.

I knew weird.

I was surrounded by it on a daily basis.

And that girl? It wasn't the fact that she didn't talk because she was nervous or just didn't give a flying rat's ass about me — I could get past that. It was the simple oddity that she wanted to.

But chose not to.

And because I was running on two hours sleep, I'd spent the past few minutes fantasizing what her voice would sound like.

Jo-Jo was waiting for me in the lobby when I jumped off the elevator.

"There you are!" she screeched loudly, enough so that my ears rang a bit while my skin crawled like I was having an allergic reaction to something. "Where have you been?"

Unlike Dani, Jo-Jo talked. A lot. And her voice? Well, the

11

only way I could relate the sound her lips emitted was to think of the nearest butcher knifing a pig.

She laughed.

Maybe two pigs.

Another laugh.

Or five.

Why was she here again?

"So…" Her nails dug into my forearm. "… my agent says we just need a few pictures to circulate. Then I'll be out of your hair, baby."

Oh, and she called everything and everyone *baby*.

It wasn't cute.

Or endearing.

Or even slightly funny.

It was irritating, like her voice, and there I was again wondering about Dani. The girl with bright eyes and soft lips.

The girl who was mute.

"I hate the ocean, fish, crowds of people, and coffee shops that try too hard to be local and quaint." I was getting jerked toward the door, and why the hell was she listing things she hated?

"Oh…" Another tug on my arm as my arm hair rebelled and pulled back as if repelled by her touch. "… and I hate any restaurant that claims to be organic yet still cooks with non-organic oils."

I was going to speak — would have, but she just kept talking.

"And I think it would be extremely off-putting for us to take a few pictures at the mall. I mean, what about the poor people?"

Because poor people had no need for food or clothing? Where else did she think they bought and paid for their daily needs?

"Listen…" I pried myself free. "… I think I forgot something back in Jaymeson's room. Why don't you text me where you want to go, and I'll meet you there."

She began to pout again, her Botoxed lips pressing together in one giant, swollen blur.

"Besides..." I coughed into my hand. "... my truck still has all my shit in it so—"

"Truck?" She spat the word loud enough for the bellhop's head to turn in our direction.

His eyebrows rose and he took a few steps back, out of the line of fire. Smart man.

"You drive a truck?"

"Yes." I nodded slowly. "I mean it's only twenty years old, hardly ancient, and sure, it has a missing windshield wiper and sometimes sputters out large plumes of exhaust at the stoplight but I got a great deal on her down at the Jalopy Jungle and—"

Jo-Jo held up her hand. "You know what? I think I will meet you, later today, maybe tomorrow even, I have a really busy schedule over the next few days, and since you'll be shooting some of your first scenes on Friday..." She kept walking backward, shoving her large Prada sunglasses onto her face. "Be in touch."

I waited until she disappeared, then nodded to the valet.

A few minutes later, he pulled up in my truck.

Not an old jalopy junker.

But a brand new, fully loaded Ford with enough bells and whistles that I actually preferred sleeping in it over my trailer.

"Will that be all, sir?" the valet asked.

"Yup." I handed him a twenty and got in the truck but didn't take off because I saw a flash of blonde hair.

Dani was walking out of the hotel lobby. Her white Converses were clean — too clean — giving off the idea that she didn't do anything outside. Either that, or she was one of those people who wiped off her shoes before they put them back into the closet.

Her skinny jeans were ripped at the knees — not in a fashionable way, but almost like she'd taken scissors in an attempt to make shorts, then decided against it.

Shoulders slumped, her black T-shirt hung loosely against her body. Did the girl eat? Did she do anything at all? And why the hell was it suddenly bothering me that she looked too skinny? That black circles marred the skin beneath her eyes. Yeah, I really needed to sleep more, because the last time I'd obsessed about a girl this much was in the fourth grade when I'd pulled Mary Bailey's pigtails and asked if she wanted my Cool Ranch Doritos.

I didn't obsess over women.

Because women surrounded me. Constantly. If I wanted one, all I needed to do was speak up and take my pick — it wasn't arrogance speaking, just a simple fact of life — which is why I stayed blessedly single and kept any relationship I had on a twenty-four-hour basis. Fun was shared, and then the shared fun ended. Both sides satisfied. Story over.

I frowned and looked at my watch. It was nearing six at night. Technically she wasn't supposed to start until tomorrow, but my schedule had just freed up.

I quickly sent off a text.

Linc: *How good are you with packing?*

Dani reached for her phone and stared at it, then texted back.

Dani: *Who is this?*
Linc: *Your new boss. Look left.*

She glanced up.
I waved.
Slowly, she walked over to my running truck, her eyes on the tires rather than my face as she methodically typed a

message.

Dani: *Hmm, I was told never to get into a car with strangers.*

I burst out laughing. "Thank God you have a sense of humor."

My phone buzzed. I looked down.

Dani: *I wasn't kidding.*

I slumped forward just as a smile teased her lips, transforming her face from sad to triumphant.

"Alright…" I laughed softly. "… get in. Promise I won't bite, nor will I tell."

My text alert went off as she climbed into the passenger seat.

Dani: *Tell?*

I tossed the phone into the cup holder and waited for her to buckle her seat belt before I answered. "That you have a really pretty smile."

Her high cheekbones flushed with color as she quickly averted her gaze.

"What?" I pulled out of the hotel and into downtown traffic. "No text?"

When we were at the stop light, my phone buzzed.

Dani: *Don't text and drive, asshole. Stop reading! The light's green!*

Naturally, the light had turned green. I cursed and dropped the phone, then stole a glance at her. "You're going to be a handful, aren't you?"

She shrugged innocently.

"I'm onto you, you know."

She didn't answer. I didn't expect her to, but the yearning was still there. Maybe because she was a challenge. And God knew I hadn't had one of those in forever. Huh, maybe since the Doritos incident?

"Just because you aren't talking doesn't mean your brain isn't firing on all cylinders. I'm sure you have some killer conversations with yourself, and, lucky for you, I'm an expert at body language. So although you may be quiet, I know your secrets."

She froze.

"I made you smile," I announced with a cocky grin. "Which means, today? I win."

THE DRIVE TO THE small apartment I was renting downtown was silent and awkward. I'd expected awkward. What I hadn't expected was the girl to literally pretend like I was the most boring person on the planet.

"Do you like music?" I blurted, turning up the volume.

She shook her head no.

I tapped my fingers against the steering wheel as nervous energy swirled around me. Silence wasn't something I was used to. Who didn't like music?

I must have said that aloud because she shrugged.

Something about my driving was making her anxious — either that, or my one-sided conversation skills needed work. Every time I looked at her, she had her hands clenched in her lap, draining all the blood from her fingers. If she kept clenching, she was going to lose a thumb, and that thumb would be on my conscience.

"So..." I gripped the steering wheel with my fingers, sweat from my palms made a sliding sound across the leather. I needed some sort of noise to keep me from going insane. "...

you like Jaymeson?"

A nod.

"Right." I hissed out a breath of air between my teeth just as I pulled up to a spot on the street and turned off the truck.

Dani's seatbelt nearly smacked her in the eye as she hurriedly hit the buckle and jumped out of the truck as if it was on fire. When her feet landed on the ground, she let out a few desperate gasps of air.

And I was left wondering if it was my truck, the company, or both.

"Can't say I've ever had that kind of reaction before," I whispered under my breath.

My phone buzzed.

Dani: *I'm mute, not deaf, you idiot, and I don't like trucks.*

"Why?" I frowned looking up from my phone.

Hand shaking, she typed fast and started walking away from me toward the apartment building.

Dani: *Because that's what hit my parents' car the night they died. A truck. It was red.*

"Shit." I glanced back at my cherry red truck, feeling like an ass for making her ride in it. But it wasn't like I'd known. *Damn it, Jaymeson!* He should have sent the girl with a manual or something!

I jogged after Dani and opened the door to the building lobby. She walked through, her eyes void of emotion.

So, clearly she wasn't impressed that we were in one of the nicest apartment complexes in Portland.

Then again, she was probably used to it.

The opulence.

She was Jaymeson's sister–in–law. The guy on his way to owning Hollywood.

We rode the elevator in silence.

We walked down the hall… in silence.

I opened my door — yup, you guessed it — in silence.

The silence was going to kill me.

Thank God I'd left the sound system on. We walked in on the newest Ne-Yo release.

I tossed my keys onto the table and nearly swallowed my tongue whole as Dani started tapping her foot, and then moving her hips to the left, right, and back again. It was cute as hell.

"So?" I cleared my throat.

She stopped dancing.

"You hate music, huh?"

Blushing, she lowered her head and lifted one shoulder.

"Only certain types of music?"

A head nod.

"Shit," I muttered, running a hand through my shaggy hair. "We have to do something about this talking. I'm not one of those guys who likes silence, probably why Jaymeson thought this would be a good idea. Hell, I'm a heckler, I hate libraries, and if I have to sit and listen to myself swallow — or breathe for that matter — for five more minutes, I'm going to lose my shit. So type out what kind of music you want and at least grunt when you nod."

I reached for my phone.

Dani: *Like this?*

I glanced up as she grunted out loud, making a noise that sounded a hell of a lot like some farmer after he inspected a cow and deemed it worthy to butcher.

"You're a shit grunter. Tell me you can at least sigh? Or moan?"

She flushed.

"Ah, so which one is it? Or both?"

Dani: *You'll never know, Hollywood.*

"Ha." I barked out a laugh at the random unicorn emoji that accompanied the text. "Fine, I'm turning up the music since apparently Ne-Yo is good, but for some reason Wiz-Khalifa is out."

Her rosy cheeks went pale.

I wracked my brain then cursed aloud. "It was the new song, wasn't it?"

Dani: *Don't worry about it.*

"But…" I leaned against the counter. "… you see, that's like the opposite of my personality — I care, I worry. I'm like a girl, only in the body of a really hot guy."

That had her smirking.

"I'm sorry…" At this rate, I was going to talk enough for the both of us and probably go hoarse. When had I ever tried this hard to communicate with a girl? Never. "… I know it must be hard to—"

Her head jerked up while she maniacally typed something in her phone, then slammed her hand against the countertop.

Cheeks red, eyes wild, she stared at me then pointed to the phone in my hand.

I glanced down.

Dani: *You don't know. You never will. Nobody does, yet everyone says it. I'm here to work. You're my boss, not my therapist.*

Swallowing, I lowered my phone to my side, then shoved it into the back of my jeans. "Fine, packing it is."

She exhaled, her body going from tight with rage to relaxed, while I was strung up like a drum.

I wasn't used to being reprimanded by anyone. *I'd like to*

think that, considering I grew up in a house with two very emotionally detached parents, it was saying a lot that I even knew how to pick up on social cues, let alone care about another human being. Hell, my parents forgot my birthday, yet threw a freaking party for the family Chihuahua.

But I'd never complained.

I felt stupid having even opened my damn mouth because I'd come from fame, money. I'd been born privileged. Lucky. Even though my parents sucked.

My sister hadn't gotten off as easy.

One addiction after another had finally landed her in rehab, thanks to Alec Daniels, one of the guys from AD2. She still hadn't confided in me the details from a few years ago, but, considering everyone was on good terms again, I could only assume he'd been the one that had gotten her the help she'd needed, which is why, when I'd received the audition for this movie, I'd known I had to try out.

AD2 was doing the soundtrack, and Jaymeson was semi-related to the guys. I knew, without a shadow of a doubt, that it would be a blockbuster hit, and after all the drama and shit from my last flick, spending a few months filming on the Oregon coast sounded like a freaking vacation.

A throat cleared.

Dani put her hands on her hips then held them wide as if to say, "So? Are you just going to stand there like an idiot or actually tell me what to do?"

The voice I had her using in my head wasn't near as sexy as it needed to be, because the girl was sexy, from that cute blonde head all the way down to her ankles.

My eyes lowered.

What was it about her ankles?

Two claps in front of my face.

My eyebrows shot up. "You can't talk, but you can clap in front of me like I'm five?" I slowly pushed her hands away, the contact brief.

She didn't answer.

I hated it.

I pointed to one of the boxes. "So, I guess we can start with the living room. I won't be here a lot since we're doing most of the filming in Seaside, but I figured it would be nice to have a place to come back to, you know?"

No answer.

"I move a lot…" I seriously couldn't stop myself from talking. It was a really unfortunate nervous habit while in the company of someone who suffered from muteness. My money was on her stabbing me before the end of the night. "… you know, because of the films."

Idiot. Of course I moved because of the films. I was an actor for shit's sake. Maybe I should take a cue from her and just not speak. Ever.

Dani started packing one of the boxes, then held up a small, blue pig that I'd gotten from my very first commercial when I was about ten, for a savings and loan company.

"That's Wilbur."

She held the pig out as if it disgusted her. Then again, it had somehow gone from a really nice aqua to more of a dingy white with weird black marks that had suddenly appeared. I'd cried over that when I was little. My mom, bitch that she was, had said my pig must have had cancer — and then had laughed. I shook away the memory, snatched the pig from Dani, and set him in the box, careful to put several pieces of newspaper around him.

"He always gets prime real estate while traveling."

My phone buzzed.

Dani: *I like pigs.*

I burst out laughing, not expecting that, and glanced up at her shy smile. "Is there a reason?"

My phone vibrated with a text and an emoji pig sitting in

mud.

Dani: *They have cute tails.*

I nodded. "I think we're going to get along just fine, Dani."

She quickly turned around and continued packing the box — but not in complete silence. Because if I listened really carefully, I could hear a slight hum coming from her lips.

Thank God for common ground.

Thank God for pigs.

CHAPTER THREE

Dani

LINCOLN OFFERED TO DRIVE ME BACK to the hotel once we finished packing. I'd agreed only because the only thing more terrifying than getting into his truck, was riding in a car with a stranger, whose only goal in life was to get me from point A to point B in as little as time as possible.

The drive back wasn't as awkward as the drive there.

Mainly because I was getting used to him, sort of. You know, if it was possible to get used to good-looking men who smiled — a lot.

He was a smiler.

I hadn't expected that.

Most of the pictures I'd seen of him were shirtless-brooding-angsty — total opposites of the guy sitting next to me. The guy who packed a pig with him everywhere he went.

A pig.

It had been on the tip of my tongue to tell him about the pig my parents had gotten me when I was little. I'd told them it was stupid to count sheep; ergo, Patsy the Pig had arrived and helped me dream only good dreams.

I still had her.

It was more common ground, something I felt like we needed, since I might as well have been an alien to him.

But the minute I'd opened my mouth to try, to really try, the only thing I could force out was a weak noise that sounded like I was trying to hum.

Totally embarrassed — that's what I did. I hummed because I didn't want him to think I had Tourette's on top of everything else. That's exactly what he needed, someone who just blurted out random noises for no reason.

I held my groan in until he dropped me off, making me promise to show up the next morning bright and early...

I waved.

And he waved back, something I wasn't used to. Typically, once people discovered I was mute, they stopped noticing me, almost like I didn't deserve the attention because I couldn't properly contribute to the conversation. It sucked. Sometimes my own sister even did it, though I knew that was on purpose.

It was also why one of my best friends, Demetri, had come up with the whole texting thing.

It had basically saved my life.

Then again, he'd basically saved my life, both he and Alec, lead singers for AD2.

It was strange, going from fan-girling over the guys to having them by my side after the accident. They would have left — should have left Seaside, but they'd wanted to put down roots, so when they weren't traveling, they lived there full-time.

Demetri lived next door to me.

He'd been there the first night things had gone dark.

I still don't know why it happened, or how...

My leg was still healing from the accident, and I'd been told I had to exercise it as much as possible.

Walking at night was my mom's and my favorite thing to do, so I went for walks and talked to the stars and sometimes, I really believed they talked back.

I didn't hear the car coming.

All I saw were lights.

And then screaming.

So much screaming I had to cover my ears because I thought my eardrums were going to explode.

Demetri was with me, not that he could have done anything to prevent it, just like I couldn't do anything to prevent the screaming.

My voice was hoarse.

Completely gone.

On the outside, I was fine.

The car had missed me just in time.

But on the inside?

I was absolutely destroyed.

I had no idea who was driving it, just that it was a black Mercedes AMG. The plates had even been a blur. Not that it mattered since the person hadn't actually hurt me.

I think I'd been hurt before that night, my emotions hanging by a thread, and then the car had acted like scissors, snapping the thread in half, leaving me falling into a pit of despair.

I hit the penthouse level again and waited, praying the elevator wouldn't do the creepy thing it had before.

A short Asian girl with dark hair ran toward the elevator. "Can you hold it please?"

I nodded and pressed the button, but the doors wouldn't re-open. They closed with her yelling "Bitch" in my face.

That was another thing that sucked about being mute.

People constantly thought I was stuck up or rude.

My own friends — friends I no longer had in my contact list — had told me I acted like a bitch.

It had hurt.

It still hurt. And sometimes I wondered if that was true, or maybe this was my punishment for not being thankful enough during high school.

The elevator dipped, then soared to the top floor and opened.

I quickly let myself into the large suite and quietly went into my room. Tomorrow we were returning to Seaside since filming would be starting.

I shivered.

Seaside used to be home.

Now? It held just about every bad memory it could.

Because, everywhere I walked, I saw my parents and every time I closed my eyes, I woke up thinking they were still alive.

Only to realize within a few seconds that it wasn't just a bad dream — they were dead.

I stuffed a few pillows behind me so I was sitting up in bed and grabbed my phone to check my text messages. I needed a good distraction.

Demetri: *I heard from a bird, also known as my brother, that you're the new assistant to Lincoln Greene? Tell me; is he as scary as his sister? That bitch still makes me want to slap a woman, and you know me, I'm all about love — no violence. It's in the songs...*

With a laugh, I wrote him back and sent a few emojis of smiley faces with hearts in their eyes.

Dani: *I can't imagine you slapping anyone. Wouldn't that ruin your manicure?*
Demetri: *Take it back!*

He sent a picture of his angry face. The guy was seriously hot. Married, taken, and completely happy — but hot. No sane girl could ignore his crazy dimples, blond hair, and crystal blue eyes. He was like a younger version of Brad Pitt and Paul Walker's love child — it was its own hashtag.

Dani: *Sorry. You're pretty?*
Demetri: *I'll take it.*
Dani: *He thinks I'm stupid.*
Demetri: *Impossible. Did the bastard actually say that?*
Dani: *No, *I* say that.*
Demetri: *Do we need to have that talk again where I make you list all my favorite things about you, little sis?*

I smiled through my tears. I'd never had brothers; I didn't count the two guys that my parents used to support down in Haiti, even though my sister often did. Demetri and Alec were as close as I'd ever gotten. I imagined they were even better than the real thing.

Dani: *No, weak moment. Sorry.*
Demetri: *Tell you what, when you get into town tomorrow I'll take you out for ice cream, and we can throw taffy at Alec when he's rehearsing.*
Dani: *One of my favorite things in the world!*
Demetri: *Mine too. Also, fair warning, he's been getting basically no sleep since the baby was born so, if he snaps at you, it's not you, it's him.*
Dani: *K*
Demetri: *You swear he was nice to you?*
Dani: *Who?*
Demetri: *Don't play dumb. You know who. Lincoln freaking let me take off my top Greene.*
Dani: *Crap, do you think I should have played harder to get?*
Demetri: *WTH?!*
Dani: *Kidding. Joke. Ha ha?*
Demetri: *Dude would be lucky to still be breathing. Don't scare me like that. I'm getting old. I have a weak heart.*

Dani: *Aren't you twenty-two?*

Demetri: *Hold on, let me get my magnifying glass so I can see this tiny, tiny typing.*

Dani: *Go to bed.*

Demetri: *Only if you go to bed and promise me you'll try this summer.*

Dani: *Try?*

Demetri: *To have fun like a normal teenager. I'm not suggesting drugs and alcohol or all night orgies. Maybe go see a movie, remember what those are? Swim naked in the ocean but don't tell your sister I encouraged said behavior. Just live, Dani.*

Dani: *It's late.*

Demetri: *Don't it's late me! Just say yes, Demetri.*

I smiled and texted back a thumbs up with a girl sleeping.

Dani: *Yes, Demetri.*
Demetri: *Good girl.*
Dani: *Good boy.*
Demetri: *Hilarious.*
Dani: *Say hi to Lyss for me.*
Demetri: *Will do.*

I set my phone on the nightstand then stood up and paced my room. Maybe he was right. I needed to do something fun this summer. After all, I was only going to be seventeen for another month. And then I'd be an adult.

Without any clue about my future or what I even wanted to do.

Every time I thought about moving away from Seaside, I started getting all panicky, yet staying there did the same thing.

It was as if no matter what I did — the anxiety would still be there.

Shaking my morose thoughts, I stripped off every inch of clothing and crawled into bed... another fun quirk. If I wore clothes to bed, I ended up sweating so much I had to change.

It was the nightmares.

The therapist had said to make sure my room was always chilled. And she'd thought that maybe my clothes brought on a panic attack because of the restriction, which caused me to sweat.

So I started sleeping without clothes.

And, thank God, it had actually worked.

Over on the nightstand, my phone buzzed again. I smiled, ready to text back to Demetri that he needed to get some sleep since he had to record tomorrow. But it wasn't Demetri. My finger froze over the little keyboard as I quickly collapsed onto my bed and read the text.

Linc: *Tell me something funny.*
Dani: *Was that in the job description? Entertaining you?*
Linc: *It is now.*
Dani: *Are you that bored?*
Linc: *Try insomnia, and Wilbur went to bed hours ago so...*

I snorted and sent him ten pig emojis.

Dani: *And he normally does that job?*
Linc: *Hell yes, he does. Clearly, you underestimate our relationship.*

Linc texted back a farmer emoji.

Dani: *I have no jokes, but I can send you a picture of Demetri Daniels getting lit on fire. Would that help?*
Linc: *You do realize I was the one filming it, right? The one from the pre-production cast party?*
Dani: *Nope. Also. Still funny, regardless of who took it or how*

many times you've seen it.

Linc: *Watching it right now. You think his arm hair grew back?*

Dani: *Last time I asked him, there was a lot of inappropriate language and middle finger flashing.*

Linc: *Still sensitive I take it.*

Dani: *He's afraid of birds, what do you think?*

I giggled as I sent over Demetri's least favorite emoji of a crow circling over and over again.

Linc: *You're kidding.*

Dani: *I hid one under his pillow thinking it would be funny and cement our friendship. He had to hide it in my house because every time he woke up, he cursed, thinking it was real.*

Linc: *Why not hide it outside his room?*

Dani: *Because he could feel it. His words not mine.*

Linc: *Ha ha, thanks for the ammo.*

Dani: *Yeah, well, I don't have jokes, but at least I can throw my best friend under the bus.*

Linc: *How did he earn that coveted title?*

I swallowed the emotion in my throat and wondered if I should answer truthfully or just joke it off.

Dani: *Easy. He understands my obsession with Sour Patch Kids.*

Linc: *So if I was to go to Costco and buy you a year's supply…*

Dani: *DON'T KID!*

Linc: *A two-year supply?*

Dani: *Demetri who?*

Linc: *I feel like I accomplished world domination just now.*

Dani: *Um, you're welcome?*

Linc: *I think I'll fall asleep with a smile on my face now… thanks for answering. One more thing…*

Dani: ?

Linc: *How old are you?*

Dani: *Had I filled out a normal job application, like a normal person, you would know that.*

Linc: *Does that mean I need to make up a bogus application just to find out? Or will you take pity on me and just say it?*

I don't know why I was embarrassed about my age. Maybe it was because he felt so much older. Not that he was. Without losing my nerve, I quickly typed back.

Dani: *Seventeen, turning eighteen in one month.*

He didn't respond right away.

I frowned at the screen. What? Had I acted younger?

Linc: *Thank you.*

Dani: *Sure.*

Linc: *Get some sleep, your boss is a real ass. Don't want him riding you tomorrow morning because you show up late.*

My face heated.

Dani: *Good night.*

CHAPTER FOUR

Lincoln

SHIT. I WAS AN IDIOT. FIRST I'd asked for her age. Then I'd nearly fallen off my bed when she texted back seven — freaking — teen years old. I'd had her pegged at nineteen. How old did that make her sister?

And why did her age matter?

It wasn't like I needed her to be of legal age to work for me.

The cool sheets felt itchy against my legs. Kicking them off, I stared at my phone again. My mind had clearly been on vacation. Had I really said her boss would ride her in the morning?

No idiot, you typed it.

So if someone hacked either one of their phones I'd be going to prison for flirting with a minor!

Great. That was just freaking great.

Why did she have to be seventeen?

I needed to get laid. Plain and simple.

Maybe that was how you knew you were bordering on exhaustion.

You start daydreaming about minors — or obsessing over something as silly as what your name would sound like coming across those lush lips.

"Hellllll…" I pounded the pillow with my fist, then covered my face with the same pillow. It smelled stale, as if it had been sitting in the moving truck too long.

I hadn't been lying about needing something to help me fall asleep.

But first days on set always brought on a lot of anxiety and nervousness.

It was like going to the first day of school all over again. Will they like me? Will I completely suck? Who do I sit with at lunch?

Groaning, I tossed the pillow to the floor and got up to pour myself a glass of wine. At least that would help me relax a bit.

And, hopefully, take my mind off the girl who had no problem texting her words, but for the life of her, couldn't speak them.

LINCOLN: *PICK YOUR POISON*.

I texted her a picture of Starbucks and waited for her to answer back.

Dani: *Sugar and caffeine — surprise me.*

I was still grinning at my phone when the barista asked for my order, and, because my brain was still on that same vacation from yesterday, my mind went completely blank.

"Uh." Great start. And I had to actually spout out lines today about true love? Kill me now.

"Lincoln?" Jo-Jo's voice was like nails on a chalkboard.

"Lincoln, is that you?" Like five hundred nails getting simultaneously dragged down the chalkboard. On repeat. "Lincoln?" Five hundred times.

"Yup?" I turned around and forced an easy smile, even though I really wanted to jump over the counter, steal the barista's apron and visor, and yell, *"Doppelganger!"*

With a very practiced pout, Jo-Jo pressed her lips together, then made a grand show of swiveling her hips as she walked toward me. "You didn't text last night."

"Fell asleep," I lied, backing toward the counter. Maybe the barista would take pity on me and dump hot coffee on my hand so I had an out clause.

"Oh." Jo-Jo frowned. "Well, I have some time this morning if you want to do something?"

"Can't." I gave her my shoulder. "I'm meeting with my new assistant then driving down to set."

"In your truck?"

What was with her and my truck?

"Yes." I mouthed *"Sorry"* to the barista, while the line tripled in size. I moved my lips to order, but Jo-Jo interrupted me. Again.

"Oh, well..." She ran her nails down my arm. "... guess we can take a selfie here. It won't have the desired effect spending the day with me would, but it's better than nothing." Before I could protest, she lifted her phone and pointed it at us, snapped a picture of her kissing my cheek, and then slapped my ass. "Great. We'll be in touch."

My ass was tingling — and not in a good way. More like a warning that it might actually cease to exist if she tried to touch it again.

"Dude, you gonna order or what?" The barista tapped his marker against one of the cups and narrowed his eyes at me.

"Yeah." I choked. "Two grande vanilla lattes. Triple shot."

I slipped him a hundred while he wrote down my order, and whispered, "For the customers behind me."

He stared at the hundred-dollar bill, then narrowed his eyes. I fumbled with my sunglasses as recognition dawned on his face. "Dude, you're Lincoln Greene!"

"Shh." I waved my hands in front of me and pasted a fake smile on my face. "Let's keep that between you and me, man. That okay?"

"Sure." He licked his lips and slid the black marker toward me. "But can I have your autograph?"

"Yeah." I quickly scribbled my name on the cup he'd handed me and went to wait for the drinks.

Portland people didn't care about my celebrity status. I'd been asked for my autograph more when I was in Hollywood. Maybe they didn't care, or maybe they really were high all the time as Jaymeson believed.

He said filming between Portland and Seaside would be like a vacation, and I was starting to believe it.

Damn, I needed one of those.

"Lincoln…" The barista nodded to me and called out my drinks. "… you're up, bro, and thanks for being so cool."

"Sure, man." I grabbed my drinks and jogged out of the coffee shop to my waiting truck, a little too eager to meet Dani and irritated that I was excited to meet my assistant. I took a misstep and nearly dropped the lattes all over the pavement.

My *assistant*.

She intrigued me.

And it wasn't because she hadn't thrown herself at me. Plenty of girls kept their distance. I mean, granted most of them were usually blind or over the age of eighty, but still. It's not like I'd never been rejected.

It just didn't happen often.

I started the quick drive back to my apartment, tapping my fingers against the wheel, nervous energy pouring out of me. It wasn't Dani. It was the movie.

And the stupid part I had to play.

My stomach clenched.

Ha, well at least I'd found the object of my nervousness. The fact that I had to play a brooding alpha male who vies for the girl's attention. I was the second half of the love story, the guy every girl roots for even though she knows he's bad… the unredeemable. Hell, give me a motorcycle and a leather jacket and I'd be all set.

I'd played that character before.

But something about this specific one, Dean Elis, bothered me. He was so… passionate. About everything. Not just about the girl but about life in general. I'd never experienced that type of passion. In fact, I was pretty sure experiencing that much passion in a lifetime was unhealthy. And I'd never been in love, not that it had ever been a problem for me to play the shit out of the part.

But sometimes, it made me feel like a fraud.

I burst out laughing. And this was why I needed coffee.

"Get your head out of your ass, Linc," I growled to myself as I braked, cut the engine, and hopped out of my truck, two coffees in hand. "You're early," I blurted to my new assistant.

Dani was standing outside my building, and her phone was held to her ear. Her lips were moving — fast.

What the hell?

What type of person faked a sickness like that? Rage boiled inside me as I stomped over to her, ready to grab the phone out of her hands and toss it into the air, feeling a bit self-righteous, because how could someone be so selfish? I mean, her poor family! And she could actually talk?

"I miss you." Her low voice was barely above a whisper making it hard to hear what her voice actually sounded like. "I start a new job today." She paused. "It's Jaymeson's fault." She twirled her blonde hair around her thumb. "I love you so much. I'm so sorry."

"Well…" I cleared my throat, not caring that I was intruding on her private conversation. "… what are you? The girl that calls wolf?"

36

Slowly, Dani raised her eyes and met my gaze. The harsh glare of the morning sun revealed her face was white as the proverbial sheet. Her mouth opened, a small squeak emerged, and her lower lip trembled.

"Oh, please," I sneered. "I heard you talking, so drop the act, Dani. God knows I'm not the type to go tattle to your sister and brother-in-law. It's not my business that you like to lie to family."

With a hoarse cry, she smacked me in the chest. I backed up as some of the coffee spilled out of the cups.

She tugged the phone from her ear and started typing.

My phone buzzed.

I rolled my eyes. "Hands are kind of full, darling. Why don't you just use your words?"

She shook her head and pointed to my front pocket.

"Let's try this again." I could feel my irritation growing. "Tell me what it is you want to say. Like an adult."

She stomped her foot.

"Oh, great." I huffed out a breath "I lose a clepto assistant only to gain an angry teenager who thinks the only way she can get attention is to act out, pretend she actually has a disease that effects REAL people, and stomps to get attention. Tell me I'm not off base."

Tears filled the corners of her eyes.

"Wow." I sighed heavily, too tired to put up with her bullshit. "Ever think of going into acting? You're probably better than your sister, and she's the best I've seen in ages."

Tears spilled onto her cheeks. She just kept furiously pointing at my phone.

I stared her down. "Sorry, sweetheart. Your family may enable you, but I'm not going to. In fact, as of right now, consider yourself fired. I don't need drama in my life. I get enough of it as it is."

She let out a little cry and grabbed my arm.

"Let go," I said in a chilled voice.

Dani shook her head then held up her phone, the screen pointed in my direction. It was the text she'd sent me.

Dani: *The only person I can talk to is my dad. I listen to his last voice message every morning, and when he's finished, I talk back.*

"Well... shit," I muttered dropping my gaze to the ground, where her knees damn near knocked together, they were trembling so bad.

I raised my head.

Her chest heaved, cheeks stained with red.

Slowly, she typed back into her phone.

Dani: *You're a jackass.*

"Shit," I said again, lifting both coffees into the air in frustration. "I know. Look, I'm sorry, I saw you talking, heard you talking, and just assumed the worst. I didn't know."

She held up her phone again.

Dani: *Now you do.*

She snagged one of the coffees, jutted out her chin, and marched away from me. Feeling like one of the biggest pricks in the world, I called after her, and, when she didn't stop, let out a curse.

"Wait!" I set my coffee down on the sidewalk, raced after Dani, and grabbed her. "Look, I said I'm sorry. I just assumed. Can't we start over?"

She jerked away from me and shook her head no.

"Dani..." Shit, I really needed an assistant, Jaymeson wasn't joking when he said my life was chaotic. I'd had an assistant since my first commercial. Not having a right-hand person was like not having my phone, or walking around

naked on set, extremely uncomfortable and unnecessary. "…
wait, I need you."

She kept walking.

"Don't make me call Jaymeson!" Low blow. I knew it, but
I was desperate.

She froze, her shoulders tensing.

"I'll do it." I held up my phone. "You don't want to let him
down, do you?"

Her fists clenched at her sides, and she glanced back at
me out of the corner of her eyes, nostrils flaring.

"I'm sorry," I repeated, only slightly distracted by the way
her chest rose and fell. *Minor, minor, minor.* "I need help. Can't
we just call it our first fight and move on?"

She threw her hands up in the air then pulled out her
phone.

Dani: *How much are you paying me?*

"Clearly not enough since you have to put up with me
yelling at you," I joked.

She didn't laugh. Well, at least I'd tried.

Dani: *I want double what Jaymeson asked.*

"Wow, tough bargain."

She turned around and crossed her arms.

"Deal," I croaked. I could afford it, but the girl seriously
had no idea how much she was already getting paid. She was
now officially one of the highest paid assistants in history — or
at least it was going to feel like it. "So I'll just deposit that
fifteen grand at the end of every month then?"

Her eyes widened.

"Kidding." I grinned.

With a scowl, she kept walking away from me.

"Wait!" I called after her. "Aren't you riding with me to

Seaside?"

She pointed at the truck, made a cutting motion with her hand across her neck, and then shook her head no.

"But what are you riding in then?"

Her hand shot into the air, pressing a button on the key ring that lit up a brand new, black Jeep Cherokee.

"Yours?"

She nodded and got into the driver's seat.

"See you at Seasi—"

The door slammed, cutting off the rest of the word.

Never had I seen a car peel away so fast. Yeah, something told me she wasn't going to be trying to seduce me or sell my stuff online. If anything, I was going to need to watch my back, just in case she switched my sugar and salt containers and flashed my number on Twitter or something.

Not the best start to our relationship.

Then again, our relationship was only going to last as long as filming. Three months, and I'd be, hopefully, a semi-non-traumatic memory she could stuff away.

Three months without actual conversation.

Great.

CHAPTER FIVE

Dani

IT WASN'T EVERY MORNING THAT I talked to my dad; I hadn't actually spoken to his voicemail in a few weeks. This morning I'd expected my voice to be gravelly, like one of those Truth commercials with the smokers, warning kids against the perils of tobacco, instead it was just as I remembered it. Light, airy. I choked back the sobs building in my throat as memories surfaced.

"Who's my favorite little girl?" My dad twirled me in his arms. I tried to fight him, but I was dwarfed by his size. He'd always been such a big man, while I was barely above five four.

"Dad!" I laughed as he continued twirling me until I was dizzy. "I'm sixteen! Stop!"

"Aw…" He stopped, placing me on my feet. "You'll always be my little girl, Dani. You know that, right?"

I rolled my eyes. "Dad, I know."

"You're beautiful." He sighed. "And remember, I'm the only one that can say that to you. If some young boy invites you into his car using pretty words, he's only after one thing."

"My flower," I said in a deadpan voice. "Message heard loud

and clear. Oh also, if you could stop cleaning your gun out front and talking about your connections with the Italian mafia whenever Elliot comes around, that would be great."

"What?" He shrugged innocently. "We're Italian."

"Ah, actually half-Hispanic…" I patted his cheek. "… but nice try."

"Mexican mafia." He snapped his fingers. "That would sound more convincing."

"You look more white than Mom, and she's actually white," I pointed out. "Therefore, probably not."

He frowned. "I'll think of something."

"Please don't." I laughed, gripping his shoulders. "You've raised a good girl, you know that. The last thing I want is to end up pregnant. I mean, I'm at the top of the pyramid, Dad. Pregnant girls can't fly."

He patted my cheek. "Neither can pigs, yet they do."

"No, they don't."

He grinned.

I rolled my eyes. "Alright, good talk as always, Dad."

"Hey…" He grabbed my hand and kissed it. "… I only threaten because I care. I love you, snuggle bug. You're my youngest."

"And some may argue brightest," I added.

"Shhh, don't tell Pris." He winked and patted my cheek again. "Just be careful. Make good choices. And if he takes off his pants, use the Taser."

"What if his pants are on fire?"

"Always Taser first — ask questions later. That's like Girl Scouts 101, sweetheart."

"You got fired as den mother."

He gasped and clutched his heart. "You were sworn to secrecy! Don't tell Mom. She still thinks it was because I was too busy counseling at church."

I made a zipping motion with my lips. "I'll take it to my grave."

"I knew I raised you right."

"Says the man who's asking me to lie."

"Omit." He nodded encouragingly. "Big difference, cuddle bug."

"Night, Dad." I opened the screen door and slammed it behind me.

"Say no to drugs!" he yelled out.

Elliot's car window was open, and he yelled back, "Only hugs!"

"No hugs either!" Dad called. "Hugs lead to sex!"

"Just like dancing!" Elliot agreed. "Good talk, Mr. Garcia!"

"Dani!" Dad called. "I like him better than the last one."

"What happened to the last one?" Elliot just had to ask.

"Buried him out back...wanna see?" Dad grinned. "You two have fun at prom now!"

I pulled over on the side of the freeway and wiped the tears from my eyes. I was usually so good at keeping them tucked away, but the fight with Lincoln had drained me emotionally.

I just wanted to talk to my dad.

He'd always been my go-to parent. Not that I hadn't loved my mom, but my dad and I had just… got each other. We'd had similar outlooks on life. He'd been hilarious and had done everything one-hundred percent. There'd never been hesitation in any area of his life. Whatever he did, he did well. It was the perfect example for a young girl. Don't try to be good at everything, don't spread yourself so thin that you accomplish nothing; rather, pick a few things and do them well. Excel in those areas and you'll excel in life.

So I had chosen cheerleading.

Academics.

Baking.

And I was good at all of them. While my other friends stressed out over playing multiple sports and sat on the bench — I was busy living, doing things that made me happy and doing them well.

It was kind of a family motto.

Do it well, or don't do it at all.

I clenched the steering wheel with both hands. My knuckles turned white, and my fingers cramped, but still I hung on. I wasn't doing anything well right now.

Except breathing. I guess I could count breathing. My therapist always said to focus on the positive. Well, at least my breathing wasn't uneven. Okay, so I was doing that well.

I continued to do that — breathe.

The tears slowly started to dry up, even though the pain was still slicing through my chest. I'd once heard that memory was just as powerful as experiencing something in the present.

Your past really could define your future, if you let it.

Every time you remembered something painful or something exciting, your body responded to it as if it was experiencing it for the first time all over again.

So every time I thought of my dad? Of my parents' death? It was as if I was back in the car, dressed in my cheerleading sweats, falling asleep to Echosmith while our car had been hit head-on by that truck.

He'd fallen asleep.

My dad.

It was my fault he'd been so exhausted that he'd drifted asleep in the first place.

A honking horn jolted me out of my thoughts again.

Seaside.

I was going home.

At least I didn't live in that house anymore. In fact, I was going to make it a point to avoid every single place I'd visited with my parents, because I was done reliving things.

I was already in a living hell.

I didn't need to add to it.

And if Lincoln wanted taffy from the taffy store or anything even remotely related to my old life, he could just kiss my ass.

I pulled back onto the freeway and cranked up the music.

Lincoln Greene would *not* be my downfall. I would not allow him to make me feel bad about myself. I was done with self-pity — absolutely done — and even though the way he'd treated me made me sick to my stomach, so sick I almost puked onto his shiny expensive shoes, his attitude didn't have to define me.

I wouldn't let it.

My cell phone rang.

Demetri.

"Hey," he said over the car speaker, "I know you won't respond, but I just wanted to let you know that Lyss and I have chocolate cake for you at our place when you get into Seaside. Oh, and she has some clothes for you too, since she's pregnant and can't fit into a damn thing anymore, so make sure you come over. Drive safe!"

I exhaled.

Cake.

Forget Lincoln Greene. Forget Seaside.

Focus on the cake.

Chocolate cake.

My therapist had said I needed goals. Well, my new goal? Eating that cake while giving Lincoln the middle finger in my mind.

I smiled.

Yeah, that would feel good.

CHAPTER SIX

Lincoln

"RAIN." I PULLED INTO TOWN FOR the second time in my life and slowly made my way toward the beach house I'd rented during filming. "Rain, rain, and more rain." It was coming down in buckets, making the dreary morning look like something out of a depressing Gothic novel.

During the summer months, Seaside was a huge tourist destination for people living in Oregon. But the winter was something less to be desired.

And it was October, meaning it was either overcast or raining all the damn time.

The novel called for wet weather.

Well, it was wet all right.

I swerved out of traffic and made my way down A Street, then B, then C. Who the hell named streets after letters?

Finally, I stopped at my destination and turned off the truck.

My new place was a six-bedroom beach house that had fallen on hard times and been recently renovated. The owners had put in a quarter of a million in updates, and were more than thrilled that a movie star was going to be their first renter.

It was white with blue shutters and had a two-story enclosed glass deck that made it possible to sit outside and barbeque without having to develop gills or wear a snorkel.

The outdoor fire pit was also under cover. The view was incredible, and the rent, even though it was high, was still cheaper than staying in Laguna.

I hopped out of my truck and ran toward the front door. The keys jangled when I jammed one into the lock and turned the knob. Then I burst into the house and looked around.

Fully furnished.

Nice.

And alone.

I checked my watch. Where the hell was Dani?

Linc: *You in Seaside? Or did you drown?*

Dani: *Here.*

Linc: *Okay…are you coming over to help me?*

Dani: *I don't recall you asking.*

Frustrated, I damn near threw my phone against the wall.

Linc: *I need help unpacking and grocery shopping. I have a list for you. I may need to laminate it with this weather…*

Dani: *Fine. Be there in five. I'm stopping over at Demetri's first.*

Linc: *How about you come here now, and we'll go there together?*

Dani: *Okay.*

Linc: *Not even a smiley face?*

Dani: *Hmm, no, sorry, fresh out of those after I was accused of lying to my family. Thanks for asking though!*

Linc: *I said I was sorry.*

Dani: *I know.*

Linc: *So I'll see you in a few.*

Dani: *Yup, but I'm driving.*
Linc: *Okay!*

A horn honked in front of my house five minutes later. I ran out and jumped into the passenger side. Shivering, I shook the rain out of my hair.

"Why aren't we moving?" I asked Dani.

She stared at the seatbelt.

I sighed. "You do realize Demetri lives about a mile away from here?"

Arms crossed, she glared, her bright blue eyes flashing.

"Right, then." I buckled my seatbelt. "Someone's prickly this morning. Then again, that's my fault, so yeah, sorry about that."

Silence.

My breathing was loud. Too loud. Damn, the girl had me wanting to hold my breath and jump out of a moving vehicle.

"So," I said once we parked in front of Demetri's townhouse. "How was the drive over—"

Her car door slammed.

"She's really gotta stop doing that," I muttered under my breath as I hurried to follow after her.

Taking the stairs three at a time, she was already inside the house before I made it to the top of the stairs.

"Dani!" Demetri shouted. "Long time no see, little sis, and why the hell did you drag this loser with you?"

"Nice to see you too, Demetri." I held out my hand.

He stared at it. "Still pissed you put that video of me getting set on fire on YouTube."

"It was funny," I pointed out. "And you would have done the same thing."

"True." He took my hand then pulled me in for a hug. "So, how lucky is it that you needed a new assistant, and Dani's a little miss smarty pants and doesn't need to go to school this fall?"

"Super lucky," I croaked out while Dani met my gaze with one of absolute annoyance. The last time I'd received a look like that was in the fifth grade because I didn't want to play spin the bottle with the girls in my class.

"Dani…" Alyssa gripped her hand. "… I went ahead and put a crap load of clothes in your room at Jay's. I hope that's okay?"

Dani nodded vigorously and wrapped Alyssa in a tight hug.

A twinge of jealousy shot through me. No idea why the hell I was jealous of two girls having a good relationship. Maybe because I'd botched whatever chance I had with Dani that morning.

"You need something to drink?" Demetri asked, stealing my attention away from Dani, and the way she clung to Alyssa as if she was her lifeline.

"Nah." I licked my dry lips. "I think we're going to head back to my place soon anyway. I'm a slave driver and all that — need to get shit done before tomorrow morning."

Demetri swiped a bottled water from the counter. "I heard Jay has a five a.m. call time. Yours just as bad?"

"Yeah." I sat on one of the barstools. "The good news is I have this crazy awesome assistant who can fetch me coffee so I don't fall asleep in the makeup chair."

Dani made a face in my direction.

"I think she likes you," Demetri joked.

"Wouldn't surprise me at all if she has a poster of my face in her room." I nodded.

Dani rolled her eyes, then stuck her finger in her mouth and made a gagging motion.

"You know, in some countries that's a term of endearment," Demetri said in an optimistic voice.

"Yeah…" I cringed. "…but in America it just means she'd run me over with her car, even if I had an orange reflective vest on."

"What did you do?" Demetri whispered just so I could hear. "She looks like she wants to actually knee you in the balls — more than once. Which isn't her typical MO. She's always been a bit gentler than that. Seriously, she saves ducks crossing the road."

"She saves ducks?" I stared at the girl as she threw her head back and laughed freely at something Alyssa said. "You sure about that?"

"Positive," Demetri said with a soft chuckle. "You must have done something to ruffle her feathers, because the last time I saw her glare at someone was never... Good work, way-ta take the sweetest girl I've ever known and make her hate men everywhere." He slapped my back.

Grimacing, I turned toward him. "I may have overheard her talking to her dad's voicemail on her phone, and I may have then assumed she was faking."

"Oh, shit." Demetri collapsed onto the barstool next to me. "You're an idiot, you know that, right?"

"It's not like anyone told me!" I hissed. "Jaymeson should have said!"

"Because Jaymeson doesn't know!" Demetri glanced behind him to make sure Dani wasn't eavesdropping. "She tells one person everything. Guess who that person is?"

"You?" I offered.

"Me, or sometimes on rare occasions, Alec, take your pick. We were there when she got hurt. She talked then..." Demetri sighed. "... and then—"

"You guys should probably get going if you want to hit the grocery store and run errands before school gets out," Alyssa called out behind us. "It gets kinda crazy downtown with all the bus traffic."

"Seaside?" I frowned. "It has traffic?"

"You have no idea," Demetri muttered. "It's ridiculous sometimes. P.S., have fun at Safeway."

"Safe what?" I repeated. "Is that a hospital?"

"Grocery store." Demetri nodded. "It has a Starbucks, though, so we forgive it for having a really small organic food section."

"Says the guy who eats French fries for breakfast." Alyssa sighed.

"Dude…" Demetri held up his hands. "…last I checked, people eat potatoes for breakfast."

"Potatoes and fries…" Shaking my head, I rose from my seat. "…not the same, bro."

"Alright, traitor to men everywhere…" Demetri pointed at the door. "… make sure to treat Dani right so I don't have to kick your ass."

I burst out laughing.

No one else joined in.

"Shit, you're serious?" I glared at Demetri. "So much for brotherhood."

"Family trumps brotherhood." He held up his hand for a high five from Dani. "Sorry for partying."

I rolled my eyes. "I promise to bring her back in the same condition I took her."

"Good man." Demetri saluted me.

I waved him off and followed Dani out of the house.

She skipped to her side of the car, appearing to be in a better mood since our car ride over. I only hoped it would last after she saw the list of things I had to get done before I was expected on set.

CHAPTER SEVEN

Dani

DANI: *DO YOU DO LAUNDRY EVER?*

Lincoln flashed me a grin as he continued putting away our groceries. "Nope, I've never had to."

Dani: *You need to learn.*

I rolled my eyes and continued sorting his clothes, most of them workout clothes, which made me curious as to what he did. Was he a runner? I stole a peek at his jean-clad legs. I wouldn't be able to tell anyway. His arms were huge, bulging beneath his gray long-sleeve shirt.

"Oh, hey." He peeled the shirt from his body and tossed it in my direction. "If you're doing a load of darks, wash this one too. Someone spilled coffee on it this morning. Not that it wasn't deserved."

Had I not already been a mute, the sight of his bare chest and abs would have done it. His abs were chunky; he didn't just have a six-pack, he had freaking rivets that dipped into delicious golden skin, trailing all the way down into his jeans. Holy crap! He was built, and he was still putting stuff away — not flexing, simply breathing — and somehow that translated into muscles flexing and making my mouth go dry.

His biceps were bigger than my head.

A large tattoo wrapped from his right arm all the way down to his wrist. I hadn't noticed it before; in fact, the last magazine cover he was on didn't have the tattoo. I wanted to ask him about it. Maybe they covered it up all the time? Maybe it was new?

"Not that I mind..." Lincoln didn't turn around. "... because I'm used to it, but since you don't talk, it almost makes it more creepy that you're openly staring at me like that."

I jerked my attention back to the sorting piles, my cheeks burning with embarrassment.

Dani: *Sorry. You just caught me by surprise.*

His warm chuckle filled the air. "It's fine. Really."
Someone please let me disappear into the floor.

Dani: *I wasn't staring at you because of your body — I was just curious about your tattoo.*

There that sounded better, right? Less creepy?

"Well..." Lincoln chose to talk instead of texting me back. "... I went on this month-long hike through the woods, tried to find myself, and on my last day, I was so dehydrated I almost died. I cried out for water just as a snake slithered in front of me, and when I looked past him, I heard a creek. That snake saved my life, so I made a promise to myself to never forget how lucky I was, thus the tattoo."

Officially the weirdest story ever.

Dani: *Um, cool.*

Lincoln burst out laughing. "I'm shitting you, Dani. I was sixteen, drunk, and stupid. I wanted to get a badass python tattoo. It ended up looking like shit, so I turned it into a full sleeve so that it actually resembled something other than a man's penis on my arm, because honestly, that's what it looked like, no getting around it."

I covered my mouth to keep myself from laughing.

"It's okay, you know…" Lincoln glanced at me over his shoulder. "… to laugh… It doesn't mean you like me, just means I'm even more of an ass than you originally thought."

Dani: *True.*

Lincoln grinned at me then stared back at his cupboard. "Shit, we forgot waffle mix."

Dani: *So?*

He shut the cupboards. "Just another thing you get to make fun of me for." He swiped his keys from the counter. "First day on a new movie always starts with a breakfast of waffles and peanut butter."

Ew, officially the grossest combo ever. I made a face.

"Is that for the waffles or the peanut butter?" He leaned against the counter, his abs flexing at me, winking at me, begging me to reach out and touch.

Dani: *Both.*

Lincoln gasped. "Well, I guess we can't get married now."

Dani: *And I had such high hopes of a quick betrothal.*

He barked out a laugh. "I can go grab the mix if you want, or you can come with me, and I can buy you another

Starbucks… maybe we can shake hands over the cup and vow to do that whole starting over thing?"

My hand hesitated over the laundry.

"Please?" His voice was too sexy for his own good.

That was the last thing I needed — to find the devil sexy. Because that's what he was. Hollywood through and through, a man who jumped to conclusions before he even knew the truth.

Demetri had already warned me.

As had Alec.

And Jaymeson, not that it mattered. A guy like Lincoln would never be interested in me, even if I wasn't mute.

Dani: *Sure.*

SAFEWAY WAS PACKED. I sent a text over to Lincoln that I'd grab the waffle mix if he wanted to wait in line at Starbucks. I knew he was thankful. Already he was getting odd looks from people. It was in the paper that filming was taking place for the next few months, and he was a dead giveaway with his Lakers hat and Ray-Bans.

I quickly weaved through the grocery-cart traffic until I reached the pancake and waffle mixes.

He hadn't specified what brand he wanted.

So I just picked the one that said organic, assuming that was probably what he'd want anyway.

"Dani?" a familiar male voice called. "Is it really you?"

Shivers ran down my spine as I turned and came face to face with my ex-boyfriend.

"You're back." He grinned, looking like an innocent boy. He looked how I should have looked at that same age… innocent, wide eyed, excited about life. "Are you going to be finishing senior year?"

I tried to speak. I wanted to so bad. I begged my stupid mouth to move. I prayed to God that I wouldn't be embarrassed or that he wouldn't think I was a total bitch, too good for him.

I made a croaking noise.

He frowned.

I tried again.

"Oh." He took a step back. "You're still sick, huh? That has to suck, not talking... have you ever tried just being better?"

Have I ever tried just being better? Light bulb! Why hadn't I thought of that? Someone give him a prize!

"I mean..." He stepped forward. "... don't you think it's kind of immature to use this to get all that attention?"

Tears stung my eyes as another figure made its way down the aisle.

"Elliot, hurry up — oh..." Amanda his new girlfriend, my ex-best friend paused mid-sentence. "Dani, you're back!"

Fake smile.

Fake boobs — compliments of her rich parents.

And by the looks of it, fake lips. Great.

"We've missed you." She reached out to hug me.

I took a step back.

Rolling her eyes, she motioned to Elliot. "We gotta run, homecoming court and all that. I'm sure you would understand if you actually stopped pretending to be traumatized and went to school."

Angry, so angry that the words wouldn't come, I opened my mouth again. This time a weird mewling noise came out, one I'd never before uttered. I sounded like a lamb caught in someone's fence.

Amanda burst out laughing. "Anyone ever told you that you could be an actress just like your sister? How is she, by the way? Knocked up by that movie star, what's his name?"

"Jamie Jaymeson," came Lincoln's smooth voice. "We'll be

sure to let him know you said hi." He wrapped a possessive arm around me and pulled me close to his chest. A war raged within me — lean on him like I actually needed him and was thankful for his save, or jerk away and embarrass myself more.

I leaned in.

He smelled like Starbucks coffee and leather.

"No way!" Amanda smacked Elliot in the shoulder. "You're Lincoln Greene!"

"Yup." He held a tight smile. "I'm sorry, and you are?"

"Friends." Amanda blurted. "Old friends with Dani."

"Well, that's weird." He shared a look with me and squeezed. "I've known Dani here for a while, and she's never mentioned you. Not once."

Amanda's face turned bright red. "Well, she doesn't talk, so maybe that's why."

Lincoln grinned tightly. "She talks."

Oh no. What was he doing!

"But only to people extremely close to her, right, baby?" He kissed the top of my head and sighed. "Anyway, we're late. Nice meeting you. What was your name again?"

"A-amanda." She jutted her chin out.

"Right." Lincoln had the whole *little-people* stare down like an expert. Even I flinched when he haughtily dismissed the two of them and steered me back down the aisle.

"Assholes," he muttered under his breath as he angrily grabbed the mix from my hands then swiped his card.

"Are you a rewards member?" the checker asked.

Lincoln stared him down.

The checker swallowed slowly. "I'll take that as a no."

I grabbed the mix while Lincoln snatched the receipt and tugged me toward the truck. He opened my door, and I climbed inside.

He didn't shut it.

I frowned as he braced himself against the door frame. "Are you okay?"

I shrugged.

He licked his full lips then grabbed his phone and started typing.

Linc: *I'll go back and publicly shame them both, just say the word.*

Dani: *Ex-boyfriend, ex-best friend. Both have ex in front of their name for a reason.*

Lincoln read the text and glanced up, his eyes locking on me. "You dated that?"

I slumped down in my seat and typed in my phone.

Dani: *He's the quarterback.*

Lincoln's face twisted into a bitter smile. "I don't give a shit. He's an asshole."

Dani: *We all deal with grief in different ways. He loved my dad. It was hard on him losing us both.*

"But you lived." Lincoln argued.

Dani: *Is that what I'm doing right now?*

He didn't answer. He stared at the text then glanced back up at me. "Jaymeson never told me. He just said you needed a job and were a selective mute. I looked it up online." He looked embarrassed. "Beyond that, I don't know your story. But I do know this. You lived for a reason. So what you do right now — even if it's as simple as getting out of bed every day — it matters."

He shut the door.

The static silence greeted me, making my body tense with a tingling awareness, almost as if someone had just pressed cold paddles to my chest and shouted, *"Clear!"*

"So," Lincoln jumped into the truck, cleared his throat and started the engine. "Jaymeson said you baked. Please tell me that includes making kick-ass waffles."

I gave a solitary nod.

"Thank God."

And that was it.

He didn't pester me about the accident or ask for details about what had occurred in the store, which bothered me, because for the first time since everything had happened, I wanted to volunteer that information. I wanted him to know.

Maybe because he'd defended me, a stranger.

Or maybe it was because he'd been blunt, almost hurtfully so, when up until now everyone had used kid gloves with me.

Maybe the hard and ugly love was what I needed.

I'd always been a hugger.

Now, I had to wonder if the accident had changed me from a hugger — to a fighter.

CHAPTER EIGHT

Lincoln

LINC: *TELL ME A JOKE.*

Dani: *Wilbur must really suck at keeping you entertained.*

Linc: *You're telling me...*

Dani: *Am I going to have to start looking up jokes in order to entertain you at night? Also, you have to be up in four hours — correction WE have to be up in four hours. GO TO SLEEP!*

Linc: *Did you just all caps me?*

Dani: *My finger slipped?*

Linc: *Finger slipped my ass. I think you just yelled at your elder.*

Dani: *Oh please. I'm almost eighteen. You're barely twenty-two.*

Linc: *Been visiting my IMDb page, huh?*

Dani: *Wouldn't your ego like to know?*

Linc: *Yes. It needs constant stroking. Quick, give me a compliment!*

Dani: *You have a killer tattoo.*

Linc: *Now that's just cruel, I'll have you know me and Bo go way back, even if he does look like shit.*

Dani: *You named your tattoo?*
Linc: *Is that not a thing? Do people not do that?*
Dani: *Maybe people in rooms with padded walls...*
Linc: *You say padded walls. I say fluffy.*
Dani: *Still an asylum.*

A yellow smiley winked onto my screen, eyes spinning and tongue lolling.

Linc: *Bo's offended.*
Dani: *Do you name everything?*
Linc: *Would it weird you out if I named my waffle maker Chuck?*
Dani: *Yes.*
Linc: *Then no, I don't name everything... *whispers* sorry Chuck.*
Dani: GO TO SLEEP!

I grinned hard at my phone. I was too nervous to sleep, not that I'd admit that to her. It helped that the next few emojis she sent were of snakes, spiders, and then a bomb going off killing them all. Wasn't sure how that was supposed to put me to sleep, but it did make me laugh.

Linc: *One joke, or maybe even a bedtime story.*

I leaned back against my pillows, waiting for her response.

Dani: *There once was a spoiled actor named Linc. He choked on Chuck while petting Wilbur, and Bo cried. The end.*
Linc: *You forgot about Penny.*
Dani: *Who's Penny?*
Linc: *Wouldn't you like to know.*
Dani: LINCOLN GREENE — *sleep. You need it. I need it.*

The world needs us to have it, otherwise I'm going to be really cranky tomorrow.

Linc: *When was the last time you yelled?*

Dani: *That's a weird question.*

Linc: *Sorry, too personal?*

Maybe I'd overstepped my boundaries. I hoped not because I really wanted to know the last time she'd raised her voice.

Dani: *Probably after the accident when I was in a wheelchair and stupid Demetri thought it would be funny to push me around downtown Seaside at epic speeds. I yelled until I was hoarse. It was a fun day.*

Linc: *I'm assuming you were in the wheelchair because something was broken, and he had the audacity to push you into objects?*

Dani: *That's Demetri for you. But it did cheer me up. Until then, everyone had been treating me like I was so breakable, so it was nice to have normal. He gave me that.*

Linc: *I'm beginning to think it's not just the Sour Patch Kids.*

Dani: *It's not.*

Linc: *I feel jealous of his ability to be your friend when I seem to offend you every time I open my mouth.*

Dani: *You're a better texter.*

Linc: *Thanks, I think.*

Dani: *Go to bed.*

Linc: *Fine. And Dani?*

Dani:?

Linc: *You aren't breakable.*

Dani: *Thanks.*

CHAPTER NINE

Lincoln

DANI: *REMIND ME AGAIN WHY I took this job.*

    Linc: *You didn't have a choice. Almost here?*

    Dani: *Yeah, I'm at Starbucks, will be over in a few.*

The text ended with a few stunned looking smiley faces, a yawn, and then the picture of the ridiculously long Starbucks line.

    Linc: *Just let yourself in.*

My flip flops made a slapping noise against the hardwood floor as I paced back and forth, back and forth in my living room. Nervous energy swirled around me as I cracked first my knuckles and then my neck.

The sound relaxed me more than the feeling.

I cracked my left hand again then my right.

Blowing air out of my cheeks, I sat on my couch and started my deep breathing. In for eight seconds, out for eight seconds, eight times.

I'd tried to stop with my first-day ritual, but the one and only time I hadn't done the whole cracking, breathing, relaxing thing, one of the lights had fallen on me during filming.

During a sex scene.

I'd been naked.

So had she.

Let's just say we both received some fun bruises in places no person should ever be bruised.

Which brought me back to the deep breathing.

I blew out my last breath, eyes closed, envisioning my first few lines. I mouthed the words then, eyes still closed, played with a few voices.

"It's so much easier..." My voice rumbled low in my throat. "... fighting for the bad... giving in to temptation, don't you think?"

No, that wasn't right. My voice wasn't raw enough; it felt forced. I tried again, this time clearing my throat.

"It's so much easier..." I started. "Shit." I wiped my face with my clammy hands. I wasn't feeling it. When had I ever been so obsessed over someone that my sole purpose in life was to bring them down with me? Bring them to my level just so I could have a taste?

Dani.

Her name flashed like a neon sign in my stupid-ass brain. Flash, flash, flash. With a groan, I licked my lips and envisioned her standing in front of me. The forbidden fruit, someone who intrigued me, piqued my curiosity, a girl who made me want.

"It's so much easier..." My gut clenched as I reached for her hand, my fingertips tingling with anticipation of caressing her skin. "... fighting for the bad." I envisioned myself take a step forward as my fingertips grazed her wrist, the erratic pulse giving way to her feelings, though she remained still, indifferent. "Giving into temptation..." I lifted her wrist to my lips and whispered hoarsely against her skin. "Don't you think?"

The sound of clapping jolted me out of my vision, causing a near heart attack to take my short life.

"Shit!" I jumped to my feet and turned around.

Dani's face was flushed as she held out my coffee and a bag of Skittles.

"That was, um…" I scratched my neck in anxiousness. "…practice. Because actors, they do that."

Hell, someone drown me in the ocean outside.

She nodded once, a smile tickling the corners of her mouth.

"Thanks." Voice hoarse, like that of an eighty-year-old smoker, I cleared my throat — loudly — and opened the bag of Skittles, avoiding her gaze. "It's tradition. I only eat the red ones."

My phone buzzed; I picked it up.

Dani: *Red is the best flavor.*

"Thank God you agree. Wouldn't want to fire you on the first day." Again. Shit.

She rolled her eyes and glanced around the living room, her face impatient, making me feel like a diva.

"Alright." I popped a few red Skittles in my mouth and chewed. The sugary tartness reminded me, yet again, what day it was. D-day. The first day of shooting.

I had to be better than awesome.

"Let's do this." I faked the bravado in my voice, straightened my shoulders, and threw on my Ray Bans like I'd done a million times on the first day on set. Nerves would always be a part of my job. The minute I was no longer nervous would be the minute I needed to get out of the business.

I started the truck and tossed my bag of Skittles in the cup holder while Dani buckled her seatbelt.

Hands shaking, I gripped the steering wheel, hoping it would somehow center me. I was still reeling from the scene I'd played out in my head.

Of her skin.

Of her freaking response.

My phone went off.

I swiped it from my front pocket.

Dani: *Break a leg.*

"Let's hope not." I winked then tossed the phone in with the Skittles. "But thanks, Dani. I appreciate it."

My phone went off again, but I knew Dani would throw a tantrum if I checked it while driving, so I waited an agonizing eight minutes while we drove to the secluded beach just outside town.

A few semi-trailers were parked in the normally deserted parking lot. Security was everywhere — walking around, talking in their radios. Jaymeson was standing in the middle of the beach speaking into his headset.

I swallowed the nerves and glanced down at my phone.

Dani: *My dad always said nerves mean you're alive. So... today, prove why you're living. Don't think of anything else other than getting that across. Movies should be reflections of real feelings, real life. Show life.*

"When did you get so smart?"

Dani shrugged and pulled the Skittles out of the cup holder then handed me another three red ones.

"Thanks." I popped them in my mouth, swirling them around with my tongue until they were tiny, chewable pieces of sugar. "Alright. I'm ready."

THE FIRST DAY ALWAYS consisted of a lot of waiting. It never helped the nerves because it gave me time to over-think and over-analyze everything. Granted, I'd already done a ton of table reads with the rest of the cast. But being in costume on set brought it up to a whole different level.

Jaymeson was the good guy.

I was the bad guy.

According to Jaymeson, we were basically retelling Nat's love story and how she fell in love with AD2. Shortly after she married Alec, she had decided to pen their story, and, because of her celebrity status, it was quickly picked up by a production company. By then, Jaymeson had already staked his claim, saying he'd always wanted to play a self-absorbed jackass — I'd thought he meant Alec. And well, that had left me to play Demetri.

Which seemed semi-weird, since he and Dani were close.

Which meant in a way I was just as close? Right?

Ha. Yeah, not even one day in, and already I was losing my mind.

I was supposed to be in love with Pris, who was playing Nat, but I seriously had a rough time feeling it — or knowing that I had to kiss Dani's sister.

I'd done it a million times before, but it just felt…. weird

Add the fact that we were filming one of our makeout scenes, on the beach, on our first day, and I was already dreaming of the word *cut* or the sentence *take five.*

"You kiss my wife and enjoy it, I remove your balls in your sleep." Jaymeson said in a chipper voice as he slapped me on the back.

"Always great working with a real professional, Jaymeson, always great," I muttered.

"Here's a tip," Jaymeson whispered in a low voice so Pris couldn't hear us. "Get it done on the first take so I don't have to cause an on-set accident where I set your trailer on fire and blame it on God smiting you for being a Hollywood heathen."

"Heathen?" I repeated with a smirk. "Isn't that the part I'm playing? I thought Demetri was hot for Nat, so doesn't that mean I need to be hot for your wife? Your very…" I glanced at Pris. "… lovely wife?"

"Bastard. I should never have cast you!"

I burst out laughing. "Jay, you know I'm messing with you. I'm professional. That's why you cast me, because in a sea of Hollywood heathens, I'm the only one who wouldn't make a pass at your wife."

He shrugged. "True. Also you may be passable in the whole looks department, or so I've been told by numerous people on set."

"Jealous?"

"Hardly." He rolled his eyes. "I'm Jamie Jaymeson. Women tattoo my name on their asses and ask me to sign their boobs."

"You signed whose boobs?" Pris asked, sneaking up on our conversation.

"My grandma's," I blurted. "She's such—" I wrapped an arm around Jaymeson and squeezed. "—a huge fan."

"Right." Jaymeson coughed. "It's always such a thrill, signing elderly ladies tits. Hey, you think I should do a nursing home tour?"

"Yeah, man." I nodded. "Dream big."

"Well, then." Pris shook her head in amusement. "On that creepy note, I'm ready." She walked off to her spot on the beach.

I nodded and started to follow, when Jaymeson gripped my arm and tugged me back. "Remember, one take."

"When was the last time you did a kissing scene in one take, man? Seriously. Ever think that if I do it in one take it means we have chemistry?"

He frowned.

I nodded and jerked free. "Exactly. Hell, you should be happy if we're here all day trying to get this scene right. I may be kissing your wife, but I'm going to be thinking of someone else entirely."

"Demetri." Jaymeson nodded. "He does it for lots of dudes."

"You're an ass. You know that, right?"

"He made me a shirt that says *ASS* with a donkey on it, so yeah, I'm well aware."

"Good talk." I saluted him and met Pris on the blanket. She lay down on the sand while I straddled her and playfully leaned forward.

"And action," Jaymeson said in a short, angry tone.

"So, Seaside?" she asked, leaning up on her elbows.

"Seaside," I repeated, trying to stare more at her mouth than her eyes, so I really could conjure up some sort of romantic feelings or lust — anything, really.

"Did I get the real story?"

"No," I whispered. My eyes fixated on her mouth as I leaned down while she arched up. Our lips met and then, somehow, for the first time since I didn't know when, I experienced my first awkward kiss — I hit her teeth. Her freaking teeth.

The clang that could be heard around the world.

She burst out laughing.

"Shit!" I hissed, my teeth a bit jarred from impact. "Are you okay?"

Pris rubbed her mouth and gave me an amused nod.

"Cut," Jaymeson yelled then marched over. "I hate to be the one to ask this, but did you have a kissing double in your other movies? Because that was absolute crap."

I leaned back on my haunches, the chilly seaside wind biting into the back of my calves. "Sorry, sand in my eye?"

"Sand, my ass." Jaymeson grumbled. "Lips meet, do a little sliding action, tongue stays inside the mouth at all times, toss in a few groans, possibly a breathy moan." He pointed to Pris. "That's on you, love..." He rubbed his hands together. "...

and things should be great. Think you can handle that, Linc?"

"Yeah." Beads of nervous sweat broke out all over my skin and threatened to freeze there as the cold wind struck me. Just wonderful. On my first day I'd managed to physically assault my co-star. "No problem."

"Great." He walked back to his spot.

I hovered over Pris again.

"Take two."

The scene was slated again. Nerves attacked every cell in my body as I managed to steal a glance at everyone on set. Already they looked irritated, from the sound tech to the makeup artist. The worst possible thing was shooting a scene in weather, either freezing your ass off or burning to death, only to have the actor forget every damn line.

"So, Seaside?" Pris asked more gentle this time, her soft brown eyes danced with humor.

"Seaside." I leaned down, like I was going to kiss her, not part of the script, but I was trying to get myself in the right state of mind, which, to me was always the breaking point before the kiss, where you're thinking about it and the person you want to kiss knows you're thinking about it — anticipation was the best part.

"Do I get the real story?"

I hesitated purposefully. Eyelids heavy, I focused on her lips, licking my own slowly, methodically.

And I felt it.

Not the lust.

But her.

Dani.

I don't know how the hell I felt her, maybe I really was losing my mind at twenty-two. Out of the corner of my eye, her grey Converse flashed next to Jaymeson's flip flops.

"No." I leaned down, my lips rubbing against Pris's. As promised, I kept my tongue in my mouth but nibbled her bottom lip like it was the sweetest delicacy I'd ever tasted in my entire existence. My tongue swiped along the seam of her lips as I dug my hands into her hair and deepened the kiss, tugging her body upward. Her hand pressed against my chest. I grabbed it then shoved it away. The kiss was supposed to be aggressive, elusive, then suddenly angry.

She moaned.

And I felt absolutely nothing.

No blood rushing into all the wrong places, which wasn't the norm at all. If anything, it was awkward as hell being turned on during a scene, but it was simple human anatomy. If you were turned on, your body was going to show it, regardless of if you wanted it to or not.

"Cut," Jaymeson hissed.

I pulled back and grinned.

"Wow." Pris wiped her mouth with the back of her hand. "Well done, Linc."

"Oh, please." Jaymeson joined us. "The first time he tried was like watching an awkward turtle on its back."

"Thanks, man."

"Any time." Jaymeson flashed a grin. "We need to set up for the next shot, so you can take a few minutes and check out your trailer while I go make sure they haven't burned the house down."

"House?"

"For the party," Jaymeson explained. "Also the set for the music video. We're going to kill two birds with one stone."

"Great."

Jaymeson frowned. "Are you alright?"

"Huh?" I jerked my head away from Dani and felt my face heat. "Yeah. Sure. Why? Don't I look alright?" *Shoot me now.*

"Showing up drunk on the first day is frowned upon," Jaymeson whispered under his breath.

"Not drunk." I started walking away and pointed behind me. "I'm gonna go take that break."

CHAPTER TEN

Dani

WATCHING HIM KISS MY SISTER HAD to be the most awkward thing I'd ever experienced in my entire life. I trembled with the wrongness of it. I mean, my *sister*.

Granted, she was married.

And they were acting.

But the way he touched her, the way he hovered over her, protected her with his massive body, his lips caressing hers… and I wanted so selfishly to be on the other side of that kiss.

No guy had ever looked at me like that.

Elliot had never kissed me like he wanted to take his time. He'd been a great boyfriend until I was too much baggage for him…

"Why can't you just be happy, Dani?" he shouted. "For once! There's more going on in the world other than the accident, alright? I know it sucks, I know it hurts, but for the love of God, it's been a few months! At least do SOMETHING!"

I flinched at his words, at the tone of his voice. He'd never yelled at me before. I hugged myself with my arms and nodded, trying desperately to just be okay. I mean, how hard could it be? I forced a smile on my face and nodded my head.

"Look..." He approached me slowly, like I was broken, he talked to me softly, like I was stupid. "... this isn't working out."

"But..." I held the tears in. God, it hurt so bad. "... but I promise I'll do better!"

"You've been promising for months, Dani. And look? We're still hanging out in the condo, shut out away from the world. You refuse to eat pancakes, won't watch TV because it reminds you of them, and the last time you even asked about my day was because I told you to."

The walls around my heart shattered. He was the last thing I had of my old life, the last person, other than my sister, who had been a part of the old Dani. The happy cheerleader without a care in the world.

Losing him felt like I was losing my parents all over again, because he was right. I didn't even recognize myself anymore. My normally highlighted hair was dark brown, the circles under my eyes matched, and the last time I had put on makeup was for their funeral.

"I get it." I hugged myself harder, imagining my daddy's arms around me, telling me everything would look better in the morning.

It never did.

If anything, in Seaside, it looked dreary — worse.

"Dani." Elliot cursed and jerked away from me as if I'd slapped him. Except I was the one dealing with the emotional blow of one of my best friends not only dumping me, but basically saying goodbye to me forever because he couldn't handle my sadness.

I didn't blame him.

Sometimes I couldn't handle it either.

"It's fine," I whispered. "Just go."

"Dani—"

"Go!" I wailed, tears clouding my vision.

He left me that day.

He started dating my best friend the next week.

I quit cheerleading and dropped out of school the week after that.

"Cut!" Jaymeson shouted.

I jerked my head to attention and watched Jaymeson interact with Pris and Lincoln. Feeling awkward to just be standing there, I shoved my hands in my pockets and waited.

My job, while Lincoln was shooting, was to make sure everything was perfect for him when he took his breaks. Did he have enough water? Was he fed? Clothed? Happy? Was he tense? Did he have his friggin' Skittles? What? The water has to be lukewarm — not too cold. Wouldn't want the star getting stomach cramps. And don't even get me started on his trailer.

There had been a list.

I got two items done on it before I was ready to shred the paper in half.

I came back to the set to ask about the list, hoping to catch him on a break.

Not to catch him cheerfully making out with my sister.

"Hey, Dani." He waved and jogged over to me. "I'm gonna take a quick break. Trailer ready?"

I made a face and held up my hand, waving it in a *so-so* motion.

"By that expression I'm going to assume you burned down my trailer, and I'm going to have to grab a lawn chair and umbrella."

I grinned and shook my head.

"Great, I just love surprises." He rubbed his hands together then blew into them like he was cold. "Did you see my kissing fail?"

I frowned.

"The first take," he explained, chuckling, "I may have knocked out your sister's two front teeth and quite possibly given her a head injury. My kiss was more enthusiastic than smooth, and I'm pretty sure if anyone gets wind of that video, I'm going to get laughed out of Hollywood."

I quickly grabbed my phone.

Dani: *You hit her?*

"Ha," Lincoln set his hand on my lower back and led me through the few trailers next to each other. "No, I hit her teeth."

I burst out laughing.

"Get it out now," he grumbled. "Glad I could amuse you."

Dani: *Is she okay?*

"You *would* care about her." Lincoln flashed me a grin. "And she's just fine, though my ego's bruised a bit. I've been kissing women since I was twelve. No idea why the simple action suddenly seemed to be as hard as solving world hunger."

We stopped in front of his trailer.

His eyes widened a fraction as he crossed his arms, uncrossed them, then tapped his chin. "Um, Dani?"

I winced.

"Why does the sign on my trailer say LG?"

I shrugged.

"Like a homie."

I shrugged again.

Sighing, he opened the door.

I went in before him and prepared myself for a temper tantrum.

Instead, he grabbed a handful of Skittles — only red ones since I'd freaking picked them out of a five-pound bag — and lay back on the black leather couch.

Still waiting for him to say something, I stayed close to the door, just in case he threw something. I wouldn't be so freaked out if I hadn't seen one of the actors do that to his assistant a few minutes before I jogged down to the beach.

The actor, whose name was so small it was ridiculous that he even thought he had the right to act so privileged, was angry because his assistant had forgotten grapes.

Grapes, people!

"Looks good." Lincoln ran a hand through his ginger hair and patted the seat next to him. "You know you can sit, right? Your standing makes me feel like I need to stand."

I grabbed my phone.

Dani: *You're not mad?*

Lincoln pulled out his phone and tossed it onto the couch. "Why the hell would I be mad?"

Dani: *The water bottles don't have your face on them.*

Lincoln burst out laughing then frowned. "Oh... you're serious?

Dani: *The list said your water bottles needed to be at room temperature and that the stickers of your face needed to be on the name brand because you hate name brands. But I couldn't find the damn stickers.*

Lincoln smirked. "I would love to hear you curse. Out loud. I have a feeling it would be a huge turn... on." He paled. "Not that, that's exactly— You know what? Let me see that list."

Did he just say I turned him on?

Embarrassed, I fumbled for the list in my right front pocket then gave it to him. Our fingers touched, just barely, enough to still feel the tingle on my skin, even though we weren't touching anymore.

"The shades must be pulled three-quarters of the way down whenever the trailer is facing east?" Lincoln read aloud in his gravelly voice. "Who the hell cares?"

I typed on my phone.

Dani: *Don't you?*

"Sweetheart, I don't even know which direction east is, at least not without going outside and checking out where the sun rose. Besides, why would it matter?"

I shrugged.

He flipped the list over. "Uh, Dani?"

I nodded.

"Wrong list." He dangled it out. "This is for Matty Rose."

"Matty?" I mouthed. It must have surprised Lincoln because his eyes locked on my lips for at least five seconds before he shook his head.

"Some punk sixteen-year-old heartthrob who thinks this is going to be his big break because he gets to play the best friend, Evan."

Dani: *Whoops?*

"Yeah, let's just hope his assistant doesn't get fired for the shade incident."

I laughed.

Lincoln watched me. Not in a creepy *I'm watching you laugh because I want to kill you* way, but like he was curious.

"Linc!" Jaymeson pounded on the door. "Ready for the party scene?"

"Yup." He shot to his feet as the door pulled open.

Jaymeson looked more frantic than usual. "Dani, I need a solid."

I narrowed my eyes.

"Please!" Jaymeson clasped his hands together. "I'll buy you a pony."

"She's seventeen, not twelve," Lincoln pointed out.

"A car?" Jaymeson shrugged.

"Her car's brand new," Lincoln said in a bored voice.

"Holy shit!" Jaymeson jerked off his headset and pointed at Lincoln, "Help a man out, mate! I'm dying here!"

I tapped his shoulder and nodded my head as if to say *"Ask."*

"Party Girl One's plane got delayed. She won't be here, and the girl I need has blonde hair." He eyed my hair and smiled brightly. "Please?"

"Sour Patch Kids," Lincoln blurted. "I say you owe her a year's supply of Sour Patch Kids."

Jaymeson held out his hand. "Deal."

I took his hand and shook it just as Lincoln asked, "Isn't Party Girl One in a scene with me?"

"Yeah." Jaymeson was already walking away from us then turned on his heel and shouted, "She's the girl you make out with at the party."

CHAPTER ELEVEN

Lincoln

SON OF A BITCH.

I'd kissed her sister and nearly made her teeth bleed because I couldn't seem to get into the scene — then imagined myself kissing her, and it had been all rainbows and shit.

And now? Now I get to kiss her.

Well, at least I wouldn't have to act — nope that would be all Lincoln Greene.

In that moment, I wanted her to talk. I needed to hear her joke about kissing me. I needed the conversation before the kiss that set me at ease. Because at least through conversation, I could maybe gain insight into her feelings. But all I had to go off was body language. And as usual, she seemed indifferent about the whole thing.

I stared harder.

Maybe she was sweating?

I eyed her neck, hoping for a racing pulse.

Instead, she jerked her head to the side and stumbled as she mouthed, *"What?"*

"Sorry." I nearly stuttered. Great. Add that to my list of

epic fails for the day. "Just, um, thought I saw a mosquito bite."

Smooth, Lincoln, smooth.

She quickly touched her neck.

"It's gone." You know, because it was never there in the first place, and I was staring at her neck like a starved vampire. Good times.

I cleared my throat and silently hoped that Jaymeson had somehow changed the scene.

The beach house was set up with at least two hundred extras. A huge lit-up stage was built right in front of it. The idea was to shoot the party scene and then have the guys do a pretend live concert so they could get footage for the music video.

"Hey!" Demetri jumped off the stage and jogged over. Had the guy been single, I would hate him with every fiber of my being. He was like a lost Californian surfer who'd somehow gotten washed up on the Oregon shore, like a freaking mermaid with magical music powers.

Yeah, I was really overthinking things. Shit.

"How's my girl?" He pulled Dani into his arms and twirled her around. "Lincoln giving you hell?"

I rolled my eyes. "Hardly."

She shook her head no then patted Demetri's head like he was a dog. He seemed to like that though. He gripped her hand then kissed it and called Alec over.

"Well, well, well." Alec jumped off the stage. His black boots hit the ground hard, and sand went flying everywhere. I was sure the extra didn't mind. In fact, she looked so enamored with the sand he'd propelled onto her leg, I wouldn't have been at all surprised if she'd collected it and put it in a jar labeled *Alec Daniels*.

I imagined that was what their lives were like. Lots of star struck people just gaping at them with awe. What was it about musicians? Bastards. All of them.

"You've grown." Alec winked, pulling Dani into his arms

then kissing her head. "Really though..." He kissed her head again, his scruff rubbing against her soft hair. "... you look good, Dani."

The familiarity they had with her rubbed me the wrong way. Not because I was jealous. I barely knew her! Maybe it was because I was pretty sure if I tried to kiss her head, she'd probably karate chop me or knee me in the balls.

I cleared my throat.

Alec turned his attention my way, his light blue eyes narrowing. "Has Lincoln been treating you alright?"

Dani shook her head no.

My mouth dropped open.

Then she grinned and winked — yes, winked at me. Knees trembling, I almost needed a moment to sit down. The last thing I needed was bad PR, and yet, the reason I was trembling? She'd freaking winked.

Damn, she was pretty when she was happy.

And maybe that was the saddest part of all — she seemed so tight all the time, like being happy was a chore, but being sad? Just the way life was.

It wasn't my job to fix it.

And I wasn't one of those guys who took on projects where I threw up those stupid self-esteem posters all over the place then told the girl to go get a makeover, and charge a new wardrobe to a credit card. Besides, she was gorgeous as it was. I just wished she would enjoy life. Hell, she was so young.

Too young to be that sad all the time.

"How's the first day?" Demetri asked.

"Well..." I nodded. "... playing you officially sucks. You do realize what a bastard you were to Nat, right?"

Alec burst out laughing. "Amazing how he just got on my good side."

"To be fair," Demetri argued, "I was high most the time so... yeah, I blame drugs."

"Sucks he can't blame them anymore," Alec muttered.

RACHEL VAN DYKEN

"HA!" Demetri shoved him. "Hilarious, and you're just cranky because you got zero sleep last night, and spilled your coffee on your favorite jeans."

"Damn it, they were Diesel!"

"Dude, they're jeans," I said.

Both guys gaped at me like I'd just announced that I liked to wear leopard leotards and tiaras.

"What?" I shrugged as my phone buzzed in my pants.

Dani: *Never get between rock stars and their jeans.*

"Uh, sorry?" I offered.

"Changes for the script." A PA walked up to our group and circled the scene with me and Dani. "You'll be kissing twice here and again in the music video."

Dani's eyes widened.

"Uh, music video?"

Demetri rolled his eyes. "Uh, why else would we be here?"

"No I mean… why am I in the music video?"

"Because you're playing me…" Demetri grinned. "… and I'm a rock god, so yeah, you're in the music video."

"But—"

"Places!" Jaymeson yelled into his megaphone, which just happened to be near Alec's ear.

To his credit, he only flinched and gave Jaymeson the finger.

I would have done a hell of a lot more than that.

"Whoa, there." Demetri grabbed Dani by her shirt and tugged her back. "That means they're going to start shooting. You can stay back with us."

Her face reddened.

Was she embarrassed she would be kissing me?

"She's with me." I gently grabbed her hand and started to lead her away.

82

"What?" Demetri's eyes narrowed. "But you're about to start the scene."

"She's in the scene."

"Dancing?" Demetri guessed while Alec and Jaymeson started arguing over something on the script.

Dani shook her head.

"Pretending to pour beer?"

Another shake.

"Tell me you're a wallflower who sits in the corner. The one with lots of clothes."

She gulped.

"Hell, no!" Alec shouted.

"I think he found out," I whispered to Dani.

She gripped my hand harder.

"It's probably best to run and get you into makeup so you don't have to witness a fight. If you witness, you have to testify."

She giggled.

We turned and took off for the makeup trailer. I only needed touch ups, but I knew they would probably put a crapload of makeup on her, because one, she was a chick, two, she was supposed to look like a slut — probably why Alec was trying to pull Jaymeson's head off — and three, she had to look smoking.

Her wide doe eyes stared back at me through the mirror; her lower lip trembled a bit as the makeup artist pulled back her hair and started the very tedious process of shading.

"You okay?" I asked.

One nod.

"Want me to stay?"

Her shoulders slumped as if she felt bad for asking me to.

"Actually..." I pulled out a chair next to her and put my hands behind my head. "... I'm a makeup pro. I even know the difference between lipstick and mascara."

"And yet he makes more than me. Imagine that." Jean, the

head makeup artist said under her breath with a low chuckle.

I fake gasped then grinned. "Jean taught me everything I know."

"Poor boy cried the first time I put lipstick on him."

"Jean," I warned.

"Bawled like a damn baby because it made him look so pretty."

A burst of laughter came from Dani's direction before she clamped her lips shut.

"Seriously…" Jean swiped some dark concealer across Dani's cheek and nose. "… finally, I had to tell him it was magic man juice that helped aid in muscle building."

"I was twelve." I held up my hands. "And you lied!"

"We caught him trying to steal lipstick from set. When the director cornered him, he started crying and said, 'I just want to be strong!'"

By now, Dani was full on laughing.

"Great, any more embarrassing stories you wanna get off your chest, Jean?"

"Had to pee his pants for a role, and when they tried to attach the pouch to him so that it would look real,, he shouted, 'No, I do all my own stunts. I got this.'"

My phone buzzed.

Dani: *Tell me you were still twelve.*

I winced. "Yeah, I may have been fourteen."

Jean chuckled.

"I should have gotten an Academy Award for that performance, and you know it!" I shouted.

Jean moved on to the airbrushing; in swift movements, she ran the gun over the front of Dani's face.

Amazing what contouring did to a woman.

Hell, it was amazing what it did to a guy.

Her cheeks were more pronounced, almost sharp. Her

nose looked a little more prominent, and her eyes full on sparkled.

And we were only on the base layer of whatever the hell they were going to do to her.

"Linc, have you heard from Wardrobe?"

"No." I licked my lips and pried my gaze away from Dani. "Why?"

"Well, they said to do her makeup heavy. I don't want it to conflict with her outfit."

"On it." I grabbed the walkie-talkie and spoke into it. "Wardrobe."

No one answered.

"Wardrobe, it's Jean and Linc at Makeup."

"Wardrobe?" a woman answered.

"Hey, we need the costume for Party Girl One."

"Can you send someone to grab it? We're all busy searching for AD2's pyro jeans."

Dani smirked as if to say, *"Told ya."*

I sighed. "On my way." I stood and dropped the walkie into my pocket. "I'll be back. Make her gorgeous, Jean."

"She already is," Jean scolded.

"Yeah…" My eyes met Dani's in the mirror. "… I know."

CHAPTER TWELVE

Dani

"HE'S ONE OF MY FAVORITES YOU know," Jean said, once the door to the trailer slammed shut. "Always such a gentleman, never complains. The only weird quirk that kid has is red Skittles."

I wasn't sure if Jean knew that I didn't talk, and I didn't want to be rude, so I quickly wrote a little text.

Dani: *I don't know if Jay told you, but I can't talk.*

Jean read it over my shoulder. "Oh, sugar, I talk enough for the both of us." She tossed her bright purple hair over her shoulder and stared at me through the mirror, her green eyes meeting mine before turning back around and spraying something else on my face.

The mist was cool against my skin — it felt good and smelled like coconut.

"You know why he likes the red Skittles, right?" She didn't wait for me to text her. "He likes the flavor, but it's more than that. His very first movie was with some famous actor who refused to speak directly to people lest their normalness rub off on him. I won't say his name, but I'm sure you know who he is. Anyway..." She spread some cream on my eyes. "... you'll have to keep your eyes closed while I do your shadow and extensions."

I wanted to hear more about Lincoln and the reason he loved red Skittles, but I couldn't see my phone to text, and when I opened my mouth to speak, again, nothing came.

Which sucked, because she made me feel comfortable, and we were alone. If I was going to speak, it would be in a situation like that, where nobody could hear or point or laugh. For some reason, speaking in front of a complete stranger, who didn't care one way or another seemed a lot easier than speaking in front of my family, stuttering something stupid, and letting them down.

"I'm just going to apply the different shadows. If you want, you can take a nap. I can lean the chair back."

I nodded. A nap actually sounded really good. Maybe it would help take the nerves away.

It seemed like seconds later, and I was getting gently tapped. "Wake up, sunshine." Jean smiled. "You're all done! I think he'll be pleased." She winked.

He who?

The trailer door opened. Linc had a dress in his hands, along with necklaces wrapped around the hanger, and tall purple heels. "So, I don't know if you want to wear all the necklaces because it's really heavy. Depending on the makeup, we can just—"

I stood and walked over to him, reaching for the dress. The short silver cocktail dress felt silky between my fingers. It had straps that went around my neck and fell into a completely open back. It was short. I'd probably have to be careful if I had to sit down, if I could sit down at all.

"Linc?" Jean's voice danced with amusement. "Everything alright?"

"Uh..." He shoved the hanger into my face. "... yeah, sorry just... had a dry throat, freaked me out, don't want to start getting sick."

"Right," Jean said slowly. "Well, I say you wear all the necklaces. I did a purple, smoky eye and straightened your hair. I'll be sure to reapply the lipstick after every take, so don't worry about that." She clasped her hands together. "Now, Linc, I know you're used to dressing and undressing around the opposite sex, but this girl isn't, so shoo." She made a sweeping motion with her right hand. "Go on. I'll send her out when she's ready."

"But—"

"Go!"

"Fine!" He flashed me a smile. "Going. And Dani, you look really good."

I returned his smile and tried to keep myself from swooning into the chair. Regardless of how I felt about actors or men in general, I'd have to be dead not to respond to his smile. He was more than pretty. There wasn't one single thing I'd change about him, but it wasn't just his bright smile or the way his eyes seemed to look at me rather than through me. It was in the simple way he walked — or stalked. It was like he couldn't help but be seductive, even the lilt of his voice had me shivering in response, which was really, really, stupid.

The only thing that brought me back down to earth was the simple fact that he was my boss. That, and the fact that he was Lincoln Greene. He dated supermodels, not seventeen-year-old mutes. No, I was the charity case he took with him to fancy dinners in order to gain good PR. Not the girl he surprised on her birthday and whisked off to the Caribbean.

"Alright." Jean rubbed her hands together. "Let's get you into this thing."

I slid out of my jeans and pulled my T-shirt over my head as she unzipped the dress.

"You're so small," Jean mused, eying me up and down.

I wanted to tell her it was because I stopped eating after my parents died — lost my appetite and had to force myself to eat ever since then. It had nothing to do with wanting to be skinny and everything to do with the fact that after a few bites, I just felt sick.

My therapist had said it was part of the anxiety.

It was why I ate cake.

Cake made me happy, just like Sour Patch Kids. Though I couldn't eat a ton, it still made me feel joy in eating again.

"There." Jean zipped me up and placed the heels on the floor. I stepped in them and turned to face the mirror.

My mouth dropped open.

"Like I said, he'll love it." Jean winked in the mirror, and fastened about twenty different gold necklaces around my neck, with charms on them, ranging from long to short. "And before you argue, I've seen the way he looks at you. You intrigue him, and that's half the battle with a Hollywood actor. He's young, but he's still jaded."

I thought on her words.

Intrigue.

Didn't that mean I was a puzzle?

Would the old me have gotten Lincoln to turn his head? Or was the reason he was so curious the very fact that I was different?

"Ready!" Jean grinned.

My straight blonde hair fell past my shoulders, nearly touching my breasts. It was shiny but still had a nice bounce to it, rather than being glued to the sides of my head — which was how my hair normally looked whenever I tried straightening it.

Dark, long eyelashes caressed my cheeks as I gazed at myself in the mirror. I could feel each blink. I had pale pink lipstick and dark eyes, but the real difference was the sculpting.

It made me look twenty-five instead of seventeen.

Well, at least I finally looked legal!

"Knock 'em dead." Jean ushered me toward the door.

Lincoln was waiting on the other side, dressed in dark, skinny jeans and a nameless band V-neck T-shirt that showed off part of his arm and chest tattoo.

"Ready?" he held out his hand.

I took it and wobbled beside him. It had been ages since I'd worn heels.

I wanted to make a joke about Bo showing on his chest. But again, the words weren't there — they just weren't. Instead, I pointed to his chest and smiled.

He looked down. "Yeah, Bo's making an appearance."

"Finally!" Jaymeson pointed at both of us. "Lincoln, show her to her mark. Dani, for this scene you're simply staring at him like you want to eat him. Think you can do that?"

I nodded.

Any woman could do that.

Most men too.

"Cue music!" Jaymeson called out. "Action."

A techno mix of AD2's latest song filled the air as the extras started dancing around us. I stayed glued to the wall while Lincoln delivered his lines to Pris, and then he lifted his head, meeting my gaze.

It's just a movie. It's just a movie.

The breath left my chest on one slow exhale as he moved toward me, his body making fluid, purposeful movements through the crowd.

My lips parted; my entire body felt heavy as he approached.

He stopped in front of me, his forehead grazing mine as he leaned in a few inches. Our breath mingled as the music and scene faded around me.

"Cut!" Jaymeson yelled.

Holy crap on a cracker! I almost experienced my first stroke — at seventeen.

"You okay?" Lincoln's eyebrows knit together in concern.

I licked the lipstick from my lips and nodded quickly.

Jaymeson approached. "Time for the kiss, remember kissing, not hockey. Clearly, you were confused earlier."

Lincoln gritted his teeth and let out a little groan.

I patted his arm and grinned, my way of encouraging him. He seemed to pale more.

My stomach sank.

Maybe it was me.

I was the problem.

Not the kiss, but me. If he'd had trouble kissing my gorgeous sister, how was he going to be able to kiss me?

"Hey..." Lincoln cupped my cheek. "... focus on me, nothing else, alright? It's only us."

I nodded.

"You ever been to a party?"

I rolled my eyes.

"Ever made out with a guy at a party that wasn't your boyfriend?"

I thought about it then slowly shook my head.

"So that's what this scene is about. It's about a guy seeing a girl from across the room and wanting her so badly that he's willing to cheat on his own girlfriend for just one taste. Granted, he's supposedly drunk and high, but that just takes the romance out of it, doesn't it?"

He released my cheek and stepped back. "Imagine you're trying to attract me, make your body as inviting as possible. Hell, just stand there and look at me, and you'll sell it."

Sell it. I repeated the words in my mind.

I could do that.

Because I wanted him to kiss me.

It made my heart beat faster.

My blood pump harder.

And for the first time since my parents' death, I was actually excited about something. Nervous, but excited.

"Okay," I mouthed.

I must have surprised him again because his eyes darkened, and then he grinned. "One day, Dani. One day I'm going to hear my name coming from that gorgeous mouth of yours, and I'm not going to be held responsible for my actions… damn the consequences."

My breath hitched.

"Quiet on set! And action!"

There was no warning. Suddenly, Lincoln's mouth was fused against mine, no teeth, just his soft lips pushing, prodding, moving slowly back and forth until his tongue slid through and made contact with mine.

Heart racing, I opened my mouth enough to deepen the kiss as heat washed over me.

He groaned and dug his fingers into my shoulders then slid his hands down my back and gripped my butt. I let out a squeak of surprise as I flicked his tongue with mine.

"Cut!" Jaymeson yelled.

I kept kissing.

So did Lincoln.

His chest brushed roughly against mine; my breasts ached at the sharp contact. I let out a little hiss at the exact time Linc let out a groan and nudged his knee between my legs.

"Cut!" Jaymeson yelled again.

Slowly, Lincoln pried himself away from me, chest heaving.

"Good enough," said Jaymeson.

"No," Lincoln argued without taking his wild, grey eyes off me, "I went off script. We need to do it again."

"The hell you do," someone mumbled. I wasn't surprised to see Demetri glaring daggers at Lincoln's back. Alec was next to Jaymeson, giving him an earful. I noted the strong tick in his jaw.

"Fine." Jaymeson waved them both off. "We'll do it again."

"Take two, and action!"

This time the kiss was slow, languid in its movements. Hot waves of pleasure coursed through my body as his tongue slid seductively past my lips. His taste, the feel of his mouth was unlike anything I'd ever experienced. Greedily, I moaned, desperate for more of him as I reached for his shirt, fisting it with my hands and tugging him tighter against my body, wanting more contact with him. I felt every plane of muscle as he slowly turned us so his back was semi facing the camera. His knee nudged my legs apart as pressure increased down the middle of my body. I hadn't really looked long at the script, but I was pretty sure that this wasn't part of it.

Not that I was complaining.

He rocked into me, my back connected with the wall. With a possessive growl, he nipped my lower lip then started kissing down my neck. Kissing in public had never been my thing — but maybe that was because I'd never kissed Lincoln.

I would kiss him anywhere.

All he needed to do was ask.

Body humming with pleasure, I let out a little gasp as his warm lips met the pulse on my neck. Then his tongue licked where his lips had just been.

His knee rose higher and higher as my body sank onto his; the first contact of his leg had my body screaming with pleasure — just a little higher, just a little more.

"Cut!" someone shouted, though it didn't sound like Jaymeson.

Suddenly, Demetri was pulling Lincoln away from me and glaring daggers at both of us. "I think you guys got the scene."

Embarrassed, I looked down, tucking my silky hair behind my ear. Did I really almost just dry hump Lincoln Greene's leg? In front of about twenty people, including my sister?

"You sure?" Lincoln asked, voice hoarse. I glanced up at

him, his chest was heaving with exertion, his lips swollen. "Because I could have sworn I messed up my lines."

"There are no lines, you bastard," Demetri muttered under his breath.

"Damn it!" Jaymeson shouted. "Hey, guys, I'm going to need you to shoot it one more time. Remember, Lincoln, you're supposed to proposition her."

Lincoln grinned smugly at Demetri.

Demetri didn't move.

I sighed and then tapped him on the shoulder and nodded my okay.

"I saw tongue." Demetri pointed at Lincoln. "We both know that's not necessary. This isn't a brothel."

I almost burst out laughing at Demetri's knowledge of the word brothel. That, mixed with his protectiveness, wasn't something I was used to from him. He was usually too easy going.

"Places!" Jaymeson yelled.

Nervous anticipation trickled down my spine as the scene was slated, and Lincoln was facing me again, his features a mask of complete and utter seduction. Throat dry, I waited for the kiss.

Once his mouth was on mine again.

I realized.

His kisses weren't the type you could physically prepare yourself for — the feeling wasn't something my body would ever get accustomed to.

Lincoln's hands cupped my face and then tilted my cheek to the side as he whispered in my ear, "We should take this somewhere... private."

A foreign moan escaped between my lips, and his mouth was on mine again, this time his tongue outlining the seam of my lips before he tugged my lower lip with his teeth, drawing my body closer to his.

"Cut!" Jaymeson yelled.

Lincoln kept an arm around me as he led me back to the guys. My legs wobbled. Alec was pacing in front of Jaymeson like a worried mother, and Demetri was in the process of pulling off his shirt and dabbing his chest with napkins.

"My scene was that hot, huh?" Lincoln teased.

Demetri glared but continued to pat his tan, perfect body. "This… this is worry sweat, not hot, lustful, *holy-shit-it's-Lincoln-Greene* sweat, you vain, slutty, little piece of—"

"Good job." Jaymeson shoved Demetri out of the way, nearly sending him colliding with one of the crew. Cursing ensued as something loud clattered to the floor. I think that something was Demetri. "I think my favorite part was when a certain retired manwhore decided to ruin the entire scene with his mental breakdown."

Demetri dusted himself off, stood, and gave Jaymeson the finger.

I chewed my lower lip, still tasting Lincoln.

"Okay, Lincoln, it's back to Pris. We'll just film her reaction, and then you run after her, got it?"

I was left forgotten, suddenly extremely uncomfortable in my own skin, my dress too tight and hot, my lips still buzzing with awareness.

Alec came by me and stood as the next scene was slated.

His anger was so tangible I felt like I was swimming in it. He waited a few minutes before talking.

"He's really good at what he does," Alec whispered.

I gulped. Yeah, I'd gotten that part. He was a god at what he did. If kissing was an actual occupation, he'd have a doctorate.

"But…" Alec reached for my hand and gripped it.

I glanced up at him.

"… it's a job, Dani. It's…" He exhaled roughly. "… it's not real, you get that, right?"

I jerked my hand away in horror. I didn't have my phone on me so I couldn't type him the message I wanted to; besides, it would have a lot of cursing in it, and I knew that would amuse him more than anger him.

"Aw, don't get pissed." Alec grabbed my hand again, refusing to let me pull away this time. His grip tightened around my fingers. "I'm protective, okay? You're important to us, and I don't want you thinking that what just happened means anything beyond this scene today. I know you're a smart girl."

Then treat me like one! I wanted to yell.

"You're seventeen," he explained slowly as if I wasn't aware of my own stupid age. "You're so young still, and he's..." Alec shook his head and watched the scene play out. Lincoln went running after Pris. "He's Hollywood — they're born cynical and get even worse as the days progress. You don't want any part of that, no matter how nice it may look, or—" His eyes met mine. "—taste."

Was Alec Daniels really having a dad talk with me? And did he just say taste? Never in my life had I been so uncomfortable.

"Here." Demetri walked up and handed me my phone. It was a godsend. I sent a group text to both of them.

Dani: *If you start talking about the birds and the bees, I'm going to punch you in your perfect face.*

Demetri frowned down at his phone. "What did I miss?"

I jabbed a finger at Alec.

Alec chuckled. "Wow. I knew I was bad at heart to hearts, but I think I just managed to piss her off more."

Dani: *Most uncomfortable situation I've ever been in! And I've walked in on Jay and my sister!*

Demetri smirked. "Probably needed a magnifying glass to see anything on Jay though. Am I right?"

I rolled my eyes and crossed my arms.

"I was just warning her," Alec said in a hushed voice.

I stood between the two of them, jumpy and extremely uncomfortable. It was like having two really irritatingly hot and protective bodyguards. It wouldn't come as a shock if they sent me to a nunnery or decided to order one of those chastity belts, not that it mattered. Who screwed around with mute girls?

Tears threatened.

That was the worst part.

That Alec was right.

Lincoln was a good actor — a great actor.

He was doing his job.

He did it well.

Because for a few brief moments, I had felt like the most desired woman in the world. The way he'd looked at me had made me think it could possibly be true. And it was probably better for everyone that Alec was blunt with me about the type of guy Lincoln was.

Because as much as I kept my guard up — he made me want to tear down that wall just to see the other side. Just to remember what it felt like to be normal.

CHAPTER THIRTEEN

Lincoln

I'D MESSED UP.

Badly.

And I'd done plenty of stupid shit in my life, shit that could have landed me in prison or at least on probation.

If there was a list of the many sins of Lincoln Greene, her name would be at the top of it, circled in red pen, with the word LUST written in giant, all-capital letters next to it.

Double-freaking-shit.

I downed the last of my bottled water and tossed it in the trash while I waited for Pris and Jaymeson to finish the rest of the house scene, where the love fest between her and her real husband, Alec, had started.

My hands shook as I checked my watch, waiting for the damn day to end. I didn't want to have to see Dani. Seeing her would cause me to do something else stupid, like tell her I wanted to kiss her again.

Or worse, actually follow through without warning and scare the crap out of her.

Who did that? Just mauled a girl because he couldn't

control himself? The last time I'd lost control like that had been in the sixth grade when someone called my mom a whore.

Granted, it had been true. It had been all over the papers. But still.

It had pissed me off, so I beat the kid senseless, and when the teacher pulled me off him, I simply shrugged and said, "Should we go to the principal's office now?"

I had been a cocky little shit.

Acting had helped me grow out of some of the anger I'd felt at having such a public life. Weird how sometimes the cause can end up having a different effect.

"Hey!" Alec jogged over to me. Great, the absolute last person I wanted to talk to. He might as well be Dani's father with how protective he was of her. Almost as bad as Demetri, just less vocal about it.

Demetri told you he was going to shoot you then pulled the trigger.

Alec pulled the trigger first then said, *"Oh, by the way, you're dead."*

"She's seventeen." His first words.

"I know how old she is." I folded my arms across my chest. "I'm also aware she's a female. That was what you were going to say next, right? She's seventeen, underage, a female, off limits?"

His gaze narrowed. "Don't screw with her."

I rolled my eyes. "I'm an actor. I acted. That's my job, Alec." The lie tasted bitter in my mouth; my body screamed in outrage at the outright ridiculousness of the words pouring out. "She's just a girl."

"Really?" If anything Alec looked surprised as his blue eyes widened a bit. "That's all she is to you?"

"I'm her boss." I swallowed and looked away again. Thank God, Jaymeson was finishing up with his last line. "She's a great girl, but she's just a kid. Now, can you please stop thinking about where you're going to bury my body?"

"Seals." Demetri said from behind me. "I had some plans drawn up, paid a pretty penny for them too. Basically, you get eaten..."

I sighed.

"... and die," he finished.

"Good talk, guys, as always."

"Where's Dani?" Demetri ignored me and looked around.

"Last I saw she was—" Shit. Definitely not watching the scene a foot away from me.

Swallowing, she tucked her blonde hair behind her ear and gave us all a timid wave, then looked left, right, almost doing a little circle like she was confused, and walked off.

"Think she heard?" I whispered.

Demetri braced as if he was going to run after her, but Alec tugged him back.

"And if she did?" Alec asked. "What's it to you? She's just a kid, remember? Or were you lying?"

"And before you answer..." Demetri crossed his arms. "... seals, remember the seals."

"How?" I pushed away from them. "All I want to know is how the hell your wives live with you."

"Easy." Demetri smirked. "We're really good in bed. Any more questions? Oh, and the answer's no, I won't be giving you pointers, but if you want to know how to piss a girl off, pretty sure you just did it."

"Can't win for losing," I mumbled then took off after Dani.

I didn't have to go far. She was huddled on the steps of my trailer. I took a few cautious steps toward her.

Dani's head jerked up, and a smile flashed across her face. She typed on her phone then stood.

Dani: *Trailer's locked, need to grab my purse so I can go home. Unless you need me for something else?*

I did.

In fact, I wanted to make a list, and at the top of it? Making out like a teenager, something I hadn't done in years. Why make out when most girls I'd been with had been so aggressive the kissing had lasted maybe five minutes, and suddenly my pants were on the floor, and their tops were flying onto the nearest piece of furniture?

There was no savoring.

But Dani? I wanted to learn to savor.

Seventeen.

"Um, no." I shoved my hands in my pockets, my fingers coming into contact with my wallet and the tickets to Newport Aquarium my publicist had given me a few weeks ago.

She'd wanted me to go when I had a day's break from filming. Something about Shamu being back, and it being good PR to be friendly to the animals.

But I had a very serious whale... thing.

As in, I was a bit terrified of them.

So I'd told her she'd have to send someone else.

Dani started to walk off without her purse.

"Wait!" I quickly ran into my trailer, grabbed it for her then handed it over, all the while wondering how I was going to get her to spend more time with me.

She turned, her eyes cautious.

"The Newport Aquarium, how far is it?"

She frowned then started typing on her phone again.

Dani: *A few hours, why?*

"We need to go."

Yeah I just said we.

Dani: *We?*

I nodded. "It's a PR thing. I don't have any filming for

two days, so I thought you could take me and help me."

Dani: *You need help driving?*

My body felt itchy as I tried to think of a good excuse.

"No." I cleared my throat. "Not like that. It's just never smart for me to go out by myself. If I'm recognized and not with someone, I usually get mauled, but if people assume you're my girlfriend…"

Her eyes went completely dead.

As in the light that I'd somehow left there after she'd overheard me call her a girl — vanished.

She shook her head no.

"But…" I licked my lips. "… I'm paying you. Being my assistant is your job, and that includes doing things that sometimes you don't want to do."

I was actually blackmailing her to go to the aquarium with me — to see a whale that had the first name Killer, and all because I wanted to make it right.

Or kiss her?

Or just spend time with her?

Hell, I didn't even know anymore.

My phone buzzed.

I looked down.

Dani: *I'm only saying yes because I don't want you to fire me.*

I groaned aloud. "Dani, I'm not going to fire you."

Dani: *Pick me up tomorrow at six. We'll take my car. Unless you wanted to hire some sort of limo to cart your ass everywhere?*

I grinned at her limo comment.

"Would that make it easier for you to ride in the car?" I asked honestly.

She hesitated then rolled her eyes and typed more on her phone.

Dani: *All cars suck. But I've never ridden in a limo so jury's still out. Tomorrow.*

When I looked up, she was already walking away.

Without missing a beat, I clicked the home button on my phone and spoke. "Siri, what's the closest limo service?"

CHAPTER FOURTEEN

Dani

DREAMING OF LINCOLN WAS SO NOt what I needed. But dream I did. I dreamt of his kiss, I dreamt of his lips, and when I woke up in a cold sweat, my body ached with something I'd never really recognized before, almost like he'd awakened some sort of untapped passion or desire. Great, just great. Not only was I unable to speak, but now I was a sexually frustrated mute.

I glanced at the clock. Two a.m. Pris would kill me if I woke her up, especially since she had a really intense few scenes tomorrow with Jaymeson, another reason Lincoln had the next day and a half off.

It was Tuesday, and he didn't need to report back until Wednesday at noon.

I lay back against the headboard, slamming my skull softly against the fabric.

Just as I reached for my phone, it went off.

Lincoln: *Can't sleep.*
Dani: *You have a pig. Stop texting me.*

I dropped my phone onto the table and forced my eyes to close.

Sleep lasted until five when my annoying, chipper alarm woke me up. Lincoln had left me a text saying he'd meet me at my house, which was good since I was already dragging my feet. I quickly showered, pulled my hair into a low, messy bun, and threw on a vintage T-shirt with a pair of ripped jeans and my Converse. I looked seventeen.

A sharp pain sliced through my chest.

It wasn't as if I hadn't known Lincoln thought that way about me, but it still sucked hearing him say it out loud.

A girl.

I may as well be in overalls and pigtails.

Ugh.

The door to my sister and Jay's room was open, lights off, I vaguely remembered them saying they had a call time of five a.m. Sucked to be them.

With a grumble, I walked into the kitchen and yawned as I poured myself a cup of readymade coffee.

"Please, help yourself," a smooth male voice said from behind me.

I dropped the hot coffee all over my hand, and let out a little cry as a burn sizzled down the back of my right hand.

"Oh, shit." The unknown man made his way around the island in the kitchen and gently grabbed my hand, flipping the cold water on and shoving it underneath. "Typically, I make a better first impression than that."

I glanced up.

Zane Andrews.

The Zane Andrews was holding my hand under the faucet. If I wasn't shaking before, I sure was now.

I tried to jerk back, too embarrassed to even exist. I couldn't talk to him. I couldn't do anything. All I could do was stare at my angry, red hand and pray that he'd get amnesia.

Zane Andrews was…

Zane Andrews. If you said his name fast enough, it sounded like St. Andrews, which is how he got the nickname Saint from all his many Twitter followers.

He was the hottest thing to hit the music scene since Ashton Hyde, or, as I knew him, Gabe, had come out of hiding and started recording again.

And that had been huge news.

As in, it had been a year, and people were still talking about him.

But Zane Andrews? He was the equivalent of...

If Madonna and Lenny Kravitz decided to procreate...

... a sexy baby rock star would be born...

... and his name would be Zane.

With pitch-black hair and eerie golden brown eyes, he was seriously every woman's fantasy come to life.

At twenty-five, he'd already won over fifteen Grammys, and was said to be vacationing with friends while he took a much needed — oh crap — break.

Was Jay the friend?

I vaguely remembered him saying a friend might stop by for a few weeks.

But it had been months ago that we'd had that conversation.

Crap.

"Hey, you okay?" Zane's smile was kind, zapping any kind of embarrassment I'd once had.

With a quick nod, I jerked my hand free and stumbled backward, nearly colliding with the fridge.

"Whoa." He held up his hands in surrender. "I promise I don't bite."

I'd have expected him to say something whorish like. *"I promise not to bite... much."*

He didn't.

I also expected him to hit on me. Rumor had it; he even hit on eighty-year-old women — because he could.

Instead, he seemed, almost… shy.

With a gulp, he made his way toward me, holding out his hand. "I'm Saint, but my friends just call me Zane."

I took his hand then quickly held up my finger and grabbed the notepad I stashed in the kitchen just in case I needed to leave a note for Pris or Jay.

With shaky hands, I scribbled out a message.

Sorry. I don't know if Jay told you, but I don't exactly talk. As in, I can't. I'm mute, but it's nice to meet you, and I'm sorry I stole your coffee.

Zane moved to look over my shoulder, his eyes taking time to read every word before he glanced back at me and winked. "It's cool. I still can't sleep without a nightlight, so we all have our issues, now don't we?"

I let out a little laugh and nodded.

"Besides…" He was still extremely close to me, so close I could feel a wave of heat emitting from his large six-foot-four frame. "… sometimes, I think messages would be so much clearer without words getting in the way."

It was the perfect thing to say.

Maybe he was a saint.

My phone buzzed in my pocket.

"So," Zane moved around the island and poured another cup of coffee then brought it over to me. "… I hear you're Lincoln's new assistant. I hope he's not being an ass."

I held up my hand and flip-flopped it from side to side, indicating *so-so*.

Zane's laugh was soft. He gripped his ceramic mug tightly, the muscles in his tattooed forearms flexing.

Meanwhile, my phone kept buzzing.

"Yeah, well…" Zane lifted the cup to his mouth and drank then set it back down. "I'm sure you're more of a handful than you let on."

I smiled at that.

An angry knock pounded against the door, and then it nearly burst free from the hinges as Lincoln exploded through as if he was ready to tear someone apart.

"What the hell!" he roared. "Dani, I thought you'd been kidnapped or something. I texted. I called three times. I had to look for the damn hide-a-key. It freaked me out! Don't ever—" He stopped yelling and glanced at Zane then without a word stalked toward him.

"Saint?" He said it like a growl, his fists clenched tightly.

Zane looked up over his coffee cup and smirked. "Mother."

The next thing I knew, the coffee cup shattered against the counter as Lincoln punched Zane in the face. Twice.

I scrambled toward them, not sure what I could do to actually stop the two massive beasts and their caveman ways, but I worried about blood getting on the carpet.

The minute I reached them, Lincoln got up, dusted his jeans off then held his hand out for Zane.

"Thanks, man." Zane grinned.

"Yeah, well..." Linc ran his hands through his thick hair. "... you knew you had it coming."

"True." Zane winced as he dabbed his lip with his finger. "But could you have at least taken your ring off first?"

Lincoln nodded seriously. "Next time."

"Awesome." Zane groaned then stole my coffee and took a slow sip.

My jaw went slack. Were they friends? Enemies? Frenemies?

"You ready, Dani?" Lincoln popped his knuckles.

I frowned then threw my hands up into the air. *What the heck!*

"Don't worry about it, coffee girl." Zane winked. "Just old business that needed settling. Isn't that right, Linc?"

"Yup." Lincoln reached for my purse and a jacket then

grabbed a cap.

"Wow, never thought I'd see the day," Zane said under his breath.

"What was that?" Linc snapped.

"It's going to be a beautiful day." Zane smiled in my direction. Then, when Linc turned back around to open the door, he winked.

A white limo waited out front, back passenger door open and attended by an elderly man in a black suit and white gloves.

"Hope you don't mind," Linc said at my side. "But since you've never ridden in one, I thought, why not try and see if your car-riding experience gets better."

Happy that he'd done something so thoughtful, I had to hold back a squeal of delight as we piled into the plus-stretch limo.

The minute my butt hit those soft leather seats, I wanted to sigh and then take a really long nap. For some reason, maybe because the shape was different, but riding in the limo didn't affect me the way riding in a car did. My anxiety hadn't shot through the roof, and I wasn't ready to scream.

Wordlessly, Lincoln handed me a bottled water. I took a hit and watched as he clenched and unclenched his fist then shook it in the air.

I typed out a text then nudged him with my foot.

He glanced at his phone and smiled.

Dani: *WTH was that?*

"That? That was life."

And what? In life you were allowed to punch people at six in the morning?

Dani: *Are you guys friends?*

Lincoln snorted and took a long sip of coffee, his eyes piercing as he stared me down. "We're... amicable."

Big word.

It sucked that he had to miss out on all my lovely sarcasm just because I couldn't say it out loud, though I was sure the eye rolling and scowling was helpful.

"My sister... you may have heard of her, Angelica Greene? She's been after him for months, finally cornered him, and he may have turned her down..."

I frowned. So? Normal people got turned down all the time.

"In front of the media, and let's just say his words weren't kind, no matter how true. Shortly after that, according to my sources, she nearly relapsed, though she's good now. He's apologized, but I told him that I still had to defend her honor, so he said I could punch him next time I saw him."

Dani: *Guys are stupid.*

He burst out laughing. "Yeah well, nobody really defends Angelica... probably because nobody really likes her, and she's a bit crazy. But I'm her brother. It's my job to be protective. So the punches? He deserved them, even if he was right to turn her down."

I frowned.

"What?" Linc leaned forward. "What's on that pretty mind of yours?"

I would *not* react to his words.

My body didn't listen as a shiver ran down my spine while I typed out another message.

Dani: *He doesn't seem to be the type to turn anyone or anything down.*

A knowing look crossed over Linc's face as his eyes met

mine. "I don't know, looks can be very deceiving. Especially in our business. I think you'd be surprised."

Hmm.

"Hey." Linc snapped his fingers in front of my face. "No. I know that look. Don't go there. He asks you out, you say 'hell, no' and run in the other direction."

I giggled and shook my head as if to say *"Yeah right."*

"I'm serious." Lincoln set down his coffee and popped his knuckles. "Don't give me another reason to kick his ass."

I huffed.

"I mean, you're seventeen." Did he know any other numbers? Seriously? "He wouldn't dream of it, but still…"

The words stole the breath from my lungs.

He wouldn't dream of it because why? Because of my age? Or because I was mute? Or was I really just being that oversensitive?

"I mean…" Lincoln crossed his ankles, uncrossed them, fidgeted in his seat then looked at his phone. "… it's illegal and… shit."

Dani: *You're making me uncomfortable.*

"Yeah, well that makes two of us," he said under his breath. "I didn't get much sleep last night. I think I'm going to lay down for a few, alright?"

I nodded.

And tried not to watch him as he slowly lay down and put his baseball cap over his face, covering up his sinful mouth.

Was he really going to sleep?

I was tired, but not so tired that I was able to sleep or be that comfortable in his presence. Instead, I was left feeling a bit sick to my stomach.

I always tried to put on a brave face. And I'd like to think I'd done a really good job with it. The car swerved a bit. I gripped the leather with both hands and tried to ignore the sting of tears.

He hadn't made me uncomfortable.

He'd hurt me, and he didn't even realize it. Every time he said seventeen, it was like he was throwing my age back into my face. Most people live their entire lives without going through what I'd gone through, not that I was feeling sorry for myself, but he treated me like a kid.

When really? Sometimes I felt like I was an eighty-year-old woman, hiding out in her house, waiting for the rest of the world to pass by.

Waiting to die.

My stomach sank even more. Because really, that was how I felt sometimes, and the guilt at feeling that was more than I could bear. I needed to be happy for Pris, for Jay, for the new little baby on the way.

My feelings *felt* selfish because they were.

And it was stupid of me to think I could suddenly just be okay, but sometimes I felt like I was only going through the motions. I brushed my teeth because I had to. I ate because I had to, which my therapist had said meant I actually wanted to live.

I left out the part that I'd started eating again because of the look of panic on Jays' face and the hurt in Pris's eyes.

I ate for them, not me.

I got out of bed for them, not for me.

I lived because my parents didn't, yet sometimes at night, when I couldn't sleep, I had to wonder if God had messed it up.

Gah. I let my head fall back against the leather a few times, bouncing up and down as I stewed. I hated self-pity. I drank more coffee and tried to focus on the positive. I was in a limo with a hot guy.

A famous hot guy who thought I was a child.

But at least I was still in the limo, and he'd ordered me

coffee, and for once in my life I got to experience a kiss, that for a few brief moments had made me feel alive again.

My phone buzzed.

Jay: *Zane said he freaked you out this morning, and you burnt your hand. You okay?*

I glanced down at my hand. It was still red, but honestly, being with Linc had made me forget all about it.

Dani: *I'm good. Hand's fine. How long is Zane staying?*
Jay: *Not sure, at least a month. We'll see how long he wants to take off. He needed an escape.*
Dani: *Great.*
Jay: *He's a good friend, didn't want him in a hotel, plus he'd get mobbed in a minute, and he hates staying alone.*
Dani: *Staying alone?*
Jay: *Forget I said that please? He'd be pissed. Have fun at the aquarium. Don't kill my star.*
Dani: *Damn, probably shouldn't have added arsenic to his eggs this morning. Oh well, we'll always have that one kiss.*
Jay: *Ha ha. And if he kisses you again, you bite his lip, love.*
Dani: *As in a love bite?*
Jay: *As in bite it off, spit it out, run like hell, and let me finish him off.*
Dani: *Thanks, Dad.*

I gasped as I realized through blurry eyes what I'd just typed.

Jay's text back was immediate.

Jay: *You know I'm going to be the hottest father in the history of the universe.*

I laughed softly as he sent me an emoji that said *Number*

One Dad. He always knew what to say to make me feel better.

> Dani: *So very true.*
> Jay: *Love you.*

I sent him a pink heart.

> Dani: *You too.*

CHAPTER FIFTEEN

Lincoln

"I'M SORRY." HANDS SHAKING, I BLOCKED my view with the brochure and pretended to be interested in the mating penguin exhibit. What the hell? "I really can't do this."

Dani tugged the loop on my jeans.

"Rip them off. See if I care."

She kept pulling.

"I've got almost a foot on you, Dani, no chance in hell. It's time to go. We've seen everything but a mermaid. Let's just go."

Her foot stomped down on the top of mine.

Sharp pain radiated upward toward my shin.

"Son of a—"

The brochure was ripped from my hands. She stood in front of me bracing for a fight. I'd never seen her look more beautiful. Face flushed, chest heaving, eyes blazing.

Holy shit, I wanted to devour her on the spot.

I suddenly forgot why I was so freaked out.

My eyes zeroed in on her mouth.

Her lips parted.

If that wasn't an invitation, I didn't know what was. I gulped, reaching for her face.

Just as a giant wave of water collided with her back and my front, nearly exposing just how much I wanted her body glued to mine.

"Sorry about that! Whales can get kind of feisty."

Oh good, something I had in common with the giant demon currently splashing its tail a few feet away.

"You guys ready?" The trainer hopped out of the water like a freaking seal on crack and giggled.

"No," I croaked. "Not. Ready." Words. I needed to find more words. Did I mention I was going to kill my publicist?

"Oh." The trainer laughed. "But the kids will be so disappointed if their favorite star doesn't at least do one trick with us!"

As if on cue, the crowd of kids in the audience cheered and started chanting my name.

"One, just…" I held up my finger. "… one minute."

Clothes drenched, I squeaked my way back toward the fence, pulling Dani with me.

"I can't do this."

She sighed and glanced back at the crowd. I really needed her encouragement right now, and the part that sucked was that she had no words to give me, nothing. I felt stupid and selfish for needing both.

"I'm scared of whales," I mumbled.

She cupped her ear.

I rolled my eyes as she leaned in.

"Scared—" I coughed into my hand. "—of whales."

Her grin had me feeling like a teen who'd just been caught staring too hard at his hot math tutor.

"Ready?" The trainer bounced back. Could someone — anyone — just shoot a whale tranq into her ass or something?

Dani reached for my hand and squeezed it. I expected her to let go, but instead, she gripped it as if she was going to go into the water with me.

Granted, we had our shoes off. It was one step.

When I told my publicist we were going to go use the tickets, she'd called ahead and let them know I'd be more than happy to do a surprise appearance during the afternoon water show. Lucky for me, I didn't have to swim with a whale.

All I had to do was feed one.

I had graphic blood filled visions of falling into his giant mouth and being no more.

"Yay!" The trainer bounced up and down a few times, making me feel nauseated, or maybe it was just the whale, Zoe, the one currently swimming around and jolting itself into the air.

"You kids ready?" Another trainer screamed into the microphone. "Let's give a huge round of applause to Lincoln Greene!"

I gave a weak wave at the crowd as Dani tugged me toward the first step into the giant whale pool.

"Here you go." The trainer held up a bucket. "Zoe's going to splash you guys again and open her mouth. You'll toss the food in, and when you're finished with that, all you need to do his hold up your hand for a high five. She'll close her mouth, chomp down on the food and do a trick."

As long as my body wasn't involved in that trick.

The bucket was shoved into my free hand. I clenched Dani harder. She leaned into my side then started humming *Jaws*.

"Not funny," I said through clenched teeth.

She hummed louder.

Great.

A giant black-and-white blob freaking flew through the water at breakneck speed, stopping right in front of us, splashed with her giant-ass fin, then opened her mouth wide.

Teeth. She had teeth.

And so many of them.

I got dizzy just thinking about them. Who cared if they're flat? They were still teeth, and it wasn't the teeth as much as it was the jaw that had me freaked.

Dani nudged me.

I released her hand and dug the small fish out of the bucket and dropped them into Zoe's mouth.

She held it open.

Hand still shaking, I lifted it into the air to make a high five.

Without warning, she splashed us again.

"Uh oh!" The trainer said in the microphone. "It seems Zoe wants a kiss!"

"Not a chance in hell," I hissed.

"Kiss! Kiss! Kiss!" The kids chanted along with the trainer as if it wasn't a legit life-and-death issue.

They kept chanting. I couldn't move.

Dani quickly knelt on her knees, soaking her jeans as she leaned over the water, holding her head so close to the whale I was freaked she was going to get bit. But the whale didn't move. In fact, she seemed to enjoy Dani's closeness.

Dani closed her eyes and rubbed her nose against the whale's skin as if to show me it was okay.

Slowly, I lowered myself to their level and leaned in. Zoe smelled like fish. Any fast movements and I was going to have a legit issue with passing out and drowning in the giant pool.

"Kiss! Kiss! Kiss!" the audience kept shouting.

Dani tugged my face down to the whale; my lips were inches away from Zoe's skin. Next, Dani shoved my face into the whale. It wasn't even a kiss as much as it was a push with my lips against its rubbery skin. She pulled me back then launched herself into my arms.

And kissed me.

I forgot all about the whale.

In the distance I heard cheering and a splash. I assumed Zoe had done her trick, but I was busy doing one of my own.

Without hesitation, I lifted Dani against my chest. Her feet dangled against my shins as I swung her around and kissed her harder, needing her more than my next breath.

Her mouth was just as I remembered, hot, sweet and so inviting it was hard to pull back.

The trainer next to me coughed. "Children present."

Dani slid down my hard body as I slowly released her and mouthed, *"Thank you."*

She winked.

"Really, you saved my life," I whispered.

She burst out laughing as the kids laughed and cheered.

"So…" Dani licked her lips. "… scared of whales, huh?"

My mouth dropped open at the same time hers slammed shut, as if she'd just realized she'd spoken out loud.

The trainer, clearly not realizing the epic moment, tried to engage us in conversation. "Thanks so much for coming and—"

"Yeah, yeah." I nodded and shook her hand while trying to steer Dani away. "Thanks again. We have an appointment."

We walked hand in hand toward our discarded shoes and socks. Dani didn't say anything. I wanted her to, but I didn't want to push her either. My heart was pounding so hard my chest ached.

Once we were away from the crowd and alone, I turned to her and said the only thing on my mind, "Your voice is the most beautiful thing I've ever heard."

CHAPTER SIXTEEN

Dani

ADRENALINE SURGED THROUGH MY BODY. MY voice! That was my voice! A voice I hadn't heard outside my head in months! I wanted to shout in victory, yell at the top of my lungs. But instead, my knees knocked together and spots clouded my vision as Lincoln lifted me up into his arms and carried me down the stairs.

I blinked my eyes as the angry, black clouds started moving in our general direction.

Cold rain splattered against my face before Lincoln walked us down into a small alcove.

Chilled, I couldn't stop my teeth from chattering as he set me on my feet directly in front of the penguin exhibit.

It was freezing in there.

But we were alone.

"Dani?" He cupped my face. "Are you going to pass out?" His eyebrows knit together in concern as he backed me against the wall.

I could almost taste him again — wanted to — but then he'd be on to me. He'd know I wanted more of his kisses.

Was it so wrong to want a kiss from someone like him? A real kiss? Not one that was forced or acted out — but a kiss made of passion and spontaneity?

I nodded my head, swallowing the dryness in my throat.

"That was..." His eyes lit up with awe. "... that was insane... right?"

"The whale or this?" My voice was barely above a whisper as my treacherous eyes zeroed in on his mouth.

Linc leaned in, pushing my hair out of my face. "Both, but for the record, I forgot all about the whale the minute I heard your voice."

I smiled at that.

"Is it hard?" He eyed me gently, almost like I was a piece of china about to teeter off a table and shatter into a million pieces.

I'd thought it would be nice to be on that side of his looks, but something in me felt disappointed; maybe it was because he was looking at me in reverence as a result of my talking, not because of me.

Then again, I've always been hard on myself.

I shrugged.

"Nope." He grinned. "Not gonna let you default. At least say 'I don't know.'"

I licked my lips. "No."

"Okay, that works," he said with a tender chuckle. "Has this ever happened before? You know, where a dead-sexy actor, afraid of whales inspires you so much that a miracle occurs, and you say your first words in—" He tilted his head in question.

I rolled my eyes, even though I was so nervous I felt like I was going to puke. Texting was one thing, talking to him was... well, difficult would be an understatement.

"Eight months." Saying it out loud made it seem so much worse than I'd originally thought. Almost as if I was finally admitting that there was this huge elephant blocking my way out of the room. My hands went to my throat. Lincoln was still staring at me in shock, so I immediately went into sarcastic, defensive mode. "And, for the record, it was probably brought on by the whale... don't go tweeting that you're magic or anything. That's not what the world needs, Linc."

His jaw went slack.

I frowned and shoved my hand into my jeans. Crap, I hoped I hadn't just taken it too far. I'd seriously turned into a really sarcastic person since I stopped talking, maybe because I was my only source of entertainment. "What?"

"Holy shit, you've been talking for three minutes, and you've already insulted me." He held up his hand for a high five.

"I'm not hitting that. Imagine the places it's been," I teased, this time my words flowing a bit easier.

"Same place as you, sweetheart. A whale's mouth." He shivered.

"I'm sure that's not the worst place." I patted him on the shoulder.

"Ha!" He gave a dry laugh and rolled his eyes. "Jealous?"

"Immensely."

"I didn't expect you to be funny."

"And I didn't expect you to be afraid of fish, yet here we are."

"Mammals," he corrected, eyes narrowing. "They're mammals."

"Look at you getting all defensive of Zoe. Should I go let her know you want another round?" I turned on my heel but was pulled back by my T-shirt.

"Zoe's sleeping."

"You sure?"

"Yeah, she communicates telepathically and made sure I got the message before almost eating me."

"That was nice of her."

"Whales are givers." Linc's gaze dropped to my lips.

My eyes darted to his.

What was happening right now?

"Seventeen," he whispered. I almost didn't catch it.

"What was that?"

"Clean." His eyes traveled the length of my body from my feet to my head. "We should probably… shower."

"Right."

"Separately."

"Because you normally shower with the help?"

"Ha ha." He choked out a strangled laugh. "Should we go?"

Lincoln walked around me and held open the door. The minute we stepped outside, a woman and three kids barreled into me, sending me sideways into Linc. His strong hands gripped my shoulders.

"Sorry!" The haggard mom blew her bangs out of her face as all three of her kids ran into the penguin exhibit. "They get kinda crazy over penguins."

"I know the feeling," Lincoln whispered, his lips grazing my ear.

I don't know how long I stayed staring at the door, or how long Lincoln held me like that, but our little moment, or whatever it was, was interrupted by more screaming, only this time it was directed Lincoln.

"Lincoln Greene!" a pre-teen squealed.

His fingers dug into my skin as he used me for a human shield. Classy.

"Think we can run?" he asked, already backing away, with me still blocking the way of the girls as they grouped together and started pounding the pavement toward us.

I didn't have time to respond as we were flooded with screams and laughter. Cell phones pointed into the air snapping pictures of us. They asked for his autograph and then, once the excitement died down, glared in my direction.

"Who are you?" One girl, who looked about ten, put her

hands on her hips and glared.

I wanted to say, *"Nobody."*

I opened my mouth and... nothing.

Deflated, I just shook my head and gave Linc a pleading look.

"She's my assistant for the summer."

Dismissed.

Like we hadn't just shared a few moments.

Why did I keep doing that to myself? Oh right, because I loved torture. I nodded emphatically and quietly stepped away so he could finish signing autographs.

The rain was coming down in sheets by the time he was done. I'd been hiding underneath an alcove while mud and water splattered my tennis shoes.

I had to give it to him. He didn't once complain, just kept taking pictures even though his shirt was clinging to his abs like a second skin, and his skinny jeans left absolutely nothing to the imagination.

It was bordering on indecent.

Even the moms were stopping now and taking pictures. I inclined my head to the side as Lincoln let out a loud laugh and signed a girl's shirt.

My breath hitched. He had a gorgeous laugh. Was there anything ugly about the man?

Even the way he walked was captivating.

And he was currently walking toward me.

It was one of those moments I prayed I looked cool and nonchalant, leaning against the trash cans that smelled like old hot dogs and wet dog hair.

"Sorry." He ran his fingers through his wavy hair, slicking it back, then shook some droplets out. I imagined it wouldn't be a stretch to see girls trying to lick the water out of the air.

I nodded.

"What? No words of sarcasm?"

Smiling, I opened my mouth to say something just as his

cell went off.

"She's fine, Jay. I'm fine. Everyone's fine," he sang, winking in my direction. "Oh." His face went from easy going to tense as his eyes darted back and forth between me and some imaginary object in front of him. "No, problem. We'll figure it out."

He ended the call and gave me a long, heated stare.

"Jay?" I offered.

"You should have been a detective in another life." He wrapped an arm around me and led us toward the exit.

"Yeah, my hearing his name had nothing to do with knowing who was on the other end of the line. I just calculated the minutes we'd been gone and divided that by the distance traveled — and boom — Jamie Jaymeson, calling to check in at exactly three in the afternoon."

"You're kind of a smart ass." Linc nodded his head in approval. "I like it. No wonder you and Demetri are best friends."

"Told you it wasn't just the Sour Patch Kids."

"That you did." He sent a quick text, I imagined to our driver, and then faced me. "So Jay wants us to stay the night."

"At his house?" I asked, confused. I mean, I lived there. Why would I need an invitation from my own family?

"No." Linc licked his lips.

I tried desperately not to follow with my hungry gaze. "Here in Newport. Apparently, a huge storm's coming in, and your sister's freaked about us driving. Flash flood warnings have already been issued, and because of the whole..." He gulped, looking away.

"Because of my parents' accident, you mean?"

Linc's eyes flashed with regret. "Yeah, she just... didn't want you to have a relapse like last time."

My cheeks burned with embarrassment. "Last time."

"You don't have to tell me."

"What's there to tell?" I looked down at my muddy shoes.

RACHEL VAN DYKEN

"There was a storm, we drove in it, I was so freaked out we were going to get into a car accident that I hyperventilated, nearly passed out, then started screaming hysterically when another car's headlights flashed us because our high beams were on." I let out a long exhale, counting to five before continuing. "It was shortly after I stopped talking, so somehow she thinks the whole car nearly hitting me then us being in that thunderstorm just compounded the whole mute thing."

Linc grabbed my hand. "You're not mute."

"Not with you. But ask me to talk to the milkman, I'd probably shriek and run in the other direction."

Linc winked. "Probably because they don't exist anymore, and seeing one out in the wild would be like a whale walking on land."

"It happens you know, whale walking," I teased.

"Right up there with milk delivery and VHS tapes making a comeback." Linc nodded. "But thanks for the visual that's going to permeate my dreams tonight."

I giggled as the limo pulled up to the front entrance.

"So, where are we staying? In the limo?"

Linc burst out laughing. "Hell no. Do I look like the type of guy who would sleep in a car?"

I eyed his wet shirt and shaggy hair then met his gaze and gave him a tentative shrug.

"So I look like shit. Message received. Let's go freshen up, then it's time for crabs."

I gasped. "I'm not that kind of girl."

Linc's cheeks reddened instantly. "Are you implying I have crabs?"

"Hey, you said it, not me." The talking was getting so much easier.

"I think I liked you better mute."

I didn't take offense to that. I knew he was kidding, and it helped that when he said it, he didn't take his eyes off my mouth.

CHAPTER SEVENTEEN

Lincoln

HER VOICE WAS REALLY PRETTY. IT wasn't what I'd expected. When I'd overheard her talking on the street in front of my apartment, it had been muffled, distorted. In all the times I'd imagined her talking since then, her voice had always sounded low in my head. I don't know why, maybe because Pris's voice was low and a bit throaty?

But Dani's? It was lyrical.

I could listen to her talk all day.

I was probably getting pneumonia from being out in the rain —the only explanation why I was staring at her mouth like I wanted to actually taste the words as she spoke them across my lips.

All the wrong parts of me twitched with excitement.

One in general that was making things... hard, not difficult, hard...

Shit.

"I've never stayed overnight in Depot Bay," she offered, glancing out the window as she tied her hair back into a low bun. Her vintage shirt rose just above her hips, giving me a glimpse of her tan skin. I barely held in my whimper as I tried to adjust the way I was sitting without her catching on.

"Me either." That was all I had to offer her. Two words and the distinct impression that, while she was turning into quite the conversationalist, I was suddenly without the ability to string full sentences together that didn't include words like lick, bite, nip.

"Linc?"

I jumped. When had she started calling me Linc? I loved it.

Hell, every physical part of me responded to my name coming from her lips as if I'd never heard a woman say my name before.

"What's up?" My hoarse voice was a dead giveaway. I prayed she was innocent enough to think nothing of it and just assume I was catching some sort of disease that would render my voice useless. Damn, where was a good head cold when I needed it? At least I'd have to stay away from her — away from temptation.

"Are you okay?" Her little bow-shaped lips pressed together, giving me the distinct impression she was trying not to say more. Damn, I would sell my soul to lick those lips.

Mute was safe.

Mute meant I didn't really know her personality or at least only knew what she felt like showing me through text and body language.

Now that she had words? A whole different line of communication opened, and with that, the freaking floodgates burst open and now I was screwed. So. Very. Screwed.

The limo pulled to a stop in front of the condo that I'd been forced to rent last minute. It overlooked the tiny town of Depot Bay. Add in the view of the Pacific Ocean as it crashed against the rock bridge in downtown, and it was idyllic, romantic, probably not the best choice I could have made, but it was private, and after today, being recognized in public was the last thing I needed or wanted.

"I'm great," I answered about five minutes later, as if I was a slow learner and had just comprehended the words she'd spoken. Things were going downhill fast, and I had to spend the night with her.

Crap. Bad, *bad* word choice. My body tingled all over with anticipation. *Down, boy.*

And no matter how many times I looked at her and thought about her age, it's like it didn't register on any level.

All I saw were her lips.

And that damn mouth as it moved, forming words, captivating every part of me and making me yearn to hear more.

Why wasn't she making a bigger deal of this? Hell, why wasn't I calling Jay and telling him that whatever had been her issue, she was basically healed?

"Sir." Our driver opened our door and helped Dani out and then me. "The key was left under the mat, and the entire kitchen has been stocked to your specifications. I'll pick you up at seven a.m. and take you directly to set."

"Great." I shook his hand. "Thank you."

He gave a brief nod and turned away.

Dani stared wide-eyed at the two-story building; her cheeks flushed as a gust of wind and rain hit her small body. "You have an ice cream parlor downstairs."

"Don't forget the store of knickknacks." I pointed to the left where a small store sat nestled between an ice cream/coffee shop.

"I love it." Eyes bright, she placed her hands on her hips. "It seems so secluded."

I snorted. "That's because it is." I nodded toward the stairway leading up to the condo. "Now let's get inside before you freeze to death, and Jay charges me with murder."

"He's not that dramatic."

"Right, he yelled at me for eating sushi in front of his

pregnant wife because that's normal. Did I forget to mention he slapped my plate out of my hand?"

Dani reached for the railing and laughed. "Yeah well, he tends to get a bit carried away sometimes."

I followed the sway of her hips, the ones I shouldn't have even been looking at, as she made her way up the stairs.

"I'm just thankful he didn't know me in high school. He would have probably tried murdering my first boyfriend."

"Elliot," I spat. Bastard needed to get in line. "Whatever. He's a kid."

"I'm a kid..." Dani turned around and glared. "... or at least that's what you keep referring to me as. It's either kid or assistant or — and this is my favorite—" She lowered her voice and drew her eyebrows together. "Seventeen."

I actually felt my face redden.

When had I ever been embarrassed?

And by a teen?

"Well," I sputtered, "you're..." My hands did a weird flailing thing in front of my body. "... young." I choked out the last part as my eyes zeroed in on her perky breasts. Great, just give me a van and let me park it outside the local high school. I pinched the bridge of my nose and let out a pitiful groan.

"It's fine." Dani smiled warmly. "I'm over it. Promise." Her grin was tight. I highly doubted she was over me insulting her, but I didn't want to push things, because, in my current state, I'd probably blurt out that I was attracted to her and end up in prison.

I was being dramatic.

Then again, I was an actor... so...

I quickly snatched the key from under the mat and jammed it into the lock, pushing the door open once it clicked.

The condo had floor-to-ceiling windows facing the ocean and a gourmet kitchen with white granite and white wooded cabinets. The floor was a dark oak stain, and every piece of furniture was a nautical theme, right down to the blue cloth couch decorated with coral pillows.

"Hungry?" I tossed the key onto the counter and shook the rain out of my hair. "I can whip something up."

"Can you?" Dani laughed. "It cooks?"

"Ha." I nodded. "Nice. Am I the *it*?"

She made a face and pointed at my mass of hair. "Well, you look a bit haggard. Maybe shower, and I'll start cooking."

"Ah, so she cooks?" I grinned. "See what I did there? *She* because you're a girl?"

"Seventeen." She winked. "Don't forget that very important part of the scenario, not that I think you're in danger of it, considering you repeat it to yourself when you think I'm not listening."

"Question." I braced my hands against the granite and leaned forward. The smell of rain floated through the room. "Have you always been this snarky?"

"Always." Her blonde head bobbed.

I fought to keep my grin small, so as to not scare her into thinking I was going to attack her or turn into the Joker, because, I couldn't stop smiling in her presence. She just seemed so... alive. And in days previous, it was as if death was a better description of the way she carried herself. "Is it getting easier?" I asked softly while she chewed on her thumbnail, like a teenager. At least she was reminding me of one, the way she was focused in on gnawing the thing off and ignoring me.

"What?" She dropped her hand and stared me down, her blue eyes penetrating mine with such clarity I averted my gaze.

"The talking." I licked my lips and stole a glance at her mouth.

"Only when you stare at my mouth like I have something on it."

Damn, I wish she did have something on it — me. "Sorry."

"It's okay," she said in a quieter voice. "So cleanup and then crabs?"

"Is this your way of getting me to change the subject?"

She pushed away from the counter and breezed past me, making her way toward the fridge. "Yeah." She poked her head inside. "I figure if I talk about it, then I may freak myself out or jinx myself. I know it's a huge deal, really. Jay and Pris would freak, not to mention Demetri. I imagine he'd dedicate a song to me or something, at least pet a bird."

It was hard to keep up. "Pet a bird? What?"

She pulled her head back from the fridge and grinned. "It's true he really is that terrified, I wasn't exaggerating."

"Noted." I crossed my arms, staring at her because it seemed so natural. Talking, being in the kitchen, making dinner.

I could get used to that. God knew I needed normal in my life after having such a demented childhood and not being able to stay in one place for any length of time.

I wanted to take her out.

But not in my truck.

I made a mental note to have my car brought up from Malibu.

"It is a big deal, Dani," I whispered.

Her hand gripped the front of the fridge, tight enough for her fingers to turn white. Hanging her head, she slowly closed the door and leaned against it, letting out a soft, "I know."

"And being scared..." I took a cautious step toward her. "... it's normal, you know? I mean, this is the first time you've spoken in a while and I can't imagine what's going through your head right now."

She let out a painful laugh. "A lot."

I reached out to her, meaning to touch her arm; I tugged her against my body and kissed her instead. "Ignore the fear. Embrace the triumph."

Her body relaxed against mine. "How do I do that?"

"Easy." I ran my hands slowly up and down her arms. "You choose to look at the mountains rather than trying to concentrate on the valleys. It's easier to glance behind you and see the peaks, but it takes actual effort to look down into the darkness of where you've been."

"Sage advice." Dani pulled away, tilting her head up toward mine. "Thanks, old man."

I knew she was teasing, but I had the sudden feeling that she was twisting the knife into me while I reached for my walker and reading glasses. Holy shit, was this how she felt when I called her young?

The thought stung, and I pulled back. "Okay, so I'll stop making a big deal out of your age if you never call me old again." I popped my knuckles.

"Careful," she teased, her eyes glinting with mischief, "you may get arthritis."

I choked out a "Ha" and shook my head. "And, for the record, I'm not old. I'm only a few years older than you."

"I know." She rolled her eyes. "My point exactly. Stop treating me like I'm still in diapers. I own a thong for crying out loud, and I'm pretty sure I can kiss the crap out of you so…" She nodded. "… no more talk about talking tonight. Let's just… hang."

Hang? How about strip? That sounded like a much better option.

Thong. Diaper. Kiss. Hell, my brain didn't know what to focus on anymore.

"I'll just… go get cleaned up." I turned on my heel, nearly running into a wood beam I could have sworn had appeared out of nowhere. Sidestepping it, I ducked through the bathroom door and slammed it behind me. Thank God, it was the actual bathroom and not the closet.

"Focus." I stared at my reflection in the mirror. "Seventeen." Yeah, that number no longer had any effect on me. Well, damn.

CHAPTER EIGHTEEN

Dani

HE'D FINALLY LEFT. NOT THAT I wanted him gone, I just needed some time alone to process the fact that, in the last two hours, I'd said more sentences than I'd manage to accomplish in the past year.

Deep breaths. That's what my therapist always said. *"And when that fails, try counting to ten while envisioning yourself walking along the beach and watching the waves."*

Sometimes it felt like psychobabble crap.

But right now? I needed something — anything — to center me. I quickly glanced out the window and started counting the waves as the tide rolled in, my hand clenching my cell phone.

I felt guilty that the first time I'd talked was with a Hollywood actor who was basically paying me to get his coffee, while I couldn't say one thing around my sister or brother-in-law, or even my best friends.

My brain hurt from trying to figure it out.

Was this just a special one-time thing? Or was I suddenly going to be completely fine? Was it the whale? Lincoln? The kissing?

Maybe that was it. He was my long lost prince, and I was the princess. His kiss was magic. Ha. Only in fairy tales. And in those, the mute girl didn't star or win the hot guy — she was usually the best friend to the princess or the maid.

My phone buzzed in my hand. A text from Demetri, because why call when he wouldn't be able to hear my voice?

"Just do it," I whispered to myself, staring down at the phone. Some part of me needed to test it to see if it was real. But I knew if I tried with Jay or Pris, they'd just freak out that I was calling. That was another thing. If I called, it meant I was basically dying.

If I called twice.

I was already dead.

Taking a deep breath, I pushed Demetri's number and brought the phone to my ear. It felt natural. Like it should. It rang, once, twice, three times.

"Holy shit, Dani. Are you okay? Just start yelling if you need me to call 911. Or play loud music. Shit, shit, shit. Clap your hands, you hear me, Dani? Clap one for ass dialing. Clap two for cops!"

"And if I clap three times?" I joked.

The phone went silent.

"Demetri?" I frowned and brought the phone down to see if I'd gotten disconnected, but he was still on the line. "Demetri."

"D-Dani?"

"Oh sorry, she can't come to the phone right now. Can I take a message?"

"You always were a smart ass." He chuckled and then laughed so hard I had to pull the phone away from my ear. "Holy shit, you're talking! I've missed that sexy voice of yours."

I rolled my eyes. "Seventeen."

"Please tell me that's not his nickname for you? Damn, I

should have backed off with the whole *seals are going to eat you if you seduce her* thing."

"Wait, what?" Sometimes it was hard to keep up with him. And now that he was talking, not texting, I found it almost impossible.

"Linc." Demetri said his name like an expletive. "I basically told him if he touched you, I was going to throw his body to the starving seals, and they'd kill him."

"Seals like fish, not humans."

"He's an actor. It's not like he's the brightest crayon in the box."

"This from the guy who cried when a seagull landed on his head last year."

"HE KNEW MY NAME!" Demetri shouted.

"*Heeee...*" I drew out the word. "...was making normal seagull noises. Not once did he utter a *D*."

"Whatever. I'm not arguing with you over that seagull. He freaking stalks me, you know this. He has white on his head."

I sighed. "All seagulls have white... You know what? Never mind."

He was silent for a minute and then, "Dani?"

"Yeah?" My heart pounded against my chest.

"Don't go away again, okay?"

Tears welled in my eyes, threatening to spill over. "I'll try not to."

"I won't ask now... but I will ask later... about how this happened, because it matters to me, and it should matter to you, but the most important thing is you're talking. Want me to tell Jay and Pris?"

I wiped the tears from my cheeks. "I'll tell them, if I can. When I get home."

"Hey," Demetri said softly, "none of that. You'll be able to. I promise."

My throat clogged with more tears, tightening so much it

was painful to breathe. "And if I can't?"

"Then we figure it out. But at least now you know one thing."

"Oh, yeah?"

Demetri laughed. "Yeah, apparently all you needed was a nice, hot kiss from Lincoln Greene to loosen those lips of yours."

"Two kisses."

Silence.

More silence.

"What the hell?!" he screamed. "That bastard! I'll kill him!"

Lincoln made his way out of the bathroom.

"Oops, gotta go. Love you!"

"He touch you? If he even lays one fing—"

I hung up on him and shoved my phone in my back pocket.

"Hey." Lincoln wiped some of the excess water from his neck and moved the towel down his chiseled abs.

Mouth dry, I didn't know where to look. If I made eye contact, it seemed like I was trying too hard not to stare at all of those tightly corded muscles just ripping around his midsection. And if I stared, then he'd know it.

I settled on an awkward flinch, a guttural moan, and turned around to watch the rain pound the window. "It was Demetri."

I knew the minute Lincoln made his way over to me; it wasn't just the smell of fresh lavender soap or the fact that he towered over me — it was him. His heat, his magnetism, his everything.

Swallowing my nerves, I turned to glance at him out of the corner of my eye. Still shirtless.

Still sexy.

I swallowed a gulp and met his amused gaze. "What?"

"I asked what he said."

RACHEL VAN DYKEN

"Oh…" Probably while I was checking him out for the second or third time. "… he was excited then started getting off topic. You know Demetri. One minute I can talk and a miracle occurs, the next he's yelling about seagulls and calling you a bastard."

"Me?" Linc's grey eyes twinkled. "Why me? What did I do? Aren't I the great healer in all of this?"

I snorted. "You wish."

"It does make me feel better about my life's accomplishments. Think I can put that on my resume?"

"Wow, never knew your ego was as big as Jay's." I pushed past him, a smile tickling the corners of my mouth.

"All things are bigger where I'm concerned," he said in a low voice.

Ignoring him and the goosebumps popping up all over my skin, I motioned toward the kitchen. "Didn't you say you were going to cook crabs?"

"Yup." He walked past me and opened the fridge door. "Didn't you see them in the bucket?" He pulled out a blue bucket and set it on the counter. Still shirtless.

I wasn't sure what I was supposed to concentrate on. His abs, the crabs currently fighting for their lives, or the buzzing sensation of my lips as they recalled his mouth in painful detail.

"Shouldn't you put on a shirt?" I blurted. "Don't want the crab to turn into some sort of nipple clamp. It may ruin your night." I pulled a barstool out.

"Or…" Linc dropped the crab and gave me a sultry glance, licking his lips. "… it may just give our night the added spice it needs."

"We're spicy enough," I said confidently, even though my mind whirled at his implication. "You know what? I think I'm just going to go—"

"Oh, sorry." He motioned toward the hall. "I had an extra set of clothes brought in for you along with some shoes. I

138

wasn't sure on sizes or anything, so if they don't fit then I apologize. I can't vouch for style or flair since it was the limo guy grabbing stuff for us, and shopping in Depot Bay is slightly... limited."

"That why you aren't wearing a shirt?"

"My shirt—" Linc shook his head and laughed. "—has a picture of a giant whale on it."

I joined in laughter. "What are the odds?"

"Right?" He put his hands on his hips.

My eyes zeroed in on the *V* of his abs.

"I'd steal yours, but I imagined sporting a seal T-shirt that was five sizes too small might get people talking, and the last thing I need is a rumor that I dress in tight women's clothing in order to get my rocks off."

Please. The T-shirt would probably go out of stock within minutes if he posted something like that. I pointed at his abs. "Pretty sure that's the last thing anyone would accuse you of."

He flexed. "Think so?"

"Right. And I'm the immature one."

"Hey, I never said immature. I said seventeen."

"I can count. And your crab—" I pointed at the counter behind him. "—is trying to make a quick getaway. I'll go freshen up while you wow me with your culinary skills."

"Shit." Lincoln reached for the crab just as it was trying to find its way off the counter and onto the floor.

Laughing, I walked into the bathroom and shut the door.

Only then did I allow myself to actually process what was happening. I was alone. In a romantic setting with Lincoln Greene. And he was shirtless.

And I was...

I sighed.

... *still* seventeen.

Still damaged, too, at least in my mind.

And still stupid for being hopeful that he would look at me and see anything but age, and the fact that I was still struggling to get over my parents' death. Still going through the stages of grief. And still trying to figure out my place in the world among the stars, when every day I felt more and more like my own star had stopped shining.

Maybe this was the beginning of something. The talking? Maybe, he was just what I needed to finally start walking back on the path I was always meant to be on, which didn't help things. If anything, it made me more nervous. I only hoped it wasn't Lincoln who held the key, because my chances with someone like him? They were laughable.

CHAPTER NINETEEN

Lincoln

"I'M IMPRESSED." DANI CLEARED THE LAST dish and loaded it into the dishwasher then grabbed a rag and started wiping down the bar area. "You can actually cook."

"One of my many talents." I tipped back the last remnants of my Corona and winced at the memory of how our dinner had started…

"You know, you can drink beer if you want to." Dani grabbed a Pepsi and pointed at the six-pack that I'd requested before I'd actually thought about it.

"Nah." I waved her off.

She rolled her eyes, grabbed a beer, and tossed it in my direction. "I'm seventeen, not a saint. It's not like I've never witnessed someone drink."

The beer was freezing. I popped the cap and took a long sip. "Does, uh, that mean you've been to lots of parties where you get completely drunk and need your sister to drive you home?"

Dani reached for her long, golden-blonde hair then pulled it back into a tight, low ponytail. "Well, back in the day, you know, when I was sixteen and still drinking milk at night and blending my food so I didn't choke…"

I rolled my eyes. *"Very funny."*

"Yes. I had one drunken episode that will never, and I mean NEVER be repeated." She shifted uncomfortably on her feet.

"What did you do? Get arrested?"

"Nope." She lunged for her seat and started piling food onto her plate.

"Strip then go skinny dipping?"

"No." A smile appeared as she grabbed a crab leg and wiped her hands on the paper napkin then glanced up at me from her dark lashes. *"Are you done now?"*

"One more." I lifted the beer bottle into the air. *"You… streaked across the beach."*

She blushed bright red. *"Yes."*

Beer spewed out of my mouth, barely missing her by an inch as I started coughing wildly and pounding my chest. Maybe it was the look of pure innocence on her face or the simple fact that she'd admitted to being naked, and my brain had no problem whatsoever coming up with vivid images that would most likely get me a nice, fancy seat in prison.

"Nice." She wiped her cheek with her napkin and glared. *"And, for the record, it's not like it was my idea."*

"Whose idea was it?" Dear God, let it have been a girl.

"Elliot."

Bastard seriously had a death wish.

"Oh yeah?" I croaked out, chugging more beer as I imagined my fist connecting with his nose. I smiled as the visual of him crying then pissing his pants floated around my head like a happy daydream.

Dani leaned back in her chair, jutting her lower lip out. *"Well, we were both drinking way too much, and he thought it would be funny. Apparently, I thought it would be hilarious… It doesn't matter. I'm not that girl anymore. I don't even know if I was that girl then. I just…"* She shrugged. *"… guess I wanted to be noticed. I was stuck in high school, stuck with this need to be something important. I know you keep saying I'm seventeen, but sometimes, I feel like I'm eighty."*

The room went deathly quiet.

"Well..." I reached over and grabbed her hand. "... I think I speak for men everywhere when I say I'm glad you aren't really eighty. Can you imagine what that would look like on camera? You bouncing around on the beach?"

Dani burst out laughing, her blue eyes crinkling at the sides, making me wish again things were different between us. "Hey, don't hate. The last 5k I ran had an eighty-year-old woman who beat my ass."

"Really?" I grabbed a warm roll. "You still run?"

The piece of crab met her lips, but then she set it down and shrugged as if she'd suddenly lost her appetite. "Not so much anymore."

"Maybe you should."

"Right now." Dani grabbed the discarded piece of crab, "My only goal is to finish what's on my plate. Small victories and all that."

"Eating is a victory?"

"For me?" She gulped. "You have no idea."

"Thanks." I jolted the conversation from my head, trying to clear the cobwebs, but all it did was make me more curious.

The thunder overhead threatened to take the roof off the condo as a flash of lightning lit up the entire room.

And then with another loud thud.

We were blanketed in complete darkness.

"Linc!" Dani's voice was panicked as I felt hands reach out and settle on my chest.

"Here." I pulled her against my naked chest. Her hot breath fanned across my skin. "I'm right here."

"I hate storms." Her lips caressed me as the words poured out of her mouth.

"I know." I kissed her head. I shouldn't have, but I did anyway. "It will be fine, I promise. I doubt they have any flashlights in here, so why don't we go into the bedroom and sit by the sliding glass door? At least the lightning flashes will help us see one another, and I highly doubt you want to go to sleep yet."

"So what? We'll just stare at each other?" she mumbled across my chest.

"Yeah? Too soon?"

Her laugh warmed me from the inside out. "Too creepy."

"Damn, and here I thought I was being so seductive. Oh, well. We can always trade Demetri stories. It's the same as a ghost story, only the ending always includes something bad happening to him."

"You really do know him well." Dani pulled back then reached for my hand, though it took her a few false finds with my abs to finally locate it. Luckily, she hadn't reached lower, or she would have been in for a surprise.

I squeezed her fingertips. "Let me lead the way so you don't end up with a black eye. That's the last thing either of us needs. Jay thinking I roughed you up in the whale tank."

"Right, because that would be his first thought."

"It's Jay. His first thought is always the wrong thought. He assumes way too much."

Dani tensed next to me.

Shit. I'd said the wrong thing again.

But fixing it meant admitting something that would get us both in trouble, so I left it, and I had to wonder... Would my relationship with Dani be one in which there was so much left unsaid, that at the end of my life, I'd always look back and wonder how the outcome would have differed had I actually said what I'd meant, rather than let her assume what I didn't?

We walked in silence down the hall. I felt my way into the master bedroom. Luckily, I'd left the curtains open so that, when the storm stopped, we'd at least have the moonlight on our side. A large, blue leather recliner was positioned in front of the glass door. Angry pelts of rain attacked the glass, causing a rhythm of fury to build up within the room.

Dani tensed beside me.

"Come on." I tugged her to the chair, sat, and then pulled her onto my lap. Not the best idea I've ever had, but she was scared, and if I couldn't at least comfort her without seducing her, then I deserved whatever hell was coming for me.

She squirmed a bit. I winced and bit my cheek to keep from doing something stupid, like going in for a third kiss or just letting out a pitiful moan. Finally, she settled back against me, her legs lying across my lap and over the side of the chair, while her body sat comfortably against mine.

The thunder rolled.

"And the lightning strikes…" I said in a country twang. "Another love grows cold—"

"On a sleepless night." She joined in with her smooth voice. "Are you really singing Garth Brooks right now?"

I chuckled. "It seemed to fit the mood."

"A song about adultery fits the mood?"

"I was focusing more on the thunder part… and just in case you were wondering, I don't have some hidden family somewhere else that I'm cheating on by being with you." I chuckled.

She laughed softly. Her fingers brushed the front of my bare chest, dancing in a rhythm I wasn't sure she was aware she was even making. "What about Jo-Jo?"

"The potatoes?"

"The girl."

"Ah." Her fingers kept tickling my chest. Damn it felt… too good. "She, uh…" Focus Lincoln. "… she's gone. Her publicist thought being seen with me would help her, since her newest movie is about to drop, and according to her, I'm Hollywood's newest piece of hot ass."

"Wow." I could feel her breath as her hair tickled my

neck. "You okay with that title?"

"Well, I do have a nice ass."

"At the risk of placating your ego... yes, you do."

"Jay know you've been looking at my ass?"

"Well, you're alive so... I'm going to say no." Dani shifted a bit.

I clenched my jaw while she sank further into my body, her heavy sighs doing really bad things to my self-control.

I'd never had to exert any sort of control over my baser instincts. If I wanted something, I took it. Maybe that made me an ass, but I was a guy, and if a girl threw herself at me, it wasn't like I was going to spout some bullshit about not respecting her in the morning.

But with Dani, every ounce of energy I possessed was going toward not listening to my body, and trying desperately to listen to logic and sound reason, something that clearly I'd been out of practice with.

The rain lightened slightly, enough that the angry white-capped waves were visible as they crashed against the rocks in front of us.

"I like it here," Dani finally said.

"On my lap or Depot Bay? You're going to have to be more specific." And then I said shit like that and just made it worse.

She could have cupped my face with her hands; we were familiar enough with one another for her to take any sort of lead in the relationship, and I'd follow. Instead, she crossed her arms and shrugged. "Both, I think."

Pride pricked. I narrowed my eyes. "So you're telling me that between beach — what with all its whaleness — and my lap, it's almost a tie."

"Hey, you're the one who doesn't like whales."

Baffled, I stared at her. Maybe too long for comfort, but I was a bit... taken aback. She was sitting with me, alone, without electricity, and she wasn't hitting on me.

I was the one trying to keep myself from pouncing on her, but she looked just... fine. As if my presence did absolutely nothing to her, when I damn well knew my kiss had affected her just as much as hers had affected me. So, why the hell wasn't she the one dying a slow, painful, arousing death?

"Tell me something." I cleared my throat and looked away from her. I had to. "If things were different. If your parents hadn't died..."

She sucked in a breath.

"If you were... happier. What would you be doing right now?"

"That's kind of personal," she whispered.

"I'm a personal guy."

Dani pressed her lips together, her eyes narrowing. "Honestly, I'd still need a summer job, so I'd probably be in the same place I am now. Only I would have begged Jay for the chance to be your assistant rather than being forced into it."

Ouch. "You weren't forced."

"Um, yeah I was." She laughed softly. "My choices were either work for you or get sent to boarding school. Okay, maybe not boarding school, but the last thing I want to do is hurt Jay or my sister, so I said yes."

Great. So I was with the one girl in the entire universe who didn't actually want to be around me? How unlucky could a guy get? And she was underage? Good one.

"Am I so bad?" I asked, voice hoarse.

"According to the tabloids, you're squeaky clean... no drugs, no partying, no late-night orgies."

"Oh well." I exhaled. "Sorry to disappoint, but I had the best orgy a few weeks ago, drugs everywhere, alcohol..."

Dani burst out laughing. "Oh, I'm sure."

"Fine. I'm tame. And boring. I like reading. And the last time I went to a party, I left early because *Outlander* was on."

"I like that." Her voice was quiet as she started running

her hands up and down my chest again. I thought it was mindless, like tapping her foot or biting her lip, but it made me crazy. "It makes you seem more... normal."

"I am normal."

"Hollywood heartthrobs aren't normal, sorry to break it to you. You forget that I'm best friends with AD2. Do you even know how many times they get bras thrown at their face? Or the amount of fan mail Jay gets in one day? It's not normal. Normal is eating a hamburger without someone taking your picture and posting it on the Internet. Trust me, I'm broken enough to know what normal looks like."

"Are you saying you're just like me? Not normal?"

Her breath hitched. "I guess so. Only I'm a freak in an entirely different way. The only time I speak after months of being mute is in front of someone I should be intimidated by, not to mention a large, ten-ton whale."

"Just to clarify, you meant I was intimidating, not the whale, right?"

Dani didn't laugh.

"I like your brand of weird, Dani. Normal's boring."

"Weird." She huffed. "I can't talk. My ex-boyfriend and best friend called me frigid before we just ended things, and the last time he kissed me he asked if I was a closet lesbian. Idiot, as if lesbians can't kiss, or what?"

"Frigid?" I was hung up on the word. "Why the hell would he say that? I've kissed you. I should know these things. The last word on my mind is frigid. In fact, I wished I thought that about you, then it would make pulling away from the kiss a hell of a lot easier."

Oh, shit! Said that out loud.

Dani froze.

"You have trouble pulling away?"

I didn't want to live my life in those moments of things I should have said. So, I decided to screw us over and admit the obvious. "Regardless of whether it's the second, third, or fourth time, kissing you, even if it's during a scene, and I'm acting. It always feels like the most real thing in my existence."

Her breathing turned heavy. "That would be a great movie line."

"Yeah, well," I croaked, "it's why they pay me so much money. My delivery is…"

I didn't finish.

Because Dani had unlocked her arms and was touching my face. Her fingers trailed over my mouth.

"Dani," I hissed between my teeth. Her innocent touch was almost painful. "You can't."

"Can't what?"

"Look at me like that and expect me to be your boss or even your friend. You can't do that to me."

"Why?" Her heavily lidded eyes screamed seduction as she licked her lower lip.

I let out a bitter curse and tried to look away.

I failed.

Instead, my mouth met hers.

And I instantly forgot all the reasons I'd been pushing her away, and for the first time since meeting her, I did exactly what I'd always wanted to do.

I claimed her.

And had to wonder if it was the last selfish thing I'd do, before the guys buried my body in the ocean.

CHAPTER TWENTY

Dani

HE WAS KISSING ME.

And he wasn't acting.

There were no whales.

Just me and Lincoln and the buzzing sensation of his mouth as it explored mine. My response should have been different.

Pulling away would have been wise.

Laughing it off, probably wiser.

But I kissed him back.

Because Lincoln Greene didn't look at me like a puzzle that needed to be solved in order for us to be friends. He didn't try to fix the pieces. He simply accepted them for what they were. Screwed up.

It was as if he saw the fear, hurt, anger — the ugly — and accepted me anyway.

His kiss deepened as he reached around my body; his hands tugged the seal shirt off. Cold air bit my back as it made its way to the floor.

Smooth lips slid past the corner of my mouth when his

hands found my waist and lifted me. Our mouths broke contact, and I grasped his biceps with my hands, steadying myself as he lifted me into the air and carried me to the bed.

The soft down comforter kissed my back as he lowered me onto the bed then stood over me, his chest heaving with exertion, his gaze pensive, as if he was waging a war within himself.

Wild grey eyes stared me down as he slowly started stripping. I couldn't help my swift intake of breath when he stepped out of his jeans. I gulped, and suddenly I did feel young, so young, too young to be with someone so beautiful, so mature, so experienced.

This wasn't the quarterback of the football team.

This was a man — all man.

He leaned over me, placing his hands on either side of me. The mattress dipped under his weight, as his mouth met mine in another deep kiss that left me dizzy. Sensations I'd never experienced before pulsed through my body. I felt Lincoln everywhere — even in my toes.

"You're beautiful." His mouth left mine, and his cheek rubbed down my neck as his lips continued their exploration. His skin was rough from needing to shave, sending chills down my body with every brush of his cheek, every caress of his tongue. I squeezed my eyes shut and clenched the comforter with my fingers.

And then, I couldn't help it anymore.

I wanted to touch him.

My hands reached out, needing to grab onto him, wanting to explore him like he was exploring me. The minute my fingers grazed his chest, then wrapped around his neck, I knew there was no going back. My body was on fire for him.

And unless there was an actual fire.

And we had to evacuate the building.

I was staying.

"You taste so good..." His lips fused with mine as his

tongue reached past my lips, coming into contact with mine. The kiss was liquid smooth. "I've never tasted anything like you…" He lifted me again, this time higher on the bed.

He broke our kiss only long enough to tug my jeans away from my body and toss them in the corner.

With a seductive smirk, he started kissing up my leg, starting at my ankle. I arched as his tongue made its way toward my knee, and then he froze.

I wiggled and looked down. "What's wrong?"

Face pale, he stumbled backward, looked up at me, then looked down at my leg.

"What?" I frowned. "Linc, what's wrong?"

"You have a tattoo."

I rolled my eyes. "That's why you stopped? Pris let me get a calf tattoo after my parents died. It was the one thing she let me do to honor them, even though it took weeks of begging." I'd wanted a set of angel wings, kind of like the tattoo Demetri and Alec had, though mine was larger, taking up a good quarter of my calf. It was black and white with red dates sprawled along the tips of the wings.

"It just…" Lincoln shook his head and then placed his hands on his hips. "… it's surprising, that's all."

I reached for him.

But he stepped away, out of my reach, both physically, and as his eyes shuttered closed, I realized, emotionally too.

"So that's it?" My words sounded heavy as they floated into the air, into the universe, waiting for him to say something that would ground the words, that would make them seem less bleak.

"Sorry." Lincoln flashed a wary grin. "Maybe this isn't smart, you know? I mean…"

"If you say I'm seventeen one more time, I'm going to push you off the balcony." My body shook with pent-up rage, and then when I glanced down, a wave of embarrassment washed over me. I was nearly naked. In his bed. And now he was turning me down? Couldn't he have at least turned me down when my clothes were still on? Quickly, I grabbed the comforter and wrapped it around my body. "You should go."

"But—"

"Sleep on the couch or the other bedroom. I'm tired."

"Damn it, Dani. Just let me explain."

"Fine." I flopped onto my side, the comforter still covering me in all the necessary places. "You have two minutes."

He gulped, his eyes trailing down the silhouette of my body.

"Ninety seconds."

"Fine," he snapped. "I don't want you like this."

All I heard was *"I don't want you."* The *this* wasn't important. The *this* didn't matter. It was just the end word that made the sentence seem less horrifying. The *don't* was bad enough, the *want*, even worse, but *like this*? That was a pity ending to the sentence. And I'd had enough pity to last me an eternity.

"Wow, Linc." I couldn't keep the sarcasm out of my voice. But at least it masked the hurt. "Didn't know you were so specific with who and what you slept with."

It was a low blow.

Especially since I knew he wasn't the type to take that type of insult without getting angry.

And angry? Was an understatement.

"Bullshit!" he yelled. "Really? That's what you have to say when I'm trying to be the bigger person here? Damn it, you really are immature if you think that's the reason I'm walking away right now."

"Funny, because you don't seem to be moving." I needed him to leave; I was desperate for it. I didn't want him to see me cry. Emotion welled in my throat, threatening to choke me. It was almost worse than when the words got caught, and, for once in my life I was upset over the fact that I could talk; my words had made things worse. Usually it was my silence. Ironic. And I hated it.

His muscles flexed as he clenched his fists and whispered in a hoarse voice, "Watch me."

He left.

Slamming the door behind him.

The sobs broke free seconds later as I cried against the strange pillow in the strange condo I should have never been in in the first place.

I didn't belong in his world.

So maybe it was good that this had happened. Because there would never be a place for me. I would have been a one-night stand, right?

So why did it hurt so much?

And why did it feel like the minute he left, he took a part of my heart with him?

CHAPTER TWENTY-ONE

Lincoln

THE SOUND OF MY ALARM WAS more irritating than the fact that somehow I'd managed to sleep wrong, and my neck was currently twisted so hard to the right it hurt to breathe. Damn couch.

I hissed out a curse as I wobbled to a sitting position and rubbed the back of my neck, memories of the previous night hitting me upside the head like a two by four.

Dani had been so upset — maybe I should have been honest about the whole thing. Seeing her face, seeing that tattoo that I could have sworn I'd seen before — it made me pause.

And that pause was long enough to allow my brain to start working. Sleeping with her after knowing her, what? A little over a week? Not a good idea. Hell, it was one of the worst ideas I'd ever had. Who cared if I'd kissed her? Who cared if I was attracted to her? She wasn't one of those girls, the type you slept with, then left in the early daylight by jumping out the window.

And I was treating her that way.

I was ashamed of myself.

And I'd hurt her in the process. Damn, if she only knew it wasn't for lack of wanting her. It was *because* I wanted her that I hadn't slept with her.

But explaining that to an overly emotional woman? It wouldn't sink into her consciousness; all she could focus on was what I didn't do, what I didn't say, when she should be focusing on the simple fact that I'd stopped something that should never have started, at least not yet. I hadn't even taken her out on a date, for shit's sake! And what? I was going to have sex with her?

I punched the couch cushion.

It didn't make me feel better.

Nor did the fact that my phone wouldn't stop going off with text alerts. Finally, I swiped the screen to find out what was so important.

Curses exploded from my mouth so loud that I must have woken Dani. She ran down the hall, her shirt barely covering her tight ass. "What happened?"

As if remembering she was still pissed at me, the concern was quickly replaced with cool anger as she crossed her arms and arched her eyebrows.

"Well..." I licked my lips. No easy way to break it to her, so I tossed her my phone. "... we made the news."

It was on every gossip website.

And trending on Twitter.

Lincoln Greene hooks up with new underage assistant.

Reading it wasn't as bad as seeing the picture of me and Dani kissing or the fact that somehow a camera caught us walking into our "love nest."

Dani set the phone on the kitchen counter then slumped into one of the barstools, covering her face. "That's... bad."

"I was thinking bleak, you know, like black-plague bleak,

at least as far as my life's concerned. If you see my shorts wash up along the beach, know it was the seals that did it."

Her laugh wasn't one of amusement, but joy at the thought of something happening to me...

"Does my death amuse you?"

"Right now?" She hopped off the barstool. "A bit. Yeah."

"Still mad?" I asked in a hopeful voice.

Dani paused, her hand on the doorway to the bathroom. She didn't turn around. "Not mad. A bit angry, slightly disappointed, and feeling a bit ashamed. I'll get over it. I've been through much worse."

The words may as well have been a physical knife manifesting itself right in front of my chest before getting plunged directly between my ribs — she even twisted. Swear, she twisted.

"Dani, I'm sorry. I'm trying to do the right thing."

"And I'm the wrong thing?" She turned, her cheeks flushed. "That's what you're saying, right?"

"Kind of." I threw my hands up in frustration. "Yes. No. Hell, we barely know each other. Why are you pissed that I'm being the good guy?"

"I didn't ask you to," she whispered.

"What was that?" I leaned in, already emotionally drained.

"You didn't ask me what I wanted. You decided for me. People do that a lot. I don't know if it's because of my age or because of what happened to me. But for once — once in my life — I want someone to care enough about me to ask before they make a decision that affects me."

The knife twisted harder. Figuratively, since, if it was real, I would be bleeding my heart all over the carpet.

And damn it, she would be right.

"I'm sorry," I croaked.

"I'll get ready, and we can leave. It's almost seven, and you're needed on set. I have a job to do. And so do you."

Maturity points officially went to her, while I backed away from the shut bathroom door and stumbled into the kitchen, wondering how my doing the right thing had turned into the worst thing I could have possibly done.

THE LIMO RIDE WAS awkwardly tense. My phone went dead quickly after I'd showed Dani the picture. Once we were ten minutes out of Depot Bay, it was finally charged enough for me to turn it on.

Demetri had sent me seventeen pictures. All of them included a seal attacking some sort of human or animal. He'd even gone so far as to put my name in a caption above a terror-inducing seal who looked about ten times my size.

Jaymeson's text was next.

Jaymeson: *I will kill you.*

Great. Just great.

Jaymeson: *Kill you dead.*

I groaned and cast a sideways glance to Dani. She'd read the text over my shoulder and was smirking.

"Glad you find it funny."

She shrugged.

"Silent treatment?"

She nodded.

"So just to be clear, you're choosing not to talk to me, even though you can?"

A middle finger was raised in answer before she tucked her feet underneath her body, laid her head against the door, and closed her eyes.

CHAPTER TWENTY-TWO

Dani

THE MINUTE THE LIMO PULLED UP to Jaymeson's beach house, I jumped out. Lincoln tried to follow me, so I broke out into a run.

He grabbed part of my shirt right before my fingers reached the door. "Dani, don't, not like this."

I sighed and turned. "Look, I'm still your assistant. But you don't need me on set today. I've already texted Pris and let her know what you needed in your trailer for snacks, your laundry's been delivered, and your truck is already waiting for you at the location. I'll pick up where I left off tomorrow, but for right now, can I please just have the day off to think? Or are you going to make me go to work with you? Especially after that picture's been blasted all over the Internet."

Linc's face fell. "Fine." He released my shirt. "But, for the record you don't have to call ahead and do all of that."

"It's my job," I said in a hollow voice. "Unless you're firing me?"

"No." His answer was quick. Even wearing that stupid whale shirt, he still looked gorgeous. His grey eyes always had the appearance that they'd been outlined in kohl. It was easy to get lost in them, easy to forget.

Until now.

Now, staring at him reminded me that we'd had something, a moment, something different, something inexplicable. And he'd just let it pass by without talking to me about it. I was so tired of being treated like a child, yet at the same time, I knew sometimes my reactions were my own fault.

But these last few days, he'd treated me like an equal.

Until at the worst possible moment, when I was at my most vulnerable, he turned into just another one of the protective guys I was somehow surrounded with.

I wanted adventure in the great wide somewhere. I wanted something. He'd made me want to feel alive, and then he had stomped out the match after lighting it.

I hated him for it.

As much as I hated myself for it being a guy who had pulled me from some of the darkness.

"Linc," I whispered, "you're going to be late."

Before I could protest, he pulled me in for a hug and kissed my head. "For what it's worth... I'm sorry."

He had no idea he was making it worse. I didn't want comfort! I didn't even want pretty words! I wanted him to kiss me! I wanted him to pick me up and slam me against the door, kiss me senseless, drive me insane. I wanted the scary. I finally wanted the scary again. Because I trusted him.

And he'd given me safe.

"Bye, Linc." I waited for him to walk away.

And then, like a teenager, because I could, I slammed the stupid door so hard I was pretty sure there would be a crack in the wood later.

"Whoa, there." Zane perked up from his spot on the couch. "I take it the honeymoon is over?"

I glared at his dark hair, easy smile, and stupid tattoos. Why was I surrounded by ridiculously good-looking men?

ALL THE TIME. He hopped off the couch, making his way toward me. Shirtless.

"For the love!" I shouted. "People wear shirts!"

"Whoa." Zane held up his hands. "Are you mad because my shirt's off?"

"Yes!" I slammed my keys onto the table. "Real people wear clothes! Not everyone's paid to take their clothes off."

"I think you have me confused with a stripper." He frowned. "I mean, it's happened at least a handful of times, but never in my own home."

"This isn't your home."

"Is now." He grinned.

"I'll be in my room." I tried to brush past him, but he caught me by the arm and spun me around; his grip was strong. Then again, he was clearly the love child of Zeus.

"Nope." His clear, golden brown eyes saw right through me. Saw too many things. "Maybe we should talk about the fact that you're using words."

"I'm not five."

"Nope. You're seventeen." He said *seventeen* in a low authoritative voice that had me slightly relaxing in his arms. "Trust me, I know all about your age. So does Linc."

At the sound of his name.

I burst into tears.

Against Zane Andrews of all people.

My tears were staining his pretty gold skin, but I didn't care. He let me cry and cry and cry.

"Want me to kill him?" he whispered into my hair. "I'm half Italian. I know people, though they live in Chicago and despise my side of the family. I think it's because we're half Irish. But still, I'd like to think Nixon owes me a favor. After all, I did save his ass that one time in the sandbox, when the other little kid tried to take his Tonka."

"So he owes you a favor…" I sniffed. "… because you saved his Tonka."

"Never underestimate a toddler's relationship with his truck, Dani. Stealing a Tonka is grounds for war."

"O-okay." I let out one last sniffle and shook my head. "And are you telling me you're related to the mafia?"

"Shhh, rats die. I like living. And you'll kill my squeaky-clean image."

I rolled my eyes. "Squeaky-clean to you. Sodom and Gomorrah to others."

"Up top." He held up his hand for a high five. "Look at you, able to make jokes and using your words. Shouldn't we be celebrating your using full sentences, and it's not just a Linc fluke? And please don't cry because I said his name again."

"I'm seventeen. May as well tattoo it on his forehead," I whispered in a hostile tone.

"He doesn't seem to be the type to forget," Zane said helpfully.

"Oh, he didn't."

Zane nodded.

"Or at least he had a momentary lapse in judgment when I had my shirt off..."

Zane winced.

"... in his bed."

His nose scrunched up.

"And rejected me."

Zane let out a low whistle then chuckled. "When Linc messes up, he does it well, doesn't he? Damn. Tell me he at least explained why he rejected you?"

I pulled away from Zane and leaned across the counter. "Yup."

Zane's eyebrows shot up as if waiting for an explanation.

Scowling, I wiped at my wet cheeks and huffed out all the reasons that Linc had listed. When I finished, Zane gave me a blank stare.

"What?"

"It's weird. Part of you, really mature." He crossed his

arms over his bare chest. "But the other part of you, the teen-girl part, is really, really stupid and immature. You do realize he was protecting you, right?"

"Do I look like I need protecting or something? I mean, what is it about me that screams damsel in distress?"

"Not sure, show me your guns." Zane pointed to my arms.

I flexed, trying hard not to smile.

"Hmm, and did you ever take karate? Self-defense? Or any of those weird dance classes at the YMCA that put crazy kickboxing moves to the beats of one of my songs?"

"'Hip Hop'?"

"Not that one."

"'Body Combat'?"

He snapped his fingers. "That one. That's it."

"No." I frowned. "Maybe it's because I've had a rough few years, but that doesn't mean I'm helpless! I can make big decisions."

"Will you marry me?"

"What?" I let out a frantic yell.

Zane shrugged. "You said you were capable of making big decisions. It was a test."

I rolled my eyes.

"You failed."

"Zane, look, I appreciate the help, but I don't really know you that well, and so far all you've done is tell me that Linc's stupid, and I'm immature for not understanding his reasoning."

Zane wandered over to the couch and patted the spot beside him.

Slowly, I walked over to the plush leather and took a seat next to him, while he propped his feet on the matching ottoman as if he lived there.

"You can try to figure it out until your brain hurts. How about you just come to the same conclusion I did the minute you walked in the door?"

"What?" I leaned further into the leather, wishing I could just disappear from his pensive gaze.

"You like him. He likes you. You're both a bit emotional right now. Give it time. If it's supposed to work, it will work. Now." He grabbed the remote and flipped on the *Discovery Channel*. "We're going to watch people build houses in Alaska, and you're going to stop thinking all about Linc. Believe me, what you need is a distraction."

"I can't." I started to get up. "I need to look at the filming schedule tomorrow and plan my assistant duties around when Linc's going to be—"

"Five a.m. he reports to set. Filming until around noon. He gets a ten-minute break for lunch. Then he'll have to go back, most likely to re-film the kissing scene. Rumor has it he knocked Pris's teeth last time."

I held in my amusement, just barely.

"And…" Zane's eyes narrowed. "… oh right, and tonight he has some sort of weird meeting."

Panicking, I ran into my room, grabbed my schedule, and read through it. "It doesn't say anything about the publicist on my schedule for him."

Zane didn't take his gaze off the TV. "Right, that little morsel of information was given to me by Jaymeson. Apparently Linc's publicist has been trying to get ahold of him most of the morning, ever since your picture leaked."

"Crap." I felt a headache coming on. "Do you think he's in trouble?"

Zane turned the volume down and gave me a *duh* look. "Honey, he was seen not only kissing you, but going into, and I quote, 'a love hut' with you. Both of which would be totally fine if you weren't A… underage, B… the director's little sister, and C… up until now? Mute."

I felt my knees weaken. "This is all my fault. He was scared of whales and—"

"Interesting." Zane turned slowly to face me, an easy smile lighting up his dark features. "I like hanging out with you. It's like getting insider information."

"We aren't hanging out."

"My shirt's off, my feet are up, I'm contemplating making popcorn, and you have the day off. We're hanging out."

"Because you make popcorn?" It was hard to keep up with him. The guy talking to me and the one I'd seen on TV were two very different people. His hypnotic eyes met mine in a teasing gesture.

"Dani, I may not know you very well, but I know women. I grew up with two sisters. If you don't hang out with me, you'll end up in your room sulking. And honestly, that makes me sad. You just started talking again. If anything, you should be celebrating the very fact that life doesn't suck as much as it used to. Now, are you going to make the popcorn, or do you want me to?"

"Do we even have popcorn?" I muttered, walking into the kitchen in search of something to throw into the microwave.

A hard, muscled body came up behind me just as I was reaching the second shelf of the pantry. Zane's hand brushed mine then jerked the popcorn down. I expected him to back up. But he didn't move.

"One more thing," he said in a hoarse voice.

Chills erupted around me. I might have liked Lincoln, but I wasn't immune to Zane's charm. Was any female with working hormones? "What?"

"Turn around," he instructed.

I did, keeping my eyes averted down.

He even had pretty feet. They were tan just like the rest of him, white flip flops only added to the golden skin that was already making me jealous that I hadn't lain out much all summer.

"I'm not going to hit on you," he said softly. "I know what my reputation says, but I'm more of the best-friend type."

I jerked my head up as my cheeks heated. "I swear my brain wasn't even going there. I mean, you're Zane Andrews."

"Right." His eyes narrowed. "I'm a freaking saint. Isn't that what they say?"

"I wouldn't know what they say." I swallowed the dryness in my throat. "And thanks for, uh... explaining." I tried to sidestep him.

"Hold on there, high school." Zane grabbed my arm and tugged me back to my original position, inches from his face. "It's not because you aren't really pretty or because you're unobtainable." His face changed from seductive to innocent. "Can you keep a secret?"

Curious, I nodded and waited in anticipation as he leaned forward, and whispered the absolute last thing I would have ever guessed in my ear.

"No." I shook my head. "No."

He grinned.

"Impossible." I crossed my arms. "You're lying to make me feel better."

"So you see..." He stepped back. "... timing really is everything. I'm telling you from experience. Sometimes a guy says no even when his body screams yes. Sometimes a guy says no for the simple principle that the girl he wants to say yes to is worth a hell of a lot more than a few cheap minutes that he isn't sure she wants in the first place."

Stunned, I watched him waltz out of the pantry and start ripping the popcorn package open. My mouth was still hanging open from shock.

Who would have ever thought it?

Mr. Zane Anderson.

Saint.

Was a virgin.

CHAPTER TWENTY-THREE

Lincoln

"Cut!" Jay shouted for the five hundredth time. "Look, Lincoln, you're supposed to be trying to maul the girl. This isn't your first kiss. You aren't asking for permission. What the hell is wrong with you?"

Several things. One being that we were shooting a bedroom scene, and I was with Dani's sister. It felt so incredibly wrong.

I'd never struggled with acting.

Not until now.

"Head in the game," Jay snapped. "Some of us want to go home for dinner tonight."

"Sorry, Jay." I shook my head, clearing my thoughts yet again as the scene was slated.

Pris was in her bra and underwear. I was supposed to pick her up, slam her against the wall, then try to seduce her, and then bail.

Ha.

They do say that the truth is stranger than fiction. What are the odds that they'd changed my schedule again, and I had to film this scene right after my issue with Dani?

With a deep breath, I focused on pushing away every thought of last night, keeping only one.

The hungry look Dani had given me.

I used that look and attacked Pris with everything I had in me, delivered my lines, and when Jay said, "Cut," I prayed it was enough.

"I'd ask you if you were sure you like women," Jay said once the scene was over, and we were semi-alone, "but clearly you do since you were hitting on my little sister last night."

"Not technically a blood relative," I muttered under my breath.

Jaymeson grabbed my shoulder and flipped me around. "What was that?"

"Hit him." Demetri's voice echoed through the set. "But don't mess him up too much. I want at him too."

"Get in line," Alec's voice added.

I groaned as both members of AD2 stalked toward me, their eyes crazy with rage, matching Jaymeson's obvious mood.

"What?" I looked between the three of them. "Are we going to rumble or something? It's not what it looks like."

"So the kiss was a figment of my imagination?" Jay asked.

"No." I swallowed uncomfortably. "But the reason for it... Look, it's not like I seduced her or anything."

"Did Lincoln Greene say he didn't seduce her?" Demetri asked aloud, slamming Alec in the chest. "He does realize that by breathing he seduces women all over the world."

"Very funny. My breathing?" I rolled my eyes. "Really?"

"A girl bought your sweat on eBay for a grand," Demetri said in a deadpan voice. "I rest my case."

"Look." I held out my hands. "I don't want to fight. You guys should at least be happy that whatever was going on between us, it's over. I messed up. She's pissed, and I'm pretty sure if I was ever to get close enough to kiss her again, she'd probably bite my face off." My shoulders sagged. "She even flipped me off."

"Ha." Demetri laughed. "That's my girl."

Alec glared. "You need to stop teaching her things."

"What?" Demetri lifted his shoulders in a lazy shrug. "Either that or knee him in the balls. Clearly she's been listening to my advice."

"Demetri and advice..." Jaymeson sighed. "... two words that should never go together in a sentence. Almost like ketchup and bunny rabbits."

"Drugs and alcohol," Alec added helpfully then winked. "Oh, I'm sorry. Is it too soon?"

"Asses." Demetri popped his knuckles. "All of you."

"Good talk, guys." I slowly started backing away. "Now if you're done chewing on my ass, I have to go meet with my publicist, and I'd like to have some ass left for her to chew off so I can actually walk home without it tonight."

Jaymeson snorted. "Believe me, she's not going to be pissed. What happened in those pictures is media gold. If I didn't know you better, I'd think you planned it."

I felt myself pale. "I would never—"

"I know." Jaymeson sighed. "I know."

Demetri narrowed his eyes at me. "I'll be watching you. I don't care that you got her talking again. You hurt her. And seals. There's more pictures where that came from."

"Hold on." Jay held up his hand. "What? Talking? What the hell are you guys talking about?"

Shit.

Demetri closed his eyes and cursed while Alec quickly flashed me a similar *oh shit* look.

"Speak," Jaymeson barked. "One of you idiots tell me what the hell Demetri's talking about."

Demetri backed away slowly. "Dani talked to Lincoln."

Jaymeson turned toward me so fast I almost stumbled backward. "What the hell, Linc? And you didn't think to tell me?" He gripped the front of my shirt.

I pushed him back. "It wasn't my news to tell."

"He's got you there," Demetri said under his breath.

"Not now!" Jaymeson snapped. "Where is she?"

I frowned. "At the house."

"With Zane?" Jaymeson said, his voice rising in pitch. "You left an overly emotional teenager alone, at my house, with Zane Andrews?"

It was as if the movie of Zane's many sins flashed before us. He'd never been seen doing things, but it had been whispered. And women didn't just adore him; they worshipped him, even said there was a magnetic pull about him that nobody with ovaries could ignore.

"Dude," Demetri's eyes widened. "I've never actually met him in person before, but even I'm not stupid enough to leave an innocent underage girl with him!"

"Shit!" we all said in unison as we ran off set and into the parking lot. I jumped into my truck just as Demetri and Alec got in the front seat. Jaymeson barely made it into the truck bed before I was peeling out of the parking lot, and driving like hell was licking my heels all the way back to his beach house.

"If this ends badly, you end badly," Alec said in a deathly hollow voice.

Great. Angry Demetri I could deal with. Even an angry Jaymeson didn't seem half-bad — maybe that was the soft English accent? But Alec? Well, let's just say I didn't want to be on his bad side. There was something very dark about him. Let's just say it seemed like he had the potential to kick my ass. We were matched in height and strength, but definitely not matched in crazy.

I pulled up to the beach house, didn't even turn off the truck, and ran like hell up the few stairs and almost through the closed front door. At the last minute, I remembered that I'd need to turn the knob unless I wanted to just burst through it and make a Lincoln-sized body-print through the wood.

Once I was inside, I yelled her name.

Alec and Demetri collided into my body from behind.

Jaymeson's many *bloody hells* clued me into him being last.

"Shhh," Zane said as he slowly, languidly, got up from the couch and stretched his arms above his head in a catlike motion. He was shirtless, and I was going to kill him and bury the body in Demetri's house so he'd get blamed for the crime. "She's sleeping."

"Zane…" I croaked out his name with death on my mind. "… if you touched her…"

Zane's face broke out into an amused grin. "Does holding her hand while she cries over accidently grabbing a burnt popcorn kernel count?"

"Huh?" Demetri asked.

"Zane Andrews." Zane held out his hand to Demetri.

Demetri stared at it like it was diseased. That was one thing I liked about Demetri. He was friendly, once you earned his trust, and only then.

"I know your kind," he spat.

I held my laugh in while Alec walked around us and peered over the couch. A smile formed across his lips as he stepped back and surveyed the kitchen, then finally glanced back at us. "She's sleeping."

"I just said that." Zane yawned and then stretched again. I'd be lying if I said he wasn't a really built dude. No wonder girls threw underwear at him during his concerts. "I drugged her."

"You what?" Jay shouted, pushing through Alec and Demetri.

"Shhh!" we all said at once, waving our hands in the air.

"You what?" His whisper was more of a whisper-yell, but whatever.

"First, I lulled her in with talk of reality TV," Zane said in a bored voice as he made his way closer to us, "then I promised her popcorn, which was followed by ice cream, chocolate, and finally we made s'mores in the fireplace." He peered back toward the couch. "Poor little thing was exhausted after all that eating..."His eyes narrowed in my direction. "… and crying."

You could hear a freaking pin drop in that room as all eyes turned to me.

"What?" I threw up my hands. "Seriously? I kiss her back, and you're pissed, then I tell her we can't—" I stopped talking.

"Can't?" Demetri tapped his chin. "Make sushi?"

"Can't… you know." I scratched nervously at my arm then sat on one of the barstools. "The point is, I'm damned if I do, damned if I don't. I'm trying to do what's best for her."

Dani made a little mewling noise in her sleep.

My heart clenched as I glanced over in her direction. It wasn't until I realized everyone was silent again that I looked at the guys.

They were… intrigued. As if they could read every damn emotion on my face, and see that being in the same room with her caused physical pain — especially since I couldn't pull her into my arms and apologize. Again.

"Don't you have a dinner meeting?" Demetri pointed out.

"Shit." I jumped off the stool. "Yes."

Awkwardly, I made my way toward the door as the guys continued talking about Dani as if she wasn't in the room sleeping. Damn it. I wanted to stay. To make sure she was okay, but most of all I wanted to double-check that Zane hadn't tried anything with her.

I wouldn't put it past him.

Then again, Zane really wasn't the type to poach on another man's territory. I groaned aloud. Was that how I viewed her? My territory?

A headache grew at my temples as I jumped into my running truck and made my way downtown.

It was only eight at night.

But it may as well have been midnight. I was exhausted and knew I needed more energy than I could muster, especially if I was going to have to deal with my publicist.

She never slept.

She rarely ate carbs, meaning she was always cranky.

And she had to whiten her teeth on a daily basis because of the amount of wine and coffee she drank to keep herself from falling asleep during the day, and force herself to fall into a drunken stupor at night.

My phone buzzed in my pocket. I read the text at the stoplight.

Cameron: *You're late.*
Lincoln: *Be right there.*

I prayed for patience as I pulled into Seaside Brewery and parked the truck. All I needed to do was make sure to jump through her hoops, then I could go home and down some Nyquil to force myself into sleep.

CHAPTER TWENTY-FOUR

Dani

THE SOUND OF A POT CLANGING against the floor jolted me out of my sleep. With a start, I jerked upward and nearly collided with Demetri's face.

"Whoa." I pulled back. "Why are you hovering, mother hen? I could have head-butted you."

His eyes glistened.

Without warning, he pulled me into a tight bear hug as his body shuddered around mine. "You're really talking."

"Wow, imagine what would have happened if I would have woken up and serenaded you."

"Birds..." Demetri released me on a sigh. "They would have been attracted to the high-pitched screeching, flown into the glass door, somehow managing to break it into a million pieces, and upon seeing my perfect face, attacked, pecking me to death, leaving only one tiny shred of clothing that they'd encase in glass and put in the Rock and Roll Hall of Fame."

I gaped. "Thought this through a bit?"

"Yeah well..." He winked. "... when it comes to birds, I have all the outcomes completely figured out."

"Scary."

"Paranoid," Alec's voice said from behind as he made his way around the couch and knelt in front of me. "Okay, Zane claims you fell asleep on him, but if he touched you, I'll rip his fingers off."

"You really need to stop watching *Mob Wives*." Demetri whispered under his breath.

I smiled at their concern. "Guys, seriously. He's harmless." I grinned at the memory of Zane's secret. "Believe me." I let out another yawn. "What time is it?"

"Midnight," they answered in unison.

"What?" I jumped up from the couch. "That's crazy! I was out all day?"

"Technically." Zane waltzed lazily into the room, still shirtless, still gorgeous, his black sweats hanging so low on his hips it was nearing indecent. "You watched reality TV with me for at least four hours before you fell asleep. Damn it." He opened the pantry then shut it. "You ate all the marshmallows!"

"And that's a crime punishable by murder?" I laughed.

Zane didn't.

"What type of weird junk-food obsession is that?" Demetri asked aloud. "Marshmallows? They're so soft—"

Zane shivered. "Talk dirty to me. Keep going."

"—and gooey—" Demetri clearly couldn't help himself as he lowered his voice. "—and… sweet."

"On that note…" Alec stood. "… I'm going to go back to the house and make sure Nat's getting some rest. The baby's been cutting her first teeth, so I think Nat's ready to lose her mind."

"See ya." I squeezed his arm and stared at Demetri. Hard. Silently telling him *"It's cool. I can sleep without you watching over me like a crazy dad."*

"Fine." He huffed. "I'll go too, but this isn't over, and… Dani?"

I looked up. "Yeah?"

"It's good to hear your voice again."

Grinning, I pulled him in for a tight hug. "Thanks, Dem."

"Oh..." Demetri snapped his fingers. "... also, Jay had to go to bed because he has another early day, but he said he's going to wake you up in the morning so he and your sister can hear for themselves."

I wanted to roll my eyes, but knew it would be rude and very... immature, and since my whole debacle with Lincoln, I was suddenly hyper-aware of every little thing I did that made me appear young, so young that he wouldn't touch me with a ten-foot pole.

"Right." I exhaled slowly. "I guess I should go to bed too."

"Don't," Zane called from the kitchen. "We need marshmallows."

"Dude..." Demetri turned on his heel. "... what is it with you and marshmallows?"

"I don't know." Zane shoved his hands into his baggy sweats. "What is it with you and birds?"

"I don't eat birds."

"You don't eat chicken."

"I meant birds like..." Demetri sniffed. "... pigeons."

Zane let out a low, sexy chuckle. "Are those edible?"

Demetri glowered. "Your abs are giving me a headache. Put on a shirt. There are children present."

I raised my hand and waved in jest, but Demetri flashed me a *stop encouraging him* glare, so I quickly lowered my hand and pasted on a demure smile.

"Stay out of trouble," he called, making his way to the door. "And get your own damn marshmallows, Zane!"

The minute the door closed, Zane turned to me and said, "If I put on a shirt, can we go to the store together? And by *we*, I mean, can I give you cash to run into the store while I hide out in the car with my sunglasses and hat on?"

I rolled my eyes and stood, taking time to stretch out my

sore muscles. "What's the point in you going if you're just going to sit there?"

"Easy." He shrugged. "I can keep you company."

"While I run your errands?"

"Hey, I'm going to wear a shirt. I thought that's how friendship worked. I do you a favor… you do me a favor." His smile grew.

"Stop that." I wagged my finger at him. "I refuse to let your charm work on me. Also, how is you putting on a shirt doing me a favor?"

"You asked me to put one on a while ago. Ergo, favor."

"Musicians. Are. So. Weird." I yawned again, my eyes watering this time. "Fine, we'll go get your marshmallows, but then I'm going to bed. I have to be up early, and my guess is you don't even have to be up until noon."

"Please, even on vacation I get up early." He winked.

"Marshmallows." I swiped my keys from the counter. "Then home. No detours. No sudden hankering for late-night taffy or ice cream."

Zane's face fell. "But what if the ice cream store's open? And the only way to save the world…" He stalked toward me, his face serious. "… is to go inside…" He licked his lips slowly. "… order ice cream… and…" His face tilted down toward mine. "… lick."

My heart slammed against my chest. I ignored it. Because he wasn't Lincoln, no matter how attractive or deadly that smile was. "Keep giving me that look, and I'm going to lick every marshmallow before stuffing them back into the bag, resealing it, and telling you they're fresh."

"Wouldn't be so bad." He shrugged.

"Correction. I'll drop them in the toilet then re-seal."

"Alright then." Zane backed away, holding his hands up in surrender. "But for the record, I just like messing with you. I've never actually had a girl not fall for it."

"Good to know I'm immune to your charm just like

Lincoln's immune to mine," I said in a bitter voice.

"Whoa there." Zane grabbed me by the wrist and tugged me backward. "Friends don't let friends say stupid shit. Trust me, he's not immune. You should have seen his face when he nearly took down the door and came in here guns blazing."

"Huh? Guns blazing?"

"Oh, right." Zane snapped his fingers. "You were sleeping. Lincoln barged in with Demetri, Alec, and Jay. He may have assumed I seduced you, based on my state of dress, and the fact that he clearly has the worst timing in the world, and it looked like I'd just tumbled you into the weekend."

"Nice." I groaned into my hands, keys jamming me in the cheek.

"Hey, hey." He pulled my hands back. "Not so bad. Like I said, the look on his face was pure murder, and it wasn't the whole *get your hands off my sister* look either. It was the *touch her and I cut off your hand for even thinking about it* look, along with a healthy dose of longing. I imagine once he gets his head out of his ass, it'll be any day now."

"Any day?"

"That he gives you the kiss."

"The kiss?"

"You gonna repeat everything I say or marshmallow me?" Zane sidestepped and opened the front door.

As I walked through, he whispered, "The kiss every girl secretly wants but never asks for."

I paused then turned. "Huh?"

Without any sort of warning, Zane grabbed me by the shoulders, slammed my body against the door, and kissed me with such ferocity that I couldn't breathe or think. My legs ceased to work as he lifted me into the air, his tongue twisting with mine, his breathing hot and heavy as he deepened the kiss, almost like he was challenging me to stop him. But I was too shocked to do anything.

He released my body, and I slumped down the wall, my

butt colliding with the hardwood floor as I looked up at him with blurry vision. "What just happened?"

Zane smirked then leaned down, offering me his massive hand. "Demonstration. You want him to kiss you like that. You're welcome. Also, next time a guy tries to kiss you who isn't Lincoln, you slap him."

"But it was you. I hardly know you." I took his hand and stood on wobbly feet.

"My point exactly. Geez, don't they teach you self-defense in high school anymore?"

"Something's wrong with you."

"Marshmallows," he grumbled. "They'll fix a lifetime of wrong."

"Alright, but no more kissing." I frowned. "I may like Linc, but a kiss like that could get a girl knocked-up, and I have no intention of being on MTV's *Teen Mom*, okay?"

"Message received." He winked. "Oh, and also, when that lands on social media tomorrow, which it will, remember to look really guilty when Linc corners you."

I didn't have time to digest what he'd just said, because he was already sprinting toward my car and waiting on the passenger side.

Something wasn't quite right about Zane, but he was also really... real, and kind of... entertaining in a pet-puppy type of way.

You know, if your puppy had a six-pack.

Or looked liked a walking commercial for sex.

Yeah, he definitely needed to not kiss me ever again.

Wait. I froze mid-step. Social media? I glanced around, frantic to locate whoever might have seen us, but there was no one else in the distance, just a good-looking musician leaning over my Jeep and yawning. "Are you coming?"

"Uh, yeah." I frowned. "Coming."

CHAPTER TWENTY-FIVE

Lincoln

DINNER WITH MY PUBLICIST WENT LIKE expected. She asked why I was screwing my new assistant, who also happened to be underage, and according to Twitter, a charity case.

I told her why, and that I'd broken things off...

She heaved a sigh. "Well, that was stupid. Think of what it could do for your image. Hollywood heartthrob obsessed with mute girl? Damn, don't be stupid. Marry the girl."

Offended, I'd only been able to eat a few bites of my pulled pork taco before I was ready to toss my beer in her direction and pray it blinded her enough for me to run out of the restaurant.

"What?" She'd shrugged her waif-like body. "It's good PR."

"So is giving money to the homeless."

She let out a loud snort. "Hardly. That shit never goes viral. But this? This is social-media gold. If I were you, I'd go back and play nice, at least until we hear back about your last audition with Spielberg. Hey, maybe they'll even make you an ambassador for the blind." Her icy-blue eyes twinkled with excitement, as I was sure her brain was making plans for my future presidency.

"The mute, you mean?" I corrected, taking a sip of my IPA.

"Deaf?" She waved her fork into the air. "All the same."

I'd never realized how horrible a person my publicist was until that very moment. Sure, she was one of the best in the business, she'd made grown men cry, and had fired her own sister over some sort of coffee machine fiasco that was still whispered about around the offices in LA.

"Head in the game," Pris teased, jerking me back to the movie set. Her brown hair fell in waves around her shoulders.

"Sorry." I coughed into my hand, careful not to touch my face. Damn, did they have to cake my face with so much makeup? Apparently, Demetri and Nat's whole love affair had taken place when Demetri was extremely tan, meaning my face felt two shades too dark for my liking. I tasted ChapStick and bronzer every damn time I licked my lips.

"Also…" Pris leaned in. "… thanks, for whatever you did."

Sighing, I leaned back. The locker door was hard and cold against my back. We were filming onsite at Seaside High, and I couldn't wait to get out of there. "Yeah well, I nearly shit myself in front of a whale. So, you're welcome, I guess."

Pris covered her face with her hands, her shoulders shaking with laughter. "She may have left that part out."

"Bless her whale-fighting little heart."

"But…" Pris's eyes twinkled with amusement. "… I assumed it must have been a big deal. I had no idea it was a whale of a whopper but…"

"Hilarious." I scratched my chest, trying to numb the pain still making its presence known right where my heart kept beating. Getting her out of my head was a near impossibility, especially when pictures had surfaced this morning of Zane and Dani in an embrace that looked a hell of a lot more than friendly along with the caption, *New Celebrity Bestie?*

Pris touched my shoulder.

I flinched in surprise.

"Hey, you okay?"

"I'm... great."

"Yeah, you look it. Great, happy, a bit too tan for my taste but—"

"You guys ready?" Jaymeson jogged over. "We only have the high school for the next few hours, so I need you to bring your A-game." He was looking right at me, as if I'd been bringing my C-game or something. I suppressed an eye-roll. *Whatever.*

"We got this," Pris answered for me.

I pushed thoughts of Dani from my head just as she happened to appear behind camera with Jay. He handed her some headphones. Great, so now she could hear all the dialogue and heavy breathing we emitted. I wondered if she could hear my heart race or the fact that the minute her eyes met mine, my breathing hitched, making me cough wildly in her sister's face like I was diseased.

Dani frowned then started madly typing in her phone. A smile broke out across her face.

That better be Demetri texting her.

As if summoned by my jealousy, Demetri appeared by her side and pulled her in for a hug. His pregnant wife, Alyssa, was with him. She quickly grabbed some headphones.

Two minutes later, Alec and his wife Nat made their way onto set; they must have gotten a sitter or something because they were rarely without their little Ella.

Great, I had a freaking audience watching me.

"No stress." Pris breathed in through her mouth, out through her nose. "We got this. It's just a kissing scene, right?"

"It's prom," I said in a bored tone. "I'm pretty sure I'm supposed to rock your world here."

The next hour went by so painfully slow that I felt like a turtle cooking in the hot sun.

"Cut!" Jay yelled.

"Dude..." Demetri walked up to me. "... you look good as me."

"Oh, I'm sorry. Are we friends again?"

He snorted, running a hand through his bleached-blond hair. "Of course we are, now we have a common enemy."

"Who?"

"Zane," Demetri seethed as Zane walked on set, his aviator sunglasses low on his nose. His eyes brightened considerably when he saw Dani rush toward him in a flourish then grab his hand, tugging him toward Jay.

The extras on set started whispering.

Why didn't they whisper around us?

"Dude, girls don't react like that to us, not anymore," Demetri said, apparently reading my mind. "Guy's gotta go. You set his car on fire. I'll lure him out to the ocean."

"And do what? Drown him?" I clenched my fists.

"I'm sorry. Did you have a better idea?" Demetri turned his blue gaze on me. "Let's be honest, you and I don't exactly scream violence like he does. He walks like he could take a hit, damn it, and my face is worth too much to risk."

I rolled my eyes. "He's just a guy. He'll get bored."

"Oh, shit," Demetri murmured under his breath. "Well done, Casanova. You just pissed her off again."

"What? What the hell are you talking about?" I frowned.

"Your girl had just put her headset back on, and my money's on her hearing only the last part of our conversation."

I looked for her, but she had disappeared.

Well. Shit.

The door to the gym slammed. I chased after Dani as if my life depended on it. She was in the middle of the deserted hallway. It smelled like pencils, bleach, and sweaty teenagers, with a lingering hint Axe body spray.

"Hey…" I touched her shoulder. "You didn't hear the whole conversation."

It was as if she didn't even hear my words. Instead, her eyes were trained on a glass case with trophies.

The main picture was of Homecoming Court the year

before.

She'd been the Junior Princess.

Standing with Elliot in the sexiest little cheer outfit I'd ever seen. It wasn't something I should probably have noticed, but I did. Her smile was huge, the crown on her head nearly falling over as Elliot's hand helped keep it on her head. His smile matched hers, it was disgusting, like a kick to the gut.

And then I saw the trophies.

So many trophies for the cheerleading squad.

And at least three for Dani for competitive cheerleading.

Back flips, pyramids, group photos. She was gorgeous in all of them; the girl in the pictures wasn't the girl I'd been spending time with. It was as if she was a completely different person.

"I miss her," Dani whispered. "I don't think I've ever said that out loud. Maybe I've been afraid if I said it, it would make my reality that much more cemented in my mind, make it last or something." She hung her head; pieces of blonde hair covered her face so I couldn't read her expression.

"I don't," I whispered. "I refuse to miss a ghost, someone I never knew."

Her shoulders slumped.

"But I do have another confession." I pulled her hair back. "I miss you. The you I know now."

She didn't say anything.

"Look, Dani, I—"

"There you are!" A voice I kind of wanted to forget existed screeched down the halls. "Jay said where to find you."

Note to self: Kill Jaymeson later.

Jo-Jo slinked down the hall, her heels like a hammer to my skull. "So, good news! I got on a few episodes of that scary, fairy tale show that films in Portland, so I came down to Seaside for the weekend."

How in the hell was that good news?

"Great, well..." I forced a smile. "... I have to work, so

enjoy Seaside."

"Whoa!" Jo-Jo gripped my bicep, her eyes glued to the muscle before she squeezed then leaned toward me. "I thought we could hang out tonight."

"I have a thing," I lied.

"Actually," Dani piped up, "your schedule's pretty clear. Should I make reservations for you guys somewhere?"

I purposefully stepped backward onto Dani's foot.

She yelped then pushed me off. "So where are you staying, Jo-Jo?"

"Oh..." Jo-Jo shrugged. "... hopefully at Hotel de la Lincoln." This was followed by screeching laughter.

I felt my entire body go rigid with dread as parts of my anatomy went completely limp.

"Wow," Dani croaked. "Okay then. I'll just finish the rest of the stuff on your list then get out of your way, Linc. Glad you won't be bored, with Jo-Jo to hang with you."

Damn it, she *had* heard me.

Dani walked off. I watched as her Converse faded from my view, and then the gym door slammed behind her.

"I thought she couldn't hear?"

Dear God, people really needed to learn the difference between muteness and deafness.

I jerked away from Jo-Jo. "I'm probably needed back onset."

"Yay! I'll watch." She looped her arm in mine, and I briefly contemplated gnawing my own arm off so that I could get free.

Instead, I said, "Can't wait," in the driest, most sarcastic tone I could muster, which to her must have been a declaration of undying love, since she let out another squeal and pulled me closer.

CHAPTER TWENTY-SIX

Dani

"WHOA, SLOW DOWN THERE." ZANE SLID my can of Coke Zero away and sat on my lap. How the hell had he found me on my balcony, and why did he always insist on invading my personal space? Ugh, first thing tomorrow, I was buying him a pack of shirts.

"Uffff." I pushed at his back. "Why are you so heavy?"

"I work on my fitness," he teased. "Also, not moving until you tell me why there's two empty cans in the trash and a third sitting here like you're trying to get drunk off caffeine, Splenda, and caramel coloring."

"Am I boring?" I asked, genuinely curious if that was what my life had come to — from life of the party to the party-ending sad girl.

"All the time," he said seriously. "But I like torture, so I hang out with you anyway."

"You have no friends," I pointed out.

He opened his mouth.

"And the marshmallow bunnies don't count. We already discussed this."

He grinned shamelessly. "You're no fun."

"See!" I yelled.

Rolling his eyes, Zane grabbed my hands and kissed them. "I've known you, what? Three days?"

"Feels like years," I grumbled, reaching for my can.

He swatted my hand out of the way and stood.

"What?" I stared at his tall form.

"You miss Lincoln, right?"

"No," I lied, my cheeks heating.

"Up you go, Pinocchio." He hefted me to my feet. "Night on the town. We're crashing whatever date-from-hell Lincoln's on, and I'm going to steal the girl."

"Jo-Jo?" I burst out laughing. "You don't want to do that, believe me."

"I've had dates with worse." Zane ran his hands through his dark hair. "Trust me, Linc may be fresh meat, but I'm newer meat. Ergo, I steal the girl, and leave you time with the guy."

"So he can what?" I whispered. "Reject me again?"

"The girl has a point." Zane tapped his chin. "Or we could grab ice cream downtown, do a strategic walk-by of the restaurant, then go to bed early like winners."

I nodded my head and laughed. "I especially like the winning part."

"So why the long face?" Zane shrugged.

"Maybe we should just get it over with. We'd be good together, right?"

"I think I'm missing a key part of this conversation." Zane opened the door that led back into the house from the upstairs balcony. "Fill me in while you find your shoes?"

"Sex." I nodded seriously. "We're both virgins, or well, technically you are, I'm not but that's not the point! My first time was horrible."

"Say that louder." Zane shushed me with his hand. "Seriously."

"Maybe it would be easier. Just get it over with."

"Nope." Zane shook his head. "Are you even hearing yourself? I should never be the guy you get it over with... with."

"But—"

"And you're better than that. I would never have sex with you. You're welcome for that."

"Shouldn't I be insulted?"

"Nope." He sighed, tossing my sandals at my face. "If there's anything I've learned it's this. You savor life. You don't jump into it and wish for it to be over, because you never know how much time you're going to be given. You should never get anything over with — no matter how scary it may be."

I grumbled and pulled on my sandals. "Fine."

"Geez, remind me never to give you life advice."

"Sorry." I grimaced. "Bad mood... too much soda..."

He held out his hand again. "Which is why we're evening it out with sugar!"

ICE CREAM WAS A good idea. Then again, most of Zane's ideas were good. I had a weird suspicion he didn't really have many friends. I rarely saw him texting anyone, and when I asked about his family, he locked up like a vault. It was weird, someone that famous not really having anyone. I had to wonder if the reason he hated staying alone was because he was lonely.

Maybe that was why I felt comfortable around him, or as comfortable as a girl could get around a mega-hot celebrity. He was so easy to be around that I forgot how famous he was, which nearly caused an early onset heart attack at the ice cream store, one of the employees started crying and actually handed over her bra.

Without breaking stride, Zane took it, signed his name on the strap, handed it back, and gave the girl a twenty-dollar tip, all the while remembering my order and getting extra marshmallows on his.

"You ever going to tell me?" I asked, nudging him in the side. He towered over me so it was more like I'd elbowed his hip.

Zane licked his vanilla ice cream as if he was making love to the spoon. "About?"

"The marshmallow thing," I answered, tossing my cup into the trash and wiping my sticky hands on the last of the napkins.

"Oh." Zane nodded eagerly.

I waited.

"Not a chance in hell." He flashed a grin and stopped walking, his gaze traveling to the outdoor patio of the Crab Shack.

Jo-Jo was sitting under the umbrella twirling a drink in her hands, while Lincoln looked ready to jump over the little wrought iron fence and make a run for it.

"He doesn't like her. At all." Zane laughed.

"I know." I giggled. "But he deserves it."

"That?" Zane pointed with his spoon. "No man deserves."

Lincoln threw his hands into the air, tossed a few bills onto the table, then left Jo-Jo pouting in the corner. Swearing, he nearly collided with another customer.

"Lincoln!" Zane yelled.

"Traitor," I muttered under my breath.

Lincoln swung his gaze in our direction, and his face turned an angry red. "Hey." His eyes raked my body in before he finally managed to give Zane a tiny nod.

"Ouch." Zane rubbed his stomach. "Wow, must have eaten too much ice cream. Can you take Dani home?"

I didn't have time to kill Zane, because as soon as the words were out of his mouth, he was already walking backward toward… *not* where our car was parked.

"Sure." Lincoln's hoarse voice pulled at something in my chest, our eyes locked, and Zane was completely forgotten.

"See ya," Zane called.

Dark circles lined Lincoln's eyes. He looked rough. "You wanna…" He squinted at the sunset. "… you want to go for a walk?"

I nodded.

We walked in silence for a while, side by side, not touching, but his body heat was an intensely tangible thing, reaching out and searing me with his nearness. Why couldn't I like a guy like Zane?

Instead, I was cursed to like Lincoln.

"Okay, here's how this is going to work." Lincoln said once we reached the edge of the boardwalk, where the sand met the cement. "I'm going to give you three seconds to run. Then I'm taking off my shoes and going after you."

"Um, what? Why?" My heart skipped a beat.

He turned his grey gaze on me. "It's a metaphor." His voice lowered. "I want to chase you, Dani."

I sucked in a breath.

"I want to capture you."

"Is this a catch-and-release thing?" I tried to tease, but my voice had turned all breathy, and the taunt fell short.

It didn't matter because he ignored me. "One."

I hurriedly flipped off my sandals and started running as I heard him yell two… then three.

I didn't make it far.

Until he was lifting me into the air and walking me away from the people and toward the sunset and… the ocean.

Once the water reached his feet, he set me down and tilted my chin toward his face, his fingers brushing against my lips. "Caught."

"Yeah," I whispered as cool water rushed over my ankles, "I guess I am."

CHAPTER TWENTY-SEVEN

Lincoln

I SLID HER DOWN MY BODY, feeling good for the first time in two days. Hell, I felt more than good.

"So now that you're caught, no more running," I whispered, my mouth meeting hers in a tender kiss.

"You hurt me." Dani pulled back.

I leaned forward wanting more. "I know." Our foreheads touched. "But it's not because I don't want you. At least let me explain my madness."

She chewed her lower lip and gave one solid nod.

I grabbed her hand and started walking with her along the shore. "It's been two weeks. That's how long I've known you, and though my playboy status isn't exactly... working in my favor when it comes to you, I want to do things right. I want to take you out on a date before I have sex with you."

Dani stopped walking and looked up, lifting one sexy-as-sin eyebrow. "Just one date?"

"Are you asking because you're eager or because you think I'm going to do one date to make myself feel less guilty then find the closest dark area I can seduce you in?"

"Uhhh." Her cheeks blushed bright pink.

"More than one date," I answered before she could embarrass herself further. "Maybe three, four, ten— Who knows? I may even like dates."

"Whoa! You don't know if you like dates?" Dani dropped my hand and peered up at me. She gasped. "You've never been on a date?"

"Where I was in control of it?" I shook my head. "Nope, you'd be a first."

"What is with you celebrities?" Dani muttered under her breath.

"What was that?" I asked, totally confused.

"Nothing." She grabbed my hand again. "I thought it was because of my age... the whole not wanting to sleep with me, or even because..." She sighed and stopped walking again. "... if I stopped talking again for some freak reason, it would embarrass you."

I pulled her into my arms. "Seriously? How could you even think that? If you never talked another day in your life, you'd still be you, just less vocal." I kissed her cheek. "You could never embarrass me."

Dani beamed.

And I couldn't help it; I had to kiss her again. It had been forty-eight hours, and I was already thirsting for another taste of her.

Our mouths met softly, and then with a laugh, I lifted her into the air and laid her down on the sand, falling with her, balancing my weight on my elbows as I hovered over her. Sand went everywhere, but it was the last thing on my mind as she responded to my kiss.

I breathed her in, tasted every part of her, and selfishly just wanted more, even though I knew it was smart to go slow, to at least wait until her birthday before I changed her life forever by claiming her in front of the world.

She broke the kiss. "I missed you, too."

Smiling against her mouth, I kissed her again, and when the breeze started turning chilly, I covered her with my body and continued heating her up with more kisses until my mouth was swollen from making love to hers.

My phone buzzed in my back pocket for the millionth time.

Finally, I lay back on my elbows and pulled it out. A few missed texts from Demetri and Jay.

"Your family." I showed her the screen. "I should bring you home before they send out a search party."

"Or…" Dani shrugged. "… you could take me to yours."

I froze, my body instantly latching on to that idea like it was the best thing I'd heard since discovering self-serve frozen yogurt.

"Jay would kill me." Yet, I was still arguing with myself about why it was a good idea. It would keep her away from Zane.

"Probably." Dani laughed as she got up and dusted sand from her jeans. "Okay, fine. Take me home before Jaymeson calls the police."

"I'm sure Zane told him where you were."

Dani gave me a look. "Kinda my point. Besides, if our picture somehow ends up getting everywhere again…"

"Shit." I rubbed my eyes, as I realized what my publicist would do. "Dani, you need to know something, and before you freak out, let me explain."

Her eyes narrowed into tiny slits.

"My publicist wanted me to pretend to be in a relationship with you because she thinks it's good for my image. I told her to kiss my ass, which I'm sure she's still pissed about, but the last thing I want is for her to think I'm using you or for that to somehow spread. You think we can…" I tried to think of a careful way to word things. "… not necessarily hide, but keep this a secret until your birthday?"

Dani's eyebrows shot up. "So, like secret friends who

kiss?"

I exhaled in relief. "Exactly."

She nodded. "So close, Linc, you were so, very, very close."

"Close?"

"You can't kiss me then ask me to keep it a secret. Either we're together or we're not. My age shouldn't have anything to do with it. Plenty of people date with an age gap. You get me now or not at all."

"Okay, first..." I jumped to my feet. "... you're overreacting."

She glared.

"Second, I understand why. It's not because I'm ashamed of you. It's because I'm protecting you. There's a difference."

Shoulders slumping, she nodded her head. "Fine, but if we're doing this whole friends-thing, we do it all the way. No kissing, no holding hands, nothing. Once we're actually dating, you can kiss me all you want. You can even chase after me in the sand all over again, but until then..." She held out her hand. I think she wanted me to shake it. "... friends."

I gripped her hand in mine. It was so small, frail. "You know the last thing I want to do is shake your hand."

She nodded.

"Stripping you naked seems like a better option."

Dani's eyes widened.

"And that—" I tugged her against me. "—is why I'm trying to protect you. Because you're young, inexperienced, beautiful and pure. And trying to keep my thoughts on the straight and narrow may damn well kill me."

"Are you saying... I tempt you?" A slow, salacious grin spread over her face.

"You have no idea." I said in a gruff voice. "But sure, yeah. Friends for two weeks. How hard can it be? I mean, you and Zane are friends."

"True."

"Why…" I swallowed. "… are you friends?"

"He's easy to talk to, and he doesn't ask me to keep him a secret."

"Low blow."

"I'm just saying." Dani swiped her sandals and started walking back toward the boardwalk. "Plus, it's easy to be friends with someone when you aren't waiting for them to kiss you, though—" Her face turned bright red.

"Dani." I stopped walking, my blood pumping furiously through my body. "Did he?" I couldn't even get the words out. "Did he kiss you? All I saw was a really close hug. Tell me it was a hug, Dani. Tell me."

"Look." Dani pointed up. "The moon."

"Son of a bitch!" I yelled, kicking the sand with my bare foot. The desired effect of having the kick cool down my anger hadn't worked. Not by a long shot. So I kicked the sand again then started pacing back and forth.

"He didn't mean it," Dani said in a bored voice. "I think in his own twisted way he was trying to help me."

I stopped pacing and faced her. "By kissing you? How the hell is that helpful?"

Dani's face broke out into a bright grin. "It got your attention, right?"

"Dani, listen to me very carefully." I braced her shoulders with my hands. "You could wear camouflage and hide out in the bushes, and you'd still have all my attention. It doesn't take much, believe me."

"Were you trying to be romantic?"

I sighed. "Sorry that the fact that Zane freaking mauled you with his mouth has me off my game, but yeah, I think romance was the goal."

"Didn't reach it, Linc," she teased.

Sighing, I released her and then reached for her hand, but she pulled back.

"Nope." Dani sighed. "Friends, remember?"

Irritated, I kicked the sand again as we made our way back to the boardwalk. "I may come to hate that word before the time's up."

"Is that my birthday present then?" Dani asked. Once we reached the cement, she dropped her sandals and kicked the sand off them.

"A date?" I asked confused.

"Or you popping out of my cake... singing..." She shrugged. "... shirtless."

I laughed. "I may as well ride in on a whale... me singing in public? You don't want that. The world isn't ready for that."

"Are you that bad?"

I leaned in like I was going to kiss her, stopping right before her lips. "Actually, I'm that good."

"I'll believe it when I hear it." She crossed her arms.

"Guess you'll have to trust me, friend."

Her eyes narrowed. "We'll see how long you last."

"Older," I added falling into step beside her, "also more mature. I can totally handle it."

"Right."

"Do me a favor?" I walked her to my truck slowly, trying to ease her into the fact that I was going to drive her home in it and hope for the best. "Leave the door unlocked tonight so I can sneak in and smother Zane with a pillow."

"No!" She burst out laughing. "He's my friend!"

"And when you say *friend* you mean it different than when you say I'm your friend... right?"

"Well..." Dani hesitated, chewing her lower lip while my heart plummeted to my knees. "I guess you'll find out."

Damn stupid idea.

CHAPTER TWENTY-EIGHT

Dani

"BY THE GIANT SMILE ON YOUR face, I take it my plan worked," Zane said the next morning, as he poured himself a cup of coffee and tossed two marshmallows on top. He turned around and stretched his coffee above his head, his ab muscles basically stretching a wave of good morning in my direction.

I'd already given up on him wearing anything but pants in the house. It was a battle just to get him to wear a shirt to the store, let alone in the actual comfort of my home, which he now referred to as his home. Part of me wondered if Jaymeson had adopted him or something.

"Yes." I swiped a marshmallow from the top of his coffee and popped it into my mouth. "It worked. But he wants to be friends until after my birthday."

"Ha!" Zane smacked my hand before I could reach into his coffee again. "Poor Linc's going to be in a world of hurt. I think I should help him by sending encouraging team-building texts like *'There is no I in team, but there is one in kiss.'* Or maybe this one." Zane closed his eyes, then snapped them open. *"'It's not the destination. It's the hot, wanton, sweaty*

197

journey.' Yes..." He nodded, and a self-satisfied smirk jacked up one side of his mouth. "... I like the last one best. Quick, take off your shirt so I can send him dirty picture texts with them."

I rolled my eyes. "Not a chance."

He pouted. "You're no fun."

"Because I won't take off my shirt?"

"A dirty text a day keeps the doc away."

"You sure you're a virgin?"

"I'm a virgin, not a priest." He rolled his eyes then went to the pantry to grab a few more marshmallows.

"Zane..." I frowned. "... maybe you should have something other than sugar for breakfast."

His gaze never leaving mine, he popped three more mallows into his mouth, chewed slowly, swallowed, then grinned. "You were saying?"

"Protein?" I offered. "What if I make you eggs?"

"Man don't need woman make eggs." He smacked his chest. "Man make own food!"

I waited for him to stop pounding his chest then grabbed the eggs from the fridge and handed them to him.

He stared at the eggs like they were born from an alien then stared at the stove. "Step aside, woman. I'm hunting and gathering here."

With a laugh, I stepped out of his way then went back into my room to finish getting ready.

I still had thirty minutes left before I would be needed on set. I grabbed a sweater because the beach always had a chilly breeze and swiped some lip-gloss on my mouth.

By the time I made it back into the kitchen, Zane had set out two plates, both piled high with eggs, and had somehow either killed a pig or discovered the bacon in the fridge and fried it up as well. Two glasses of orange juice were set on the counter, and he'd buttered toast.

"You can..." I pointed. "... cook?"

"What made you think I couldn't?" He gave me a look of disbelief. "Damn, are my abs that distracting?"

"You eat marshmallows for every meal," I said in exasperation. "I've been worried about your nutrition for three days!"

"Please." Zane rolled his gorgeous eyes. "Just because I don't eat when you're around doesn't mean I don't eat. How else could I look this good? Marshmallow diets don't produce muscle, high school. Don't schools teach you anything anymore?"

Ignoring him, I sat down, grabbed a piece of toast, and nearly screamed in protest when he dropped a marshmallow on my eggs for "added texture."

"Seriously." I pushed the mallow away with my fork. "What is with you and these things?"

Zane went still beside me, his face pale as he stared down at his plate. Jaw rigid, he gripped the countertop with both hands as if he was thinking about splitting the granite in half. Then he very slowly turned to stare at me. "I don't talk about it."

I'd never seen Zane look so haunted, so serious. "Maybe you should."

He hesitated, staring down at his plate briefly before saying in a hoarse voice, "They were her favorite."

I reached across the table and gripped his hand. "Who?"

His entire body shut down as he gave my hand one squeeze before releasing it and attacking his eggs with fervor. When he was finished, he was still tense.

I wanted to ask him where *she* was, what had happened to her, but I was already going to be late, and something told me that he wasn't about to open up and have a therapy session with a girl he hardly knew.

"Go." Zane sighed then flashed me a happy smile. "I'll hold the fort down here. Any special requests for dinner?"

"Are you cooking for me?"

"Well, I'm assuming I'm cooking for both you and Linc, considering he probably wanted to murder me last night."

"Smother you with a pillow actually."

He waved me off. "Details."

"Spaghetti," I answered.

"Messy for a date meal, but okay."

"Not a date," I corrected. "Friends, remember?"

"Oh, I really can't wait, Dani." His grin was evil as I ran out the door and toward my Jeep.

Fourteen days was nothing. I knew I would be fine. Besides, my day was going to be insane since Jay had asked if I could assist him as well.

"DANI!" JAYMESON YELLED MY name over the radio. I'd been toying with the idea of tossing the irritating black object into the ocean for the past hour. Being Jaymeson's assistant was worse than being Linc's. At least Linc liked order; he made lists for crying out loud. Jaymeson didn't know what he needed until he needed it, and it was always right then, in that moment. But paging me while I was using the restroom was an all-new low. He did a freaking countdown over the radio until I made it to his trailer, thankfully without toilet paper attached to my sandal.

"What?" I heaved in exertion as I burst into his trailer, only to see him calmly eating Chinese food with chopsticks and barely managing two grains of rice per bite.

"I'm hungry." He yawned. "Chinese food sucks, but that's all Pris wants now that she's pregnant. I think it's the salt, which is really bad for you, but when I said that to her, her face got very red, and I felt fear tremble in my—" He winced. "Let's just say pants. See how I'm learning to censor myself when it comes to you? Bloody brilliant of me."

"Oh, you're bloody something," I said in a terse voice.

"Question..." He lifted a chopstick into the air. "When you weren't talking, were you thinking all those snarky things?"

"Yup."

"Feel good to say them out loud, does it?"

"You have no idea." I sighed. "Jay, I still haven't gotten lunch for Linc, and he actually pays me. Did you need anything?"

Jaymeson frowned. "I led with that... I'm hungry."

I pointed to his rice bowl. "You have food."

"I want a hamburger!" he growled. "No more rice. Rice is for pregnant people with no taste buds. I'm a man. I demand beef."

I counted to three then lifted my hands in the air. "Fine. I'll have a burger and fries delivered to your trailer, just stop paging me. I need to eat too, you know."

"No." Jaymeson dropped his chopsticks into the bowl and set it on the counter. "If I keep you busy enough, you won't be spending as much time with Lincoln, meaning he keeps his dirty hands off you."

A slow burning fuse of anger lit inside me. "And if I want them on me?"

Jaymeson gave me a pointed glare. "What if...?" His shoulders hunched. "Damn it. I'm already turning into a father."

I exhaled and took a seat beside him. "How do you figure?"

Jaymeson glanced up, his eyes sparkling with tears. "What if you stop talking again? What if I can't reach you? What if he hurts you? I worry about these things constantly, as if I'm not already at my wits' end, sanity-wise."

I took Jaymeson's hand in mine. "Don't focus on it. I try not to. If I think about not talking, I can almost feel the block coming up again, my tongue feels heavy in my mouth, I start sweating... panic sets in. Honestly, I'm trying not to think about it or what triggers it. I just want to live. You should too. Besides, he's already hurt me, and I still had words after the fact. They were mean ones too. I think he even flinched."

"Did you yell?" Jaymeson's gaze turned hopeful.

"Loudly." I nodded. "A smart man would have taken cover."

"But he's not smart."

"He kissed me instead." I smiled at the memory. "Which was probably a better choice, considering had he just walked away, I would have thrown my shoe at his head."

"I forget how mature you are." Jay grinned and pulled me in for a side hug. "Fine, go assist him, but if he asks for..." His cheeks reddened as he coughed into his hand. "... you know, that sort of... help, just say no."

"Oh, so when he asks for a massage, that's code word for sex?"

"Always." Jaymeson nodded.

"And when he asks if I want to take my shirt off so he can see what the lighting's like in his trailer?"

"WHAT?" Jay jumped out of his seat.

"Kidding." I smirked. "He would never do that. We're *friends* now." I spat the word like poison.

"Yeah, right." Jaymeson growled. "And I'm a virgin school girl. I highly doubt this whole friend-charade will last long. He's a man."

"One who has nerves of steel and patience to match." I tried to keep the pout out of my voice.

"If he can't wait for you," Jaymeson whispered, pulling me in for another hug, "then he doesn't deserve you."

"Thanks, Jay."

"Now..." He squeezed my body one last time. "... go get my burger."

CHAPTER TWENTY-NINE

Lincoln

I DIDN'T REALIZE HOW MUCH OF a creature of habit I was until Dani started working for me. It was semi-embarrassing to give her daily lists of my weird quirks that, up until now, I'd never realized were even odd.

I only wanted my blinds open in the morning. I had to have them closed, blanketing me in darkness around six at night if I was still on set. The Today Show always had to be playing when I walked in. And coffee needed to be available at all times.

Not too bad, if you asked me, but then, the whole Skittles thing was next on the list. I needed Skittles at all times. And if my bowl for some reason became empty, I felt… panicked. Great, so Skittles were my comfort food.

Add in only two brands of bottled water I'd drink.

And the special laundry detergent, and I seriously felt like a freaking diva. I was trying to rewrite my list for her for the next day, crossing things out, trying to make myself seem less like a tyrant, more easygoing, when she burst into my trailer with a bag of hot, steaming food.

"Please," I said in a hoarse voice, "let that be a hamburger and fries!"

Dani gave me a tired smile and placed the brown sack on the table. "Go crazy." With a huff, she sat on the couch and held her head in her hands. "Hey, if I asked for a thirty-minute break, would you fire me?"

"You haven't taken a break all day?" I glanced at the clock on the wall. "Dani, it's nearing two in the afternoon. You started work at six and haven't stopped moving since."

She let out a quiet yawn. "I know, but Jay needed me today."

"Come again?"

"My brother-in-law," she repeated, "needed me because his assistant's sick or something."

"Jay's assistant—" I laughed. "—isn't sick."

"No?"

"No. Because Jay's assistant doesn't exist. He's never had an assistant."

"No!" Dani let out a pitiful groan. "No, no, no." She punched the couch. "So I've been at his beck and call for no apparent reason? I kept praying his assistant would have a miraculous recovery! I was on my knees, Linc!"

I burst out laughing. "Seems to me like he's trying to keep you too busy and tired to be with me."

Dani curled up on the couch and laid her head on the pillow, tucking her hands under her cheek. "Well, he succeeded. I'm exhausted and hungry."

With a sigh, I opened the bag of fries and lifted one to her lips. "Eat."

She opened her mouth.

And ended up eating my entire lunch.

Not that I cared. Feeding her was… kind of nice. In fact, just having her near me was nice. It calmed me better than any sort of yoga shit or alcohol. Her presence alone was enough to make my head clear.

"Thanks, Linc," she whispered, her eyes closed. "You didn't have to feed me."

"But I wanted to." I kissed her forehead, my lips lingering, tingling with the need to taste her, lick the salt from her lips, do anything but pull away and go back to work.

"Small nap?" she asked, eyes still closed.

"Take as long as you need. I pay you. Jay doesn't." I kissed her one last time and made my way out of the trailer, body aching, heart clenching. When had it happened? How had a small, seventeen-year-old girl wiggled her way into my life in the short span of two weeks?

Panic set in when I realized we'd only film for another two months, and then I'd be out of Seaside.

I glanced back at the trailer. Something told me that wasn't going to happen, and that Seaside was going to claim one more from Hollywood. Huh, maybe there was something in the water.

"SPAGHETTI." I STARED DOWN at the plate later that night. "You cooked for us?" Zane was currently shirtless, sporting a pink apron with cupcakes splattered all over it.

"Why does everyone assume I'm without domestic skills?" Zane asked aloud. "It's somewhat offensive."

"I don't know, man." I eyed him up and down in hesitation, "Maybe it's the skull tattoos on your arms and the pierced nose?"

"What, this old thing?" Zane pointed to the stud in his nose and heaped a pile of pasta onto Pris's plate that doubled the size of Jaymeson's. "Eating for two."

It was probably the last meal any of us would have together before filming ended. Our schedule was going to be insane over the next few weeks, which I was semi-thankful for, considering, whenever I had any free time, I just wanted to maul Dani and steal her away from society.

"Thanks, Zane." Dani reached up and squeezed his hand.

Sparks of jealousy surged through me as I eyed their hands. I knew Zane wasn't the type to try to seduce her away from me, but it was still Zane. The same guy who, while walking down the street, gave an elderly woman a heart attack, then upon noticing her not breathing, started chest compressions and saved her life. He was once given the keys to the small town he was recording in.

He was known for his looks and talent as much as his crazy sexcapades. The last thing I wanted was a shirtless Zane walking around the house.

"So..." Jaymeson cleared his throat. "... I know all of our schedules have been intense, and things are about to get crazier with Pris pregnant."

Pris touched her still flat stomach, beaming in my direction.

"And with Zane needing some time off, we thought it just made sense to have him stay here a little longer and help out."

"Help out?" I squinted. "What as? A manny?"

"I'd be a badass manny," Zane said in a serious voice. "I raised my sisters. Literally."

He had sisters?

I exchanged a confused look with Dani while Jay kept talking.

"So, we're extending Zane an open-ended invitation to stay as long as he'd like. Of course, you need to pitch in, but it may inspire your new album. Plus, going back to an empty home in Malibu..." Jay's voice trailed. "... doesn't sound like the most inspiring thing I've ever heard."

"Climb Everest," I interjected. "There's your damn inspiration."

"Oh, I did that..." Zane met my gaze. "... twice."

"Prove it."

He did.

By pulling out his phone and showing the entire table pictures. Dani was so engrossed I nearly fake-choked in order to gain back her attention.

Friends. They were just friends.

Like us.

Shit.

My palms started to sweat.

He'd never told her she was too young.

He'd never made her feel small and stupid.

NO, because freaking Zane Andrews was a saint.

Double. Shit.

"Dani." I said her name a bit loudly.

All eyes turned to me as I officially lost my train of thought. The only thing on my mind was *Marry me, go to Vegas, leave all thoughts of Zane behind before I murder him.*

"What?" She leaned back against me.

Finally.

Zane smirked.

"Nothing." I sighed kissing her head. "Sorry, just tired."

"I'd love to stay." Zane said loudly. "You guys are like family, and it's always great to have..." He eyed Dani like she was dessert. "... friends."

"Slumber party." Dani winked at him. "Perfect."

"The last one was my favorite," he whispered.

"You're having slumber parties?" I shouted. "Jaymeson, do something! He's — he's — he's—"

"Being nice?" Pris finished. "Dani still gets nightmares, you know."

"No." I felt stupid and ashamed. I hadn't known. And I felt like an ass for being jealous, but mainly I felt like a selfish ass because I wanted to be the one comforting her, not Zane.

"You can come to our next one," Zane said, all seductive glances void. "Promise."

"Do you paint toenails?" I asked, trying to lighten the mood.

"Only mine." Dani laughed. "And Zane's when he falls asleep."

Zane rolled his eyes. "One time."

Just how many damn slumber parties had they had together?

"Thanks, guys." Zane stared into his glass. "For the invitation. I really like it here. You were right, Jay." He and Jaymeson shared a look I couldn't decipher as Jaymeson's face softened, like he felt sorry for the bastard.

"Happy to have you, man." His voice even broke. What the hell?

I glanced back at Zane, hoping to clue in to the underlying message that wasn't getting spoken out loud, but he was back to shoveling food in his mouth, and I was left wondering if there was more to the guy than I'd originally assumed.

CHAPTER THIRTY

Lincoln

THE NEXT TEN DAYS FLEW BY in a blur. Even if I'd wanted to seduce Dani, I wouldn't have had the energy. It took all I had to even shower at night. I was putting in fourteen-hour days along with Pris. The only reason I ate was because Dani was incredible and made sure I always had snacks in my trailer. She even had a few extra sets of clothes brought in with essentials from my rented house, since it seemed stupid for me to go back to the house and sleep for one hour before being needed back in makeup.

The schedule was wearing on me, wearing on everyone — even Jay, who rarely raised his voice at the actors. The last person who'd forgotten a line got complete silence, which meant Jay was about ready to lose his shit.

The weather wasn't cooperating, probably because we were shooting what was supposed to be taking place in the summer, in the fall. The tourist season had been way too busy for us to chance it; plus, it would have been basically impossible to block off part of the public beaches for filming, and the last thing we needed was teenagers with camera phones leaking footage.

I finished my last line with Pris. Her eyes were tired. Hell, it was probably harder for her than it was for anyone. She was at least pregnant. Jaymeson's only excuse was that he was both directing and starring.

"Cut," Jaymeson said in a tired voice. "Linc, for this next shot, can you turn toward the camera more." I shifted my feet to the right. "Stop, right there, great, okay, deliver those same lines."

It started to rain.

"We're filming through it!" Jay shouted as the mark was set.

"Action."

"What do you want me to say? Pick me? Over my brother?" I ran my hands through my hair; the rain started pouring, water dripped from my eyelids down my cheeks as Pris reached for my wrist.

"Please," she begged. "Don't make me choose. I can't. I love you both."

"Bullshit!" I yelled, jerking away from her. "That's impossible, and it's sick. Shit, it's like the past is on repeat." I turned toward the camera, my eyes locking with Dani's as she handed Jay a water bottle.

"The past?" Pris placed her hand on my shoulder. "Talk to me. What do you mean?"

I snorted in disgust. "You should ask my brother."

My shirt stuck to my body like a second skin as I clenched my fists and delivered the last of my lines, not taking my eyes off Dani.

"I love you. Not that my love means anything. Not when you compare it to his, but..." My voice broke. "... I love you."

"Cut," Jaymeson said quietly.

The entire set was silent.

I wasn't sure if that was a good thing or bad thing. It could really go either way. Thankfully, it went the right way as Jay stood, clapped twice, and nodded his head in approval. "Good job, Linc. That was brilliant. Really, really brilliant."

"Thanks." My emotions were all over the place. I was overtired, overworked, soaking wet, and I wanted — no I *needed* Dani.

She eyed me up and down, her hungry gaze drinking me in.

And I lost all ability to stay back. When her eyes locked on mine, I just snapped. There was no other way to explain it. Blood surged through my veins, and my eyes struggled to take in her beauty as her hooded eyes damn near closed. Her body, even from this far away, I could tell, erupted in head-to-toe goose bumps. Her thin white tank top was drenched; a pink bra peeked through, teasing me beyond my control.

"I'll be back," I called to whomever would listen as I stomped toward Dani, gripped her by the wrist, and pulled her behind me. I weaved us between a series of trailers until I knew we were alone.

I looked left then right.

"Linc, what are you—?"

"Screw friendship," I growled before I slammed my mouth against hers in a rough, desperate kiss. Rain pelted off our bodies as I sucked her lips, licked, then angled my head so I could taste her more — get more. I just wanted more, damn it.

Dani wrapped her arms around my neck, interlocking her fingers and tugging me closer to her little body. I still wasn't close enough. Every kiss became no more than a tease. I gripped her shirt with my hand, twisting it to pull her closer, exposing her skin. My hand met her hot flesh, and I did the unthinkable, something I'd never been accused of in my life. I freaking blew the whole spectrum of PDA out of the water and tried to remove her shirt.

In a parking lot.

Clearly, she wasn't about to stop me either with the way

she rocked her body against me. She might be young, possibly innocent, but she made up for it with enthusiasm, and damn, that enthusiasm was going to kill me.

I broke the kiss, and took a step back, chest heaving.

Dani reached for me just as I reached for her again.

My mouth was back on hers in an instant, clamoring to drink her in, begging for any sort of release she could give.

"Well, well, well." A male voice chuckled in the distance. "I certainly don't kiss my friends like that."

Slowly, I pulled back from Dani and turned to my left, where Zane was standing, holding a box of donuts and a coffee. "Thought Dani might need a break, but I think she's going to like your break more than mine."

"Damn right," I muttered.

"Lip-gloss." Zane pointed to my mouth. "Some pink right on the corner. Other than that, I'd never know you were just mauling Jaymeson's little sister."

I glared.

"In between two trailers." He grinned. "In broad daylight."

"I know what time it is," I spat. "Can't you be charming elsewhere?"

"Of course." Zane nodded. "I'm like the good fairy of charm, just waving my… wand…" He winked at Dani. "… all over the place."

"Keep your wand in your pants, you bastard," I snarled.

"Hey, Dani, is it your birthday yet?" Zane ignored me. "Because, by my calculations, we still have three days."

Dani reached for my hand then squeezed. "Three days sounds right."

"Hmm." Zane didn't move an inch.

Rolling my eyes, I grabbed the donuts from his hands as well as the coffee. "You can go now."

"Sorry." Zane shrugged, not looking the least bit sorry. "But I've just nominated myself chaperone."

"Good, because I just nominated myself to the task of beating the shit out of you."

"You find them?" Jay rounded the corner. "Thank God, I thought my star actor had drowned or something. You're needed on set. We're going to re-shoot the last scene one more time at a different angle." Jay gave me a pointed look. "As in, right now. Today."

"Run along now, Linc. I've got this." Zane winked.

Cursing under my breath, I pulled Dani in for a chaste kiss on her cheek then whispered, "Leave your window open tonight, Rapunzel. I'm climbing in."

Her cheeks turned pink, but she gave me an affirming nod before I walked off, leaving her yet again in Saint's clutches.

CHAPTER THIRTY-ONE

Dani

HE WASN'T COMING.

It's not like he specified a time to shimmy up my drainpipe, but I assumed it would be before midnight. It was already 12:05. With a sigh, I shifted to turn off my lamp when a small stone clattered against my window. Giddy, I jumped out of bed, hurried over to my window, and pulled it open.

There he stood, looking up at my window, face sexy and gleaming in the moonlight. *Be still my heart, my pulse, my body... Heck, be still everything.* He was so gorgeous it was unfair. "Hey, Romeo." I laughed. "What brings you by my window so late?"

"I was hoping to get lucky." Linc winked.

I started to close my window.

"Joke!" he yelled. "It was a joke!"

I popped my head out and crooked my finger. "Aren't you going to climb up?"

Linc was wearing a hooded black sweatshirt; he pulled the hood over his face and shoved his hands into his pockets. "Actually, I was hoping you'd come down."

"It's midnight!"

"Actually…" He checked his watch. "… it's nearing 12:08, but who's keeping track?"

I was. Embarrassingly enough. "Why do I need to come down there? In the cold?"

"I built a fire."

"You're from LA, so when you say you built a fire, you have to understand that I assume you hired someone to dig you a hole, throw firewood in it, and light a match."

"I'm a guy. Playing with matches is basically right up there with discovering your hand can make the shape of a gun."

He had a point there.

"So?" He held open his arms. "Don't leave me hanging. Plus, I have a surprise."

"Really?"

"You'll never know unless you come down."

I chewed my lower lip. Jaymeson would kill me if I was caught out with Lincoln, especially since he'd warned me that very night to keep my distance, and when I asked why, he'd said, *"Because I said so, that's why."*

It was literally like my father had possessed Jaymeson's body. He even used the dad voice and stomped off like it was my fault he was getting gray hair or something.

"Fine," I called back. "Give me a few minutes."

I threw on a pair of skinny jeans and a sweatshirt, pulled my hair back into a ponytail, and hid the blonde locks under a Yankees cap. I'd discovered how to sneak out the day I moved in; it wasn't hard. Each level had a balcony with stairs, so all I had to do was make it to the balcony, about a two-foot jump, and I was already running down the stairs and into Lincoln's arms.

"Ooof!" He let out a curse as I tackle-hugged him. "Wasn't expecting you to pack such a punch."

"Stronger than I look."

He paused, cupping my face with his hands. "Yes, you really are."

"So..." I cleared my throat so I wouldn't focus on the tender way he was looking at me, or the way my heart did cartwheels in my chest. "...where's my surprise?"

"Follow me." He gripped my hand and led me down to the rocky cliffs that lined the beach. We carefully found the main trail as the sound from the ocean grew louder with each step.

"This..." Lincoln stopped in front of a giant bonfire, complete with two lawn chairs, enough blankets to keep us warm during a blizzard, and what looked like snacks with a canister of either coffee or hot chocolate.

I started toward camp, but he jerked me back. "Not so fast."

"What? Why?"

"We never celebrated, you know." His voice was barely above a whisper. The ocean threatened to drown him out. "You talking, you being able to talk instead of having to text everything. Nobody speaks about it. It's almost like you've been talking this whole time, but I feel moments like that deserve to be mentioned, they deserve to be celebrated. So tonight... we're celebrating."

Tears welled in my eyes, because he'd found the one vulnerable spot that I'd pushed back into my subconscious, ignored, because paying attention to it freaked me out with worry that it would come back, only worse this time.

"Thanks—" I held a sob in. "—for doing this."

"And..." Linc dug into his pocket and pulled out a necklace. "...since milestones are supposed to be remembered, I had this made."

It was a small gold-chained necklace with a little plate anchoring the front. On it was the date I started talking again.

"I can't believe you did this." I grabbed the necklace; it was heavy in my hands. Holy crap, it had to be real gold. No guy had ever gotten me a present before. "It's beautiful."

"Yeah well, I won it at the arcade downtown, and wouldn't you know? It was the exact date I was looking for." He winked. I loved that about him, his ability to make light of something that had been nothing but darkness for so long, it was hard to remember light had even existed in the first place. "Want me to help you put it on?"

Nodding, I handed him the necklace and turned as he slowly fastened it then kissed my bare neck. "Perfect."

He was perfect.

Or pretty dang close.

"So, what's on the menu?"

"Oh that?" He pointed to the canister. "Alcohol, so I can get you drunk and have my way with you."

I rolled my eyes.

"Or..." He nodded. "...hot chocolate, though they were completely out of marshmallows at the store.

I smiled to myself. "Yeah, I think I know why."

"Good looking, I'll give him that..." Linc started pouring the hot chocolate out of the thermos and into two cups. "... but odd, don't you think?"

"Eh, we all have our things. You have Skittles. He has marshmallows."

"Having a candy obsession is completely normal," he said defensively.

"It's all sugar. All weird." I took my mug from his hands and sipped. "Hmm, homemade?"

"Yes, I slaved over a stove, boiled water, and added those little packets into the water, then stirred. Blood, sweat, and tears sweetheart."

"It shows." I nodded seriously as I tried to keep the smile from my face.

He held up his hand. "Paper cut to prove my worth."

"Aw," I grabbed his outstretched hand and kissed it. "Better?"

217

"Always." His eyes flashed, and I thought he was going to kiss me. Instead, he glanced back at the fire and dropped my hand. "So, how are things?"

"Small talk?"

"Yup." He sipped his hot chocolate.

"Really?" I was a bit surprised he wasn't already kissing me and telling me all the reasons we shouldn't be together, yet making it impossible for us to be apart.

"Friends have small talk... and friends that kiss... well, they need to fill the time with something other than kissing so that *friends* doesn't turn into something else before one or both are ready." It felt like he was saying that more for his own sake than mine.

"I'm ready."

"You're... not." He frowned, staring into the fire. "So, I'll ask again. How are things?"

"Things are... good." I nodded, trying to play along. I'd always been bad with small talk, especially after the accident, when words were so much more than things you tossed into the cosmos just to hear yourself talk. Words held meaning; they held power.

"You hesitated." When I looked up, Linc was staring right through me.

I tucked my hair behind my ear. "Did I?"

"I really want to know."

I let out a huff of breath. "Things are fine, except when I go to sleep. Then, not so good." Just thinking of last night's nightmare of the accident had me shivering all over again. This time I was in the driver's seat, and it was my fault we hit the other truck head on.

"How so?" He scooted closer to me, then, as if giving up, pulled me into his lap and covered us with a blanket.

I cuddled into his chest, feeling more secure in his arms than I'd ever felt in Elliot's. "I go to bed happy that I've been talking all day, relieved that when the old lady at the crosswalk asked me what the time was, I didn't completely freak out and then, when I close my eyes, it's like I'm either experiencing the accident all over again or—" I gulped. "—I try to talk to you and fail, and you walk away."

"If I was going to walk away, I would have walked," Lincoln said simply. "I'm here. Right. Here." His arms braced me harder. "As for the no-talking thing, I think it's normal for you to have that fear. It makes sense to me. You literally just started talking again, and you're afraid that it's going to get ripped away from you, stolen."

Just like my parents were.

But I didn't voice that.

He tensed beneath me as if reading my thoughts. Maybe with Linc I didn't need to voice things like that because he knew me well enough to know what was going through my head, which admittedly, sounded crazy considering it had only been around three weeks. But he was one of those people, the type that had such a magnetic, yet familiar, pull that you were powerless to stay a stranger for longer than twenty-four hours.

"You'll never be able to move forward," he whispered, "until you stop looking behind you." His lips grazed my neck. "You know that, right?"

"Is that life experience you're speaking from... or just wisdom because you're old?"

His good-natured laughter vibrated against my back. "Just promise me you won't put me in a home for my twenty-second birthday..."

"Dang it! I knew I should have hidden those brochures for Seaside Manor!"

"Very funny." Linc kissed me softly down the right side of my neck; his lips lingered over my pulse. "And I'm speaking, from... experience."

I tilted my head and glanced up at him, raising my eyebrows.

"Why, Lincoln, what do you mean?" he said in a ridiculous falsetto that was meant to represent my voice. "Tell me your deepest, darkest secrets."

I rolled my eyes.

"You were thinking it. I was just voicing it for you." He smiled as I made myself more comfortable in his embrace while keeping his face in sight. "Sometimes it seems stupid to share my story, like it isn't tragic enough to be important to anyone but the nine-year-old kid who had to live through it, you know?"

"Yeah." I played with the thread of the blanket, twisting it around my fingers until my circulation started to get cut off. "I still feel like that. I mean, my parents died, but at least I had parents."

Linc grunted. "Some days, I wished my parents would get in an accident. At least one bad enough that my grandma would have to come take care of us, or better yet, we'd be able to go live with her." He looked disgusted with himself. "It's horrible, admitting that out loud. Confessing that my prayers at night were for my parents not to come home, while your prayers were for them to come home unharmed. Twisted in a really sick way."

My body tensed; I couldn't help it. "Did they hurt you?"

Linc's eyes didn't meet mine. He watched the fire as he spoke. Maybe the memories were too painful; maybe he was afraid that if I looked into his eyes I'd run or see too much. "Our skin wasn't marred by physical abuse. Our souls, well, that was an entirely different thing. It's sad when you break your kids so much on the inside that they wish you would just break them on the outside so they could at least explain to their teachers or other family members how bad it is. But as a kid, it's always your vote against the adults, and with no bruises, no scars... who's going to believe you? I can't even count how many times my parents would say that to us. 'Who's going to believe you?'"

Feeling sick to my stomach, I almost didn't want to ask. But Linc kept talking, and for once, it was nice to hear about someone else's pain, not because it made mine hurt less, but because I was honored to share it with him. Pain recognizes pain, and his was suddenly so evident on his face that my heart threatened to break. Had I really been that blind? That wrapped up in myself that I no longer recognized when someone else was struggling? Better yet, when someone else was stuck in the same pit I was and trying desperately to claw his way out?

"It wasn't bad at first. When I was little, they bought my love. As I grew older, I realized that having the latest in technology was a crappy substitute for a mom's hug. I can still remember asking her for a hug, the look on her face. Damn, I may as well have asked her for a pet alien. She laughed and told me only good boys get hugs. I asked her how I could be a good boy, a better boy, and you know what she said?"

I shook my head.

"Figure it out."

I gasped.

"I was five, and because money was such a big thing in our house, I figured that the best thing to do, to be a good boy, was to earn my keep. I started doing chores around the house, got a job delivering newspapers, and for my mom's birthday, I bought her the most expensive necklace I could find. I even convinced my sister to pool her money with mine so we could surprise her. The day of my mom's birthday, we ran into her room, so excited to give her the present, only to find our mom in bed with another man and another woman. My dad was away on business."

I covered my face with my hands. "What did you do?"

"Well, she yelled..." Linc flinched as though hearing it all over again. "... and told us to get the hell out, which we did. Later that morning, when she was finally sober enough to speak to us without yelling, we gave her the present, and she threw it in the trash." His voice shook. "My parents… are both, quite possibly, the most selfish human beings in the history of L.A., and that's saying a lot. If it hadn't been for my grandparents, I'd probably be just like them. As it is, my sister, well, she takes after my mom, while I'd like to think I favor my grandfather."

"Linc…" My voice was heavy, emotional. "… I can't imagine a mother treating her son that way. I mean, why even have kids?"

"Tax write-off?" he suggested in a joking tone. "I asked my grandmother that, and she said it was a competition thing. Having kids was about keeping up appearances, showing everyone how perfect and rich she was."

"Linc, no offense, but your mother should be shot."

"Ha." He lowered his head then looked at me out of the corner of his eyes. "Probably. Then again, she'd probably survive and somehow get a medal made in her honor for going through such a difficult trial. If anything, it would make her more popular in her circle of friends, and that's the last thing this world needs — for her selfishness to spread its ugly tentacles throughout society, choking the life out of more people by just being touched by her poison."

I was silent.

"Sorry." He swore. "That was uncalled for. No matter how horrible of a person she was or is, it's no excuse to put her down. That makes me just like her, and the last thing I want is to be associated with a monster."

"Why acting?" I asked after a few minutes. "I mean, don't get me wrong. You're really good at it."

"Remind me to sign your bra later," he joked.

I smirked. "Well if I was wearing one…" I froze. Where had that come from?

Lincoln's entire body went taut. "Are you trying to kill me?" Swearing, he adjusted me on his lap. "Play with fire long enough, Dani. Just remember I gave you fair warning."

"Sorry."

"No, you aren't," he growled, "but for your benefit, I'll just keep talking about myself so I don't think about you or the… bra situation." He cleared his throat. "So, acting…"

"Yeah." I leaned back against his chest as he wrapped his arms tighter around my body. The heat from the fire was nothing compared to the heat emitting from him. It was enough to set me on fire — in the best way possible. I'd only ever read about this type of feeling or seen it on TV, and, quite honestly, I never thought I'd experience it in such a real way, but there I was, sitting on Lincoln Greene's lap in front of a roaring fire, dreaming about a future, thinking about a future for the first time in months. It felt so good; I wanted to live in that moment forever. As it was, I knew I would treasure it even longer.

"My grandparents finally clued in to my parents' insanity, but they knew if they came down hard on my parents, they'd just make it so we couldn't visit anymore, so they basically enrolled us in every single summer camp you could possibly think of. When I was seven, I did one of those local drama camps. I was immediately scouted by an agent, who stupidly contacted my mom, creating stars in her eyes like you wouldn't believe." Linc sighed. "The good news was that I actually liked the escape. Acting's kind of like reading. For one brief moment in time, you can be somebody else. You can feel their pain or rid yourself of yours. You experience life in a completely different way. It was my therapy," he admitted. "It still is."

"And your parents?" I couldn't help but wonder. "What did they think about it?"

"Ah, my parents." Linc's tone was bitter, detached. "They freaking loved it. Suddenly, I had all the attention I'd never gotten but had always been desperate for. Within a few years, I was making more than my parents combined, and that's saying a lot. Let's just say Angelica quickly learned the easiest way to get attention was to do the same thing, so that's our Cinderella story of how we got started in the entertainment industry." As if stuck in a memory, his voice took on a faraway sound. "I think that's why Angelica acts the way she does now. Any attention is still attention, you know?"

"Wow." I thought on his words, hesitant to ask him anymore, since I could tell by his rigid body language that his family was a sore subject, for good reason too. "I'm glad." I kept my voice peaceful, calm, even though my heart broke for him. I hated pity. I figured he would too. When you've been on the receiving end of stuff like that for so long, you realize how much it sucks, how much you really just want someone to say, *"Wow, that blows"* and move on. "No matter how you got into acting, it's your calling. So really, if your parents weren't so crazy…"

"I wouldn't be sitting here. In front of the fire. With the most beautiful girl in the world."

"Laying it on kinda thick," I murmured.

Lincoln shifted me so that I could see him again. The outline of his face was seductive in the flickering firelight, his full lips so close to mine I yearned for a taste. "It's not a line, Dani."

Self-conscious, I tried to duck into his chest, but he gripped my chin with his hand, tilting my face toward his. "You are… absolutely gorgeous."

"Oh…" I swallowed my nerves. "… so that's what attracted you? And here I thought it was my inability to speak."

"I've had enough whiny women to last me a lifetime." He chuckled softly. "So if you ever stop talking again, know I'll be okay with it."

"Are you calling me whiny?"

"I would never accuse you of that." He smiled, his white teeth flashing in the darkness. It was a tie between burning up from the fire or the way he looked at me as though he meant every single word he was saying. "Besides, you're more of a negotiator."

Nodding, I let out a weak laugh. "I'm okay with that."

We both fell silent. My body leaned toward his, and his mouth descended toward mine.

"I don't want to be your friend anymore," he whispered, his lips brushing against mine. "But I kind of feel like a weak ass going back on my word."

"Weak ass," I repeated. "I like it." I licked my lips in invitation.

"Really?" He let out a low growl. "Stop tempting me, or I'm going to take a bite."

"Good."

"Aghhhhh." He let out a few curses before pulling away and helping me to my feet. "I'm going to ignore those seductive eyes and get you back to your room before I do something stupid."

"Am I the *stupid* in this scenario?"

"No." He took another look at me and groaned. "That would be me."

"Linc…" I grabbed his hand. "… I like you."

"Oh good, because for a second there, I was worried about your feelings and really didn't want to have one of those awkward conversations where I asked to be your boyfriend."

"Boyfriend?"

"Way better than Elliot, I can promise you that."

"You've met him once, and already I have this weird suspicion that if you met him for a second time, he'd have an accident or something."

"I was thinking something freak, nothing fatal. You know, like, *'Oh shit, sorry that you ran into that pole, man, I really didn't mean to push.'*"

Laughing, I picked up the blanket. "You sound like Zane. He likes to toss out threats too."

"Zane." Linc spat his name. "Can you find a new friend?"

"I don't have that many, so I can't really be picky. Besides, he stays up at night with me—"

"I'll do it." Linc said quickly. "How hard could it be? Guarding your dreams?"

"Hard." I swallowed nervously. "Especially when I see that stupid car again."

"The car?"

"The one that scared me right before I stopped talking. I remember every vivid detail. Demetri too. I know it wasn't the car's fault; I was just spooked, but still. I see that black car in my dreams, and it's like I'm reliving it all over again, I wake up thinking I'm going to stop talking again."

"Dani…" Lincoln tossed some sand onto the fire. "… I say next time you see the car in your dream, you throw something at it. Attack what makes you afraid. It's the only way to conquer fear. You run at it."

"If only I could control myself in my dreams."

Smiling, he pulled me in and nestled me against his body. "Let's get you home, and maybe, if I stay the night, you'll dream of me instead."

"Taking guard duty seriously, aren't you?"

"I take everything regarding you very, very seriously." Linc kicked sand over the fire, extinguishing it as he wrapped an arm around me and kissed my forehead.

"Thanks," I whispered. We walked hand in hand back to the beach house. It was easy getting back into my room, and Linc was tall enough that all he had to do was take a long step and he was at my balcony, making himself comfortable in my room.

"So…" His eyes fell on the bed. "… sleep."

"Yeah." I yawned. "But I sleep naked, so turn around?"

"What?" He hissed through his teeth.

"Kidding." I patted him on the shoulder. "I'm going to go throw on a pair of really baggy sweats."

"Doesn't work if I'm already thinking about what's

underneath," he grumbled.

"Sleep," I said again, probably to convince myself as much as him.

Linc let out a long exhale. "Right, I mean it's not like I've ever slept with a girl and not... *slept* with her."

My eyebrows rose.

"I can do anything. Really, I'm not Zane, I have self-control."

The joke was on him, considering out of all the guys I'd met in my life, Zane clearly deserved a medal in that department.

"We only have a few hours until we're needed on set anyway." I shrugged. "Let's put them to good use."

"By sleeping," he said for the third time.

"Is it easier if you keep saying it out loud?"

"Hell yes." He ran his hands through his hair. "Right, okay." More nodding. "Good."

CHAPTER THIRTY-TWO

Lincoln

"One," I grumbled softly to myself. "Two."

Things were bad; you knew they were bad when you were actually counting pigs in order to fall asleep. I saw Wilburs float over my head one after another. I named them, I numbered them, and when that didn't work, I put them in funny clothes, all for my own bored amusement.

I'd be lying if I said it was easy being next to Dani while she slept. My eyes were wide open, staring up at the ceiling that, honest to God, made me want to puke.

Zane had put a poster of himself above her bed.

His way of guarding her from bad dreams, apparently. According to Dani, he said his poster was like an Indian dreamcatcher.

It only bothered me because it was Zane, every female's dream. Something about the way he walked, even his voice, drove women insane, my sister included. I just didn't want Dani to be another.

I'd never suffered from jealousy.

Because I'd never had to fight for what I wanted.

Until now.

Even though fighting sucked, it was a hell of a lot better fighting for something than getting it without earning it in the first place.

I turned on my side. I wanted to earn her in the worst way possible. I wanted it to be hard, because I knew if it was easy, it wasn't real.

And it felt real.

Too real.

I'd never let anyone in before. I was a loner by heart. Acting day and night, making money, pouring my soul into my roles and living a detached life of meaningless sex.

In retrospect, I had no idea how the hell I got through life without going on antidepressants. Money only lasted for so long; and sex, well, it was great in the moment, but when I looked back on the last few years, I couldn't even count the real friends I'd had.

Now I had Dani.

And by association, AD2, the wives, Jaymeson, and Zane since he was apparently now adopted into our weird little family.

It felt so damn good, but my only fear was ruining it. Pushing Dani too hard, not being able to control myself and just selfishly taking her before she was ready.

It wasn't the number anymore that bothered me.

It was the fact that, at my age, I was in an entirely different place and the last thing I wanted was to project that onto her. Damn it, she needed to go to college, do stupid shit, make mistakes, all without the watchful eyes of me and the guys.

Offering her freedom would come at the cost of my own heart, I felt like a complete nut job for even contemplating things like that while she lay next to me, her soft breathing all but making me want to whimper and punch something.

My body screamed for her.

And my heart, well... it kept reminding me that I needed to keep hers intact, and if I had any hope of doing that, I needed to go slow.

Like a snail.

Be the snail. Ha, my new motto. Shit.

Dani turned on her side, then yawned and opened her eyes. I froze, hoping she wouldn't slap me, or worse yet, scream and wake up Jaymeson because I was staring at her like a wide-eyed, horny teenager.

"Can't sleep?" she asked, voice husky. The moonlight spilled onto the bed, casting a silver shadow across her hair, making her look like some immortal being.

My body responded immediately, so I scooted away, giving us space between our bodies. "Not really. I tried counting pigs, but you know how that goes. Maybe if you were texting me, I could get to sleep. I miss my texts. Promise me that just because you can talk now, you won't stop texting me."

Rolling her eyes, she reached for my face. "Promise. Now sleep."

"I can't just... sleep," I grumbled. "I feel... every little noise you make, and I may actually die staring at you." Groaning, I turned on my back. "Pretty sure things just got creepier. Didn't think that was possible after being caught staring at you while you slept, but I've slumped to new lows."

With a sigh, Dani threw off the covers, moved to straddle me, and lifted her shirt off her body.

"Uhhh." My hands went to her sides as if beckoned by her skin. I didn't let go, but I also didn't move. "What are you doing?"

Dani didn't answer.

And I really, really needed her to say something before I did the unthinkable.

She moved against me, taking the lead by pinning my hands above my head. What. The. Hell. I was trapped, and I wasn't sure if I should fight back or just kiss her, or die on the spot from pleasure as she leaned down, giving me the most amazing view of the valley between her breasts.

"Linc." Her tongue snuck out, licking the outside of my ear before her hot mouth trailed kisses down my neck. "Sometimes, thinking is overrated."

"No." Why the hell was I still fighting?

She nibbled a bit harder and then pulled my shirt off.

I let her. I was too weak to fight anything, probably too weak to even have sex with her, but maybe that was a good thing. I'd been spending so much energy trying to keep my hands off that I was officially defenseless. "You don't know what you're doing. You'll regret it in the morning." Words. I needed more convincing words. "Dani, Jaymeson will kill me."

"He won't know," she whispered against my mouth. "Give me one good reason we should stop."

"Prison," I moaned against her mouth. "Not that I think you'd turn me in, but I wouldn't put it past Demetri, Alec, or Jaymeson. Hell, they'd probably frame me."

"You're not going to prison." She laughed, her breath hot on my chest. "Stop being weird."

"The first time," I blurted, "is really... difficult." Holy shit, I was pretty sure I just quoted the video from my middle school health class. Damn you, Mr. Resik!

A man can only take so much. It's true. I never planned on being seduced; I should have thought of it, but instead I'd spent all my energy on practicing self-control, even making sure my kisses were brief.

Ha, the joke was on me.

Dani paused over me, then slowly unzipped the jeans I'd been uncomfortably sleeping in.

"Dani..." I grabbed her hands. "... I uh—"

Her eyebrows shot up. "You what?"

"I'm a virgin?"

"Nice." She actually laughed in my face.

"I'm scared of being nude?"

"A never nude?"

"Damn, I think I may love you for referencing *Arrested Development* right now."

"Ever wonder how they had kids if he always wears the short jean-shorts?"

"Daily."

Dani smirked then continued to unzip. I'd never really paid attention to the sights or sounds of being intimate. I was more of a *get in, get it on, get out, send them home.* But the sound of a zipper? Damn near impossible not to hear that. I was afraid Jaymeson could even hear it.

And then getting jeans pulled off? They scratched against my legs, against the bed.

It was loud.

Not at all quiet.

I gulped once my jeans were tossed onto the floor and nearly had a seizure when Dani dropped her white shorts to join them. I was suddenly thankful she was only joking about the sweats; the white against her tan skin was... jaw dropping.

Closing my eyes didn't work, because the minute I laid back against the pillows, she climbed back onto me, grabbed my hands, and basically forced me to touch her.

The thread had snapped.

The control was officially gone.

I waved goodbye as it floated away from my consciousness. I embraced Dani, swearing to never let her go.

"We do this, you leave me, I will chase you," I growled against her mouth. "And I mean that in the most threatening way possible. I'm not letting you go."

"Good." Her eyes watered with tears.

"Doing this with you can't be about scratching an itch. I was that guy once, but with you? I want to savor." I brushed a kiss across her mouth. "Do you understand that?"

"Just... don't hurt me," she whispered, all traces of

seduction gone.

I tried not to read into it too much but was too damn curious for my own good. "Has someone hurt you before?"

"Elliot." She pushed me back down, laying her body across mine as I cupped her at the waist and pulled her close across my skin. "After my parents died, I thought it would make me feel better."

"Killing him," I said in a serious tone, "would probably help me sleep better at night. The bastard probably didn't even know what to do with you, did he?"

She scrunched up her face. "It hurt and was over in like three minutes."

"What an idiot." I swore violently. "Tell me he at least held you afterward or told you it was going to be okay."

"He put on his clothes and left."

My fingers dug into her arms. "No offense, but you slept with a boy."

"I know," she said, her voice sounding confused.

I kissed her mouth hard then pulled back. "I'm a man."

She nodded and then very shyly murmured, "Care to prove it?"

"Thought you'd never ask." I captured her mouth again and again, each kiss going deeper and deeper as our bodies slid against one another. Minutes went by, maybe an hour while we kissed; while I made sure she understood the very meaning of the word *savor*.

Lips bruised, she came up for air then tugged me by the hair back down. With a low growl, I did the best I could at keeping things slow; at making sure she felt every caress of my mouth. Every time my body came into contact with hers, I paid special attention to the moment, adding as much pleasure as I could with my tongue and hands.

"Nightstand," she whispered against my mouth. Our bodies were sticky with sweat as the air in the room turned erotic with our tangled breaths.

"Huh?"

She blushed and averted her eyes, mumbling, "Protection."

"I'm torn between yelling at you for having condoms and embracing you for being smart. But calling it smart means it's okay for you to engage in sexual activities, and at this point, I'm pissed you even know the definition of the word."

"What?" She shook her head in confusion. "Why are you suddenly turning into Jaymeson?" Oh good, mentioning her *brother* in bed was already bad enough.

"Protective," I growled nipping at her lips. "And you're mine, so... any other guy touching you really pisses me off. Hell, he just went through puberty!"

"Killing the moment."

"Good, because I'm going to kill him," I snarled, slamming my fist into the pillow then kissing her hard on the lips. "You know, we don't have to do this."

"Yeah, we do."

"No..." I pulled back. "... we really don't."

"For once—" She locked eyes with me. "—I want to do something on *my* terms. Not because my therapist tells me to, not because people are worried about me or feel sorry for me. I want this. I want you. Don't tell me I can't have you. Don't tell me I can't have the one I love."

Stunned, I could only stare at her and pray I'd really heard what I thought I'd heard.

"Did you say love?" I barely managed in a choked whisper.

Dani nodded slowly, her eyes never leaving mine. "That sounded selfish."

"Kind of," I agreed softly. "But since I'm part of the selfishness, I'm really in no position to complain."

"Make love to me."

I stared. Hard. And in one kiss, sealed both our fates. "Okay."

CHAPTER THIRTY-THREE

Dani

HE WAS NOTHING LIKE ELLIOT. ELLIOT had been... a boy. Lincoln was all muscle, a man who had filled out in places I didn't even know guys filled out. I was desperate for him, not because I wanted to make things go away, but because I felt alive with him. I felt like me.

The me I used to know.

The one that smiled, the one that laughed, the one that talked. He had seen the mute, but he'd also seen the girl before the muteness, the one I'd missed so much it brought tears to my eyes.

But most of all, he embraced them both.

Something that nobody had done until now.

It was freeing, giving myself to someone so completely.

"Dani," Linc whispered, his mouth meeting mine in another searing kiss that had my body trembling. Sensations rocked through me as he flipped me onto my back, bracing himself over me, the muscles in his neck twitching as his arms flexed, his body weight being held up so he wouldn't crush me.

Lincoln Greene. Was. Gorgeous. Stormy grey eyes locked with mine. His lips twitched into a seductive smile.

And then I felt him.

All of him.

And suddenly decided it wouldn't work. I was insane, right? This would not work. At all. Nope. Not happening.

He must have noticed my panic because he pulled away and kissed me again, making me forget everything, including my own name.

With a whisper of devotion, his body moved against mine. With one quick thrust he tugged me against him, filling me, claiming me with such completeness that I gasped aloud.

He went still. "Are you okay?" The concern in his eyes was my undoing, breaking my heart that he was so opposite of Elliot and any other guy I'd ever known.

With a nod, I reached up to kiss him, causing a blindingly good sensation to build within me as he pulled me closer to him and slowly moved with purposeful strokes, as if taking his time.

Savor.

He'd said savor.

And I think I was finally understanding what the word meant.

I closed my eyes.

"Nope." He chuckled wickedly. "Open."

"Huh?" Disoriented, only able to concentrate on the feeling building inside of me, I shook my head and squinted at him. "What?"

"Keep them open," he commanded softly. "And on me. Watch me watch you so you know when this is over, that you'll have nothing to regret, because the look I'm giving you now is the same one I'm going to give you after, and the day after that, and the day after that."

Tears pooled in my eyes as our mouths fused together in a hungry kiss. My body shuddered uncontrollably as he thrust one last time, leaving me boneless, weak.

Chest heaving, he kept our positions tangled like a pretzel and locked his gaze on mine again. "Are you okay?"

I nodded, not trusting my voice.

"Good," he smirked, "because we still have a few hours."

"What?" I nearly shrieked, "You mean—"

"You're mine," he said simply. "And I'm yours. That's what I mean. If you thought this was a one-time thing? Or that I'd leave and forget your name? You have another thing coming. I don't say words just to hear myself talk, and I don't make fake promises."

My face broke out into a grin that hurt my cheeks. "You're kind of great, you know that, right?"

"Not nearly as great..." He kissed me with exquisite tenderness. "... as you."

"WHAT THE SHIT?" THE screaming sounded a lot like Jaymeson.

I jerked awake, my blurry vision taking in the tossed clothes in the room: mine, Linc's, and then my bra, proudly displayed at Jaymeson's feet.

By the look of rage on his face, I guessed we were screwed, and I was going to find Linc's body belly-up in the ocean.

"Linc." I elbowed him in the side. He was lying on his stomach, hugging the pillow.

With a yawn, he blinked his eyes open. "Hey there." He reached for my head and pulled me down for a kiss.

"Release the minor," Jaymeson said in an eerily calm voice that literally sounded like he'd channeled a forty-year-old dad and was currently being possessed.

Linc's eyes widened in panic before he very slowly turned over, then pulled the blanket up to cover the fact that he was naked and waved.

Right. He waved. At Jaymeson.

He may as well have pointed a gun.

Jaymeson lunged for the bed but was pulled back by a very calm Zane, who was cheerfully holding a bowl of Lucky Charms in one hand while clutching Jaymeson's shirt in the other.

"Should have locked the door," Zane said under his breath, releasing Jaymeson and dipping his spoon into the bowl. A few marshmallows tumbled from the spoon. I imagined the freak had picked out all the healthy parts of the cereal and tossed them in the trash.

"You bastard!" Jaymeson pointed his finger at Lincoln. "She's a child!"

"Bullshit!" Linc shouted right back.

I flinched at the loudness of his voice. "She's an adult, and she's been through a hell of a lot these past few years. Damn it, let her make her own decisions!"

"Right!" Jaymeson stomped toward us. "She's been through hell and back. Do you really think she's in her right mind to make such big decisions? And you come rolling up into Seaside like some bloke whose shit doesn't stink, and you think I'm going to let you? Seduce her? My SISTER?" The sister part was said on a shriek.

Pris charged her pregnant self into the room, took one look at the situation, and yelled, "Out! All of you."

Jaymeson turned to glare.

She glared right back. "Jaymeson, so help me, if you ever want to see me naked again, you will get out of this room. Now."

"Ha..." Zane shoveled another bite of cereal into his room. "... I think I'm going to love Seaside."

"Bloody asshole." Jaymeson stomped off, shoving Zane through the door then slamming it behind him.

"Linc, you have exactly five minutes to get your clothes

back on, jump out that window before my husband sees you, and make it to the set all in one piece," said Pris, holding out his jeans. "Think you can do that?"

Linc pulled me close. "I'm not going to just abandon Dani."

Pris's face softened. "You aren't abandoning her. You'll see her later today. I'm not cursing your existence and banning you from our house, though I'd appreciate it if you actually walked through the door so we could supervise all bedroom activity before it happens, but I'm too late for that. So right now, just let me talk to my sister and please... leave."

Linc kissed me on the temple then slowly got out of the bed, snatching his jeans from Pris's outstretched hand. Sighing, she turned around while he quickly got dressed and made his way over to the window. "Do I really have to go out this way?"

Pris's eyebrows rose. "The window means you live to see another day. The door means you may get shot. Jay lives in America now. He bought a gun and doesn't understand what the safety's for so..." She lifted one shoulder in a show of unconcern. "... your choice."

"Window, it is," he muttered, giving me one last comforting look before lowering himself to the balcony.

When he was gone, I wanted nothing more than to hide under the covers. But Pris very quietly walked over to me, sat on the bed, and burst into tears.

I didn't know what to do.

I was the one in trouble, right? The one who should be crying? Not that I regretted anything except for the fact that Jaymeson had walked in on us.

"Pris..." I grabbed her hand.

"I'm so sorry," she sobbed. "I should have been there more. I should have been present, instead of just..." She waved her hands into the air. "... been the sister. Damn it, I'm the mom now, and I'm going to be a mom, and I'm messing up with you. How am I supposed to do it right with our child?" Her eyes were red-rimmed already.

"Whoa, whoa." I pulled her in for a hug, keeping the sheet wrapped around me. "Pris, this isn't about you."

"You had sex!" she wailed. "With a Hollywood heartthrob who's leaving in a few months, and you love him, or at least you think you do, and he got you talking again, which is great, and I love him for it, but I hate him for leaving. He's going to leave, and you're going to be heartbroken, stop talking, and maybe stop eating again, and we're going to be left picking up the pieces that he trail blazed through. Damn it, Lincoln Greene!" She punched the mattress with her hand.

I snapped from my dumbfounded state. "Pris, geez! At least take a breath. You're turning blue and that's bad for the baby." I shook my head and grabbed her hand, but the words just kept tumbling from her. Words like heartbroken, rich, playboy, bastard. Pris had never been one to overreact, so I knew part of it was her hormones and the other part guilt. I knew guilt well. Oh, did I know it. I squeezed her hand and whispered. "He's not like that. Do you really think he'd risk everything? His career? His relationship with Jaymeson? Just so he could sleep with me?"

"Yes." She nodded, wiping away a few tears. "That's exactly what I think, Miss Forbidden Fruit."

Guilt gnawed at my chest. I felt bad for letting her down and guilty that I was more upset about getting caught than anything. But I was old enough to make my own decisions, right?

He wouldn't leave.

Lincoln might be a lot of things, but he wasn't that guy.

I refused to put him in that category. The Elliot category, the one who took what you offered and then dumped you the minute things got hard.

"Right now..." I gripped her hand tightly. "... I don't need a *mom*. I need a sister. I need a friend. You can't undo what's been done, and I wouldn't want you to in the first place. He... You're right." Tears welled in my eyes. "I love him."

"That's great." Pris's voice was weak. "It really is. And I'd love to sit here and support you, but I have a bad feeling about him. Don't take me wrong. I don't think he's a bad guy, I just... What happens if things go back to the way they were? I couldn't care less about him. I care about you. I want you happy, and I can't handle losing you again."

"Then don't push me away because I slept with the man I love," I said softly. "And trust me to make my own choices. Can you do that?"

"No." She laughed through her tears. "But I'll try. You know... sex with an actor, not the smartest choice."

"Um, you're married to one."

"Married," she said softly. "I married him first."

All the blood left my head. "You — you what?"

"Jaymeson and I... we were married first. Committed. After Dad died, there was this weird unsaid thing, us being a pastor's daughters. Jaymeson couldn't do it. He just... felt like he was doing things wrong every time he kissed me. Like if Dad was still alive, he would have asked permission to date me. He would have done things right. I was so broken after their death, so worried about you that the last thing he wanted was to add more guilt. So... we eloped."

"I didn't know that," I said more to myself than to her.

"You didn't need to..." She shrugged. "... but you're right. What's done is done. I just... I hope you know what you're doing. You're seventeen, you have a whole life to live, things to experience, but if you're sure he's what you want, I won't stand in your way. Just don't let a person ever have that type of control over you, where you're so invested in them that, if or when they leave, you lose a part of yourself. Okay?"

My lower lip trembled. "Okay."

She was quiet for a minute. Then a smile crossed her features, softening her face. "Now..." She sighed. "... I'm going to play the part of the best friend." Pris crossed her arms. "How was it?"

I hid under the sheet then let out an "Amazing."

CHAPTER THIRTY-FOUR

Lincoln

I EXPECTED JAYMESON TO FIRE ME. Hell, I would have fired me. Did I have any regrets? No. But it was his sister-in-law. His underage, gorgeous, sister-in-law, whom he referred to as his little sister. Damn it, what had I been thinking?

In his house?

Under their roof?

And it wasn't like I could say she seduced me, even though, if I was one to place blame, I'd be pointing my finger in her direction. She straddled me! Naked! What was I supposed to do? Sing nursery rhymes and close my eyes? Hold my breath?

I was in and out of the makeup trailer within minutes.

We were back on set at the local high school. The movie was being filmed in weird chunks, so technically, even though we'd been filming for a few weeks, we were just now filming the opening scene, where Nat saw Alec and Demetri for the first time.

With a sigh, I made my way onto the set and sat in my chair.

I was there for maybe two seconds before a hand slapped me in the back of the head.

"What?" I jerked to attention and glared as Demetri crossed his arms and stared daggers through me. "Why'd you do that?"

"You know why," he whispered.

I narrowed my eyes. "No, I really don't."

"You're too stupid to live, then. Which means I'm going to have to let Alec kill you."

"Why Alec?"

"He'd do better in prison."

"As opposed to you?"

Demetri puffed out his chest. "I'm too pretty."

"Why are you here? On set?"

"I volunteered." He sighed heavily. "And Dani's afraid Jaymeson's going to kill you then bury the body somewhere in the woods out past the old Smith place, under the cabin by the fifth tree."

"That's..." I coughed. "... scary descriptive."

"He may have let the location slip."

I tensed.

"Like five times when he texted me and Alec to bring shovels."

"She's old enough to make her own decisions. Seriously," I growled. "And it's not like I'm going to leave her. She isn't like that. I'm not like that. It wasn't a bang and high-five moment."

"Bang and high five?"

"You know," I shrugged, "Bang, then give positive reinforcement by a high five before leaving."

Demetri stared, then very slowly, with judgmental eyes shook his head. "To think, bigger whores than myself actually still exist in the wild."

"You?"

"Reformed." He nodded. "But you..." A finger jabbed at

my chest. "You're not married. Therefore, you're a slippery fish, one that can flap out of her grasp and swim off into the ocean, leaving us to pick up the..." He frowned. "Not sure where I was going with that metaphor."

"Me either," I muttered, giving him a side-eye.

"I can't believe I actually agreed to help protect you."

"What are you going to do? Take a bullet for me or something? No offense, but if Jaymeson wants to end my life, I highly doubt you standing in the way is going to do anything."

"Half brother." He nodded seriously. "He'd never off his own family. Besides, he's English. Violence to him is forgetting to say sorry."

I burst out laughing.

Jaymeson plopped into the seat on my other side followed by Alec, who, arms crossed, stood in front of me, blocking the view of the rest of the crew that, by the temperature in the room, had all but shuffled away from our little group. Great, no witnesses.

"You're lucky she likes you," Jaymeson said in a low voice. "And you're lucky my wife said not to kill you."

I resisted the urge to tug at my collar. "I'll have to write her a thank you card."

"You won't write her shit." Jaymeson elbowed me. "And you'll do well to remember to keep your hands off my little sister under my roof."

"Sorry." I sighed. "I really am, that was..." I shook my head. "... disrespectful, and I do regret that part."

Alec visibly relaxed in front of me.

Jaymeson still looked ready to spit nails at my face, but instead, he gave me a long, very hostile look before standing up, grabbing his headset, and barking orders. "Extras needed on set."

I let out the breath I'd been keeping in.

Alec hadn't budged from his spot in front of me. Instead, his eyes narrowed. "I'm not one to pass judgment, believe me."

His blue eyes were icy in their stripping of all of my comfort. "But if you break her heart, I will find a way to break at least one or two bones in your body. Understand?"

"Yeah." Was it wrong to respect them more after being threatened? She deserved that type of family, the type that didn't give a shit about who I was or what I represented.

It was oddly refreshing.

"Lincoln!" Jay shouted. "Don't make me tell you twice. Or do you need a minute before we shoot the next scene?"

"Nope." I stood quickly. "I'm good."

Demetri grabbed my shoulder, pulling me back. "Remember, in this scene I walk with a dead-sexy swagger." He slapped my ass. "Make me look awesome."

"Watch and learn," I said under my breath as I mentally prepared myself for the next scene. There were no lines, but sometimes, those were the hardest scenes, ones where you had to let your body language speak for you.

For some reason, I was so keyed up, so energized, that I was nearly bouncing on my toes waiting for the scene to be slated.

And then Dani appeared behind Jaymeson. She winked and then slowly licked her lips. Little seductress.

Hell yes, I could walk with swagger, because I was walking toward the camera, toward her.

Up until then, I'd been distracted, a bit more hesitant in my work, but as Jay said "Action," I had an epiphany. I was walking toward her, the girl I cared for, the girl I could fall in love with. A girl who I would do anything to keep.

So I walked.

And when I finished, I landed a deadly smirk in her direction, and clenched my fists as Jay said "Cut," and Demetri said loud enough for everyone to hear. "Holy shit, that was hot." And then, of course, "I knew he could do me."

"No more talking." Alec shook his head at Demetri while Jay leveled me with a respectful nod.

"Good." Jay relaxed. "That was really good."

Coming from Jay? That was like landing on the moon and doing back flips onto Mars.

I met Dani's gaze one last time before we moved to the next scene.

If I had her waiting for me at the end of the day, I really had everything, didn't I?

CHAPTER THIRTY-FIVE

Dani

FILMING WAS GOING LATE AND I was exhausted after being kept up most of the night, so I grabbed the last of the Skittles, poured them into the bowl, made sure that Linc had the water he wanted, double-checked the blinds to make sure they were closed, then went to let myself out of the trailer.

The door opened right before I touched it, and suddenly Linc and I were chest to chest.

My breath came out in a little gasp as he lifted me into his arms and kissed me soundly across the mouth, while simultaneously locking the door behind him. I didn't have time to respond as he walked me back into the small bedroom then tossed me onto the bed. His shirt went flying, then shoes, jeans... gone. And he was standing before me much like he had the night before, naked.

"Good day?" I breathed, sitting up on my elbows.

"It just got better." He licked his lips, eying me up and down before crooking his finger.

Slowly, I got off the bed and approached him, lifting my hands into the air as he pulled off my T-shirt, then fused his mouth with mine.

"Good day?" He repeated my question.

"It's looking up." I tugged his head down to mine again, my hands tangling in his long hair, pulling hard as I angled my body against his.

Laughing, he tossed me back onto the bed, leaving me to pull off the rest of my clothes. Then he joined me again, all traces of laughter gone as he kissed a trail down my stomach. I laced my hands into his hair again.

"I have…" He kissed then licked the ticklish spot next to my belly button.

My legs shook, while my body jerked toward him.

"… five minutes."

"We can be fast." I assumed he meant sex so I tried tugging his body back toward mine.

"Five minutes," he repeated, his head lowering farther and farther.

My eyes widened as I realized where he was going.

"But, sweetheart, I only need two."

Actually, he got it done in one.

But that was beside the point.

"Tell me," I asked, my body still wracked with tremors. "Do you put that on the back of your head shot? 'Cause it's a skill. It really is."

"I figured it would be presumptuous, and then what would happen if a casting director asked me to prove it?" he joked, tossing me my shirt.

I quickly put on my clothes, but it was so hard; each time I put on an article of clothing, he pulled me in for another kiss.

"I don't want to leave," he grumbled, "but Jay wants to get this scene, and the tide's out and—"

I shushed him with another kiss. "Go, I'm gonna head home anyway."

A regretful look crossed his face. "I'll try to hurry."

"Art never hurries," I corrected in my best Jaymeson

voice.

"Accent needs work." He winked then pulled me in for another kiss. "I probably won't see you until tomorrow. Then again, that's your birthday party... so damn it, when am I going to have alone time with you?"

"We'll work it out." I laughed. "It's not like you're leaving tomorrow or something."

He tugged my body roughly against his. "Thank God for that."

"Have fun, except when you're kissing my sister. I hope those scenes suck."

His eyebrows knitted together as he gave me a concerned squeeze on the shoulder. "Does it bother you? I'm sorry, I swear it's acting. It's not—"

"Linc," I said, allowing some irritation into my tone, "I live with actors. I know the way it works. Don't worry about me."

"I do." Voice earnest, he kissed the top of my head. "So much."

"I know." I scrunched up my nose. "Now go before Jay adds another reason to kill you to his list."

"Right." He hesitated, kissing me one last time before leaving the trailer. I swallowed a giddy shriek and flipped off the lights, then made my way home.

"SO..." ZANE TOSSED A marshmallow into the air, caught it between his teeth, chewed, and swallowed. "... you had a fun night. Care to share intimate details of how you seduced poor Lincoln out of his designer jeans? Or is that a secret?"

I tossed the pillow at his face. "I didn't seduce him."

"Ha." Zane wagged a finger at me. "For shame, lying to your best friend."

"Demetri's my best friend."

"Right, but we talked last night, and you said now it was a tie because I'm so good-looking."

"I was drunk."

"On hot chocolate?" Zane cackled. "Oh, high school, I'm going to miss you when you marry Linc on your eighteen birthday, move into his love shack, and start having little children. I really am."

"Married?" I repeated, incredulous. "You're high."

"Never done drugs. I have too addictive of a personality. Besides, why do drugs when they cost so much damn money?"

"You're rich."

"Right. And I'll stay that way because I don't do drugs." Zane glanced at the TV, and his expression fell, like something had just sucker-punched him. I tried to look in time, but he'd already changed the channel. "So, details, or am I going to have to play back the nanny-cam I put in your room?"

I felt my face pale. "Zane…"

"Fine." He handed me a pink marshmallow. "So if there really was a tape, which there isn't, because I'm not a freak like Demetri…" Another jab at my best friend, because he apparently thought the position was open for negotiation. "… I wonder if it would be Lincoln attacking you with his tongue, or poor, innocent little Dani, seducing the shit out of him, basically dragging him by the hair into her king-size bed." A satisfied smile crossed his features as he sat back against the couch and crossed his arms.

"You'll never know," I said, tossing my head in a show of confidence.

He raised an eyebrow. "I already do know. Because I know Linc, and the last thing he would do would be having sex with you while Jaymeson's next door. That's like asking to get a bullet to the ass."

"I may have…" I waved my hand in the air. "… encouraged…" I almost choked on my spit. "… a little bit."

Zane grinned.

Man, he was pretty and, of course, still shirtless. One day a girl would housetrain him, and she'd use little marshmallow trails to do it.

"Look at you, growing up, making big girl choices. Man, it's like one day you're speaking in full sentences, the next day you're grabbing a man by the—"

"We're home!" Jay shouted.

"Do *not* finish that sentence," I warned Zane, horrified.

"Dad!" Zane jumped off the couch. "How was work?"

Jay groaned. "Zane, seriously. Wear clothes."

Zane looked down. It hadn't occurred to me how many clothes he wasn't wearing until he stood. Boxers? No shirt? But he was wearing wool socks and still, *still* he looked good. "What's wrong with my uniform?"

"Uniform?" Jay and Pris said in unison while I watched the exchange with vested interest. If they were concentrated on him, they weren't thinking about me. And then, it hit me.

"Holy crap, we're siblings!" I said aloud.

Zane winked. "Sis."

"Ew, my brother kissed me!"

"YOU KISSED HER?" Jay shouted.

Pris grabbed Jaymeson. "We don't know that. Don't accuse until we know the details."

Zane burst out laughing. "Aw, shit, I really love you guys. I know I keep saying that, but…" He offered Jaymeson a marshmallow. "… it's true."

Jaymeson looked like he was about one second away from choking Zane with the spongy treats.

"Accident," I piped up. "Zane was, uh, proving a point."

Zane turned, his eyes evil as he added, "Why yes, I was teaching young Dani the perils of letting a celebrity seduce her. Well, don't say I didn't try, guys."

I narrowed my eyes. "Traitor."

He tossed me a marshmallow like that would make everything better.

Pris, very wisely, kissed Jaymeson, whispered something in his ear that clearly distracted him enough to leave us alone and go upstairs to their master suite.

"You're welcome." Zane joined me back on the couch. "Now, *Housewives* or *Game of Thrones?*"

We shared a look then said in unison, *"Thrones."*

I fell asleep halfway through the first episode and woke up a few hours later in bed.

Zane.

One day.

Very soon.

I hoped he'd find someone who took care of him the way he took care of everything and everyone else in his life.

He'd stocked the kitchen, not just with marshmallows, but with food in general. He'd labeled plastic containers, had basically force fed me breakfast, and had always made sure I was okay.

He was perfect.

Not my perfect. Not for me.

But... perfect.

Which meant he was trying really hard to either hide a flaw or ignore whatever had caused him to land in Seaside in the first place.

CHAPTER THIRTY-SIX

Lincoln

I WOKE UP WITH A REALLY bad feeling. It continued throughout the day — Dani's birthday. I couldn't shake it, maybe because for the first time in my life, I was happy. That had to mean something was going to go to hell, right?

Filming was short for me that day, which was good since I wanted to get ready for the birthday bonfire on the beach. My car had finally arrived from Malibu, which made me less stressed. I knew she hated my truck, so I was glad that I could finally drive her places where she wouldn't be white-knuckling the door the entire time, thinking we were going to get hit.

My cell phone buzzed in my pocket.

Dani: *You like?*

Attached was a picture of her in a short black dress; she was turned, showing me the scooped back.

I frowned and expanded the picture. Her tattoo seemed so familiar. I'd seen it the night in Depot Bay, it had looked like random shapes and letters. It was in a weird place, right above her ankle and below her calf in the back. Impossible to see unless she was wearing something short and was turned around, unless you knew it was there. The last time she'd worn a dress, her heels had straps that wrapped around her legs, gladiator-style, so I hadn't noticed it. And every time we'd been together I'd been distracted — by her mouth, breasts, neck, basically every damn thing about her.

I stared harder at the picture. Why the hell did it look so familiar? And why did it bother me that it looked familiar?

Shrugging, I typed a text back to her.

Linc: *Sexy. Think Jaymeson's going to let you out of the house?*

Dani: *Oh, don't worry. I asked Zane to spike his soda tonight. He's super… happy right now.*

Linc: *Drunk Jaymeson is my favorite. When I got the part, we took shots with Jaymeson until he started playing the air guitar, then sang to a house plant, thinking it was Pris. I haven't seen him drink since then.*

Dani: *Ah yes, the house plant. She threw it out after the, er, gestures he made toward it. The plant was Ralph.*

Linc: *Ralph was violated?*

Dani: *Jay tried to kiss Ralph, flashed him, then peed on the plant.*

Linc: *Poor Ralph.*

Dani: *Poor me! I witnessed the first half.*

I frowned, staring at my phone before typing.

Linc: *You were home? When I visited?*

She responded right away.

Dani: *Probably. I tended to be holed up in my room a lot back*

then. And I would remember meeting you.
    Linc: *Same.*
    Dani: *See you in a few!*
    Linc: *Okay, beautiful. And happy birthday!*
    Dani: *EIGHTEEN!*

I let out a sigh of relief. I knew I wasn't going to go to prison, but it still freaked me out she was underage; at least now it was legal, and I didn't have to feel as guilty when thoughts of her naked body crossed my mind a billion times a day.

Taking one last glance in the mirror, I straightened my tie, grabbed her gift, then headed toward the beach.

The party was in full swing by the time I arrived. Alec and Nat must have gotten a sitter for their one year old. She was sitting on his lap nursing a beer and talking animatedly to a girl I'd never seen before. She had long, red hair and really pretty skin. Curious, I walked toward the group. A tall, big guy, who looked like a football player, wrapped his arm around the redhead. I stopped in my tracks.

"No shit," I mumbled under my breath.

"I know," a male voice said to my right. "Still pisses me off too. Do you even realize how much protein I take in on a daily basis to look like that guy?"

Frowning, I turned and burst out laughing. "Gabe?"

"Live and in the flesh." He returned an easy grin and pulled me in for a hug. "How you been, man?"

"Good." We walked toward the group. "I didn't know you and Jay were close..."

"More like me and Demetri," he corrected with a chuckle. "I flew in last night to do the final music video for the sound track with the guys. After touring with them, the fans basically demanded we do another song together, so here I am."

Gabe Hyde, or Ashton as some people still called him, was one of the biggest pop stars on the planet. He'd gone into hiding for reasons I still didn't know, and had appeared back on the scene a little over a year ago. He'd toured with AD2, gotten married, and had basically been splashed on every tabloid since then. Sometimes he even gave Zane a run for his money, which was saying a lot, since Zane was everywhere.

"So..." I pointed to the built guy with the blond hair. "... is that Wes Michels?"

"Star quarterback for the Seahawks," Gabe huffed. "Hell, yeah. I had the guy write me down his exact workout routine along with his diet. I lost weight, and he put on twenty pounds of pure muscle." He sighed. "Sometimes at night I want to kill him."

"Wow, violent."

Gabe laughed then crooked his finger at a short girl with dark, wavy hair. She weaved her way through the crowd and jumped into his arms.

"Saylor..." He set her down on the sand. "... this is Linc—"

"Lincoln Greene." Her grin was huge. "I know exactly who you are. The last movie you were in—" She shook her head. "—I swear I cried for two days when you died."

"Thanks..." I laughed. "... I think."

"Hated you." Gabe looked heavenward. "She watched the movie five damn times, and each time I had to console her and remind her that it was a movie, that you weren't really dead."

"Alive." I winked. "Promise."

"Well..." She sighed. "... it was really good. I got really excited when I found out you were going to be part of this movie series."

I glanced around the fire as Demetri and Alyssa roasted marshmallows. Zane was apparently explaining the perfect twist of the stick. Wes and the redhead laughed at something he said, while Jay and Pris took seats next to Dani, who was concentrating a hell of a lot harder than anyone else on her marshmallow. "Yeah... I'm really thankful."

At that moment, Jaymeson locked eyes with me and

stood, shouting. "You steal her away to sex her, I kill you."

Gabe backed up. "Dani?"

Dani rolled her eyes and shoved her stick into Jaymeson's face. He barely caught it before it met a sandy death. But she was already running toward me barefoot. I caught her midair and kissed her long and hard. "Happy birthday."

"Now it is." She kissed me again.

Gabe and Saylor both stared at me like I'd lost my mind.

"Yeah, yeah. I know. I break her heart... you break me." I rolled my eyes. "Message received."

"Actually..." Gabe cleared his throat. "... I was going to say you break her heart, I tell Wes and his team to break you, but to each his own."

Wes waved us over, his grin huge as he glanced between me, Dani, and Jay. "So... how long has this been going on?"

"Under his roof." Zane coughed into his hand.

I glared.

Wes burst out laughing. "I don't know you, but I think I really like you right now."

I held out my hand. "Lincoln Greene."

The redhead blushed. "Remember that movie, Wes, the one I cried over."

"Oh..." Wes's smile fell. "... that movie."

"Look, I'm sorry!" I threw my hands up.

He burst out laughing. "I'm kidding. Great flick, wanted to kill you for making my wife cry and actually contemplated burning the damn thing, but..."

"A toast!" Zane stood on a stump. "To family."

Dani quickly handed me a cup of something, and I lifted it into the air as we all made a toast.

"And to the birthday girl," I said after we drank. "Eighteen. How's it feel?"

She glanced around the fire. "Perfect."

CHAPTER THIRTY-SEVEN

Dani

"WALK ON THE BEACH WITH ME?" Linc held out his hand to me. With a giddy laugh, I grabbed it and followed him down closer to the shore, while everyone behind us was being serenaded by AD2 and Gabe. A few years ago, if someone would have told me that my sister would be married to Jaymeson, and on my eighteenth birthday I'd have some of the most famous celebrities in the world singing around a beach fire in my honor, I would have laughed in their face or thought I was hallucinating.

Their voices were drowned out by the roar of the ocean as we made our way to the shore. My bare feet squished against the cold wet sand. Linc didn't say anything as we walked hand in hand for what felt like a mile. Finally, he stopped and turned; his eyes lit up like he knew a secret.

"Do you want your present?"

"You walked me a whole mile from the warmth of the fire to give me my present?"

He lifted my hands to his lips, kissing both of my wrists before dropping them and reaching one hand into his pocket.

His reddish-brown hair blew in the wind, casting a shadow over his face. I shivered, partially because I was cold, and partially because he was so beautiful. I'd always thought so, but seeing him standing before me, no secrets between us, nothing but excitement over what could happen in the future, did something to me. Butterflies spread throughout my stomach as he lifted a long jewelry box in his hand.

A small box would have freaked me out.

But this one seemed too big to have something like a ring in it.

Cautiously, I reached for it, but he jerked it back and shook his head. "A kiss, and then you get your present."

"Oh, so I have to pay for my own gift?"

"Yup." He leaned down, brushing a kiss across my lips. "Okay, your debt's paid. Open your gift."

Tentatively, I pulled it from his hand and slowly lifted the lid on the black box. Inside was another box, this one blue. Tiffany blue.

"Oh?" I glanced up. "Tiffany's?"

"I had to hide it so you wouldn't know right away." He nodded as if he was brilliant.

I pulled the lid back and gasped. A small silver charm bracelet caught the moonlight.

"It's a charm bracelet," he said in a low voice, "with a purpose. I hope you don't mind, but I talked to your sister about..." He gulped. "... about you before the accident, about the things you liked, what you were involved in. Cheerleading was obviously a big deal." He pointed to a megaphone charm. "And I added the crown because you were a princess. Still are, if you ask me." The crown dangled next to the megaphone. His voice broke. "I added the car as a way to show how you survived through a huge trauma in your life." He pointed to the next chain. "This is a cross, representing your parents — what they did, what they stood for."

Tears blurred my vision as he kept talking.

"I added the pen to represent your muteness and your ability to text and write notes, which far surpasses anyone I've ever met."

I choked on a sob.

"And finally..." He pointed to the last charm, an open-centered heart. "I added the heart... the one you gave me the minute you said yes. Symbolizing that I'm giving you mine too. I, uh..." Lincoln cleared his throat. "... I was hoping to bridge the gap for you. Combine your life before the accident with your life now."

I had no words.

And, for once, I didn't want them. I wasn't trying to speak, embarrassed because I couldn't. Because, sometimes, words were the last thing you needed, especially when they couldn't do your feelings justice. I jumped into Linc's strong arms and kissed him with all the passion I'd been keeping inside, wrapping my arms around his neck, drinking him in, making love to him with my mouth.

"So," he said gruffly, pulling back only enough to talk, though his lips moved against mine. "I take it you like your gift?"

"I love it." I kissed him again and again. "It's perfect."

"Zane got you a pet pig. A real one," he pointed out jokingly.

I burst out laughing and kissed both cheeks. "Right, that's like an eighteen–year-old's version of a pony. I get it, but this..." I hopped out of his arms and held out my wrist while he slowly fastened the bracelet. "... is absolutely perfect." I grinned up at him. "You're perfect."

"Hardly." He shook his head, his tone serious.

"You are!" I said in a convincing voice. "Now, let's go show Zane how awesome you are."

"Oh, can't wait." Linc picked me up and started running. I squealed as my body slammed against his the entire way back to the bonfire.

"Wow..." I nearly fell over when he set me back on my feet. "... good cardio. Remind me never to race you."

"Showing off again?" Zane looked up from the guitar he was holding and winked at me.

I blushed, mainly because it was Zane, and I just couldn't help it. "He's always showing off."

"Is it true Jay caught you guys?" Gabe asked, as conversation fell completely silent, and he was pinched in the side by his wife. "What?" He looked around. "Demetri said to—" He glared. "See if I invite you for Christmas now."

"You have to." Demetri grinned shamelessly. "Your wife likes my mashed potatoes better than yours."

"You spiked mine," Gabe explained in an angry voice. "With salt."

"I can't help it if you can't use measuring spoons."

Alyssa, Demetri's wife, rolled her eyes and covered Demetri's mouth with her hand.

I smiled at her then covered my yawn with my hand.

"Early day tomorrow." Jaymeson stood, glaring at Linc behind me. "We have to be on set by four."

Groans were heard around the campfire.

"Wait." I raised my hand. "Everyone's on set at four?"

"Yeah." Pris gave me an apologetic look. "The final music video shoots tomorrow morning, and the weather's supposed to be crap in the afternoon. We need sunlight."

"Wrong city," I pointed out, while everyone chuckled and started cleaning up.

"So..." Demetri approached us and wrapped an arm around me. "... your gift is an Apple watch, because I'm that badass, but I left it in my car. I'll walk you and Linc out so I can grab it, alright?"

"Sure." I waved goodbye to everyone and fell into step between Demetri and Linc.

They both towered over me.

And were equally matched in size and strength.

It almost felt like I was getting escorted back to the parking lot by body guards instead of my two best friends.

Why did I always have guys as best friends anyway? I glanced up at Demetri who was giving Linc the evil eye twitch as if to say, *"Grab her hand... I slice it off."* And Linc seemed to be as casual as ever, hands stuffed in his pockets, though his arm kept colliding with mine.

"Guys..." I stopped walking. "... can't we all make up and be friends?"

"*He* slept with you." Demetri spat out the word *he*.

"And you're a saint?" Linc burst out laughing. "Please! All I need to do is Internet-search you and—"

"Hey!" Demetri yelled. "We aren't talking about my past here!"

"But mine's up for debate?" Linc's eyebrows shot up. "How is that fair? Did Alyssa's parents freak out over your reputation? Did Nat's? Hell, did the principal even bat an eyelash?"

"Several..." Demetri smirked. "... actually."

"Cocky ass," Linc muttered. "No wonder I play you well."

I burst out laughing as I looked between them. They were even standing the same way. It would be hilarious if they weren't at each other's throats.

"Guys, I love you both."

"YOU *LOVE* HIM!?" Demetri shouted.

While I groaned into my hands.

"Present," I finally said. "Give me my present so you can go kiss your wife and blow off some steam."

"And I will be the only one doing that this eve!" Demetri nodded seriously then pointed between the two of us. "She's still... like..." He pinched the bridge of his nose. "... she's like a sister, man... Just..." He glanced at me, his face sorrowful. "... just don't hurt the only sister I have."

"You have Pris."

"Shh." Demetri waved his hand at me.

"And Nat."

"Dani!" I expected him to stomp his foot. "Not now! We're negotiating, alright?"

I held up my hands.

"I won't," Linc said in a serious voice. "I swear it."

"Alright." Demetri's voice lost most of its venom as he started walking toward his new white Escalade, a present he'd bought for Alyssa when he found out she wanted to start a family.

Once he pulled my gift out, he very slowly walked over to me then held up the Apple watch. It was the gold one.

The expensive gold one.

That had been sold out for months.

"Dem—"

"Nope!" He held up his hands. "No give backs. Plus, it's easy to spend money, but gifts that come from the heart..." He pointed at my charm bracelet. "Those mean the most. Besides, your old watch was shit, and you're always late."

"Am not!" I argued.

"Are too!" the guys said in unison, their voices nearly identical.

This time I did bust up laughing, while Demetri and Linc hid their smiles behind their hands.

"Friends?" Linc held out his hand to Demetri.

Demetri examined it like it was diseased but finally shook it firmly and left us alone, whistling as he jogged back to the group on the beach.

"He's..." I shrugged. "... something else."

"He's a good friend." Linc pulled me close. "You should get to bed. Plus, I heard from a very reliable source that there's chocolate cake waiting for you on the counter."

"From you?"

"Bingo." He kissed my nose. "But if it's covered in marshmallows by the time you make it home, just remember, those aren't me."

"Zane." I laughed then frowned as Linc started walking toward a black Benz AMG. A memory flickered in the furthest part of my mind.

I stopped walking, my eyes squinting as Linc got closer and closer to the car. Then the lights flicked as he unlocked the doors. He turned around and frowned. "You okay? I thought you'd be happy I brought my car back from Malibu so you wouldn't have to ride in the truck."

The shrieking sound of tires peeling out of a driveway hit me hard between the temples. I covered my ears with my hands and squeezed my eyes shut as my mind went back to that night…

"Dani!" Demetri shouted. "Wait up. You forgot your phone." He jogged toward me just as a tall figure got into a nice black Mercedes with California plates.

I glanced but thought nothing of it. Jaymeson always had people visiting him from out of state. I was having movie night with Dem and Lyss because Jay had some sort of meeting.

I frowned as Demetri caught up to me. My eyes were still on the car.

"Damn." He whistled. "That's an expensive one."

"Hmm." I shrugged and tried reaching for my phone, but Demetri held it above his head. "Gotta catch it!"

"Oh, I'll catch it," I threatened as I jumped, somehow lost my footing and tumbled down the small hill that opened up into Jay's driveway.

"Hey!" Demetri yelled over the hill. "Are you okay? Did we spike your juice box again?"

"Ha ha!" I called back, trying to stand, and then the lights to the Mercedes flashed, reminding me of the accident, of the moment before my life shattered right in front of me.

It was like I was back in the car again.

And my dad was driving.

"Dad!" I screamed.

The car swerved.

But I was too late. If I would have woken up sooner, I could have saved him. I could have saved Mom.

But I was too late.

"No!" I shrieked as the black car surged toward me, its lights blinding me as I turned and cowered on my stomach in the grass. Was that my scream? Why was I screaming? It wasn't like the car was going to hit me. But it was so loud, so bright.

"Dani!" Demetri reached me. "Dani!"

But he was too late.

Trauma always comes back. It always comes back. And it's up to you to either let it win or fight.

"Dani!" Lincoln shouted my name over and over again, but I couldn't hear him. I couldn't hear anything but my own scream as I covered my ears and stared at the tear-stained sand in front of me.

"What's wrong?" Demetri was at my side. I could feel his hands on my back, while Linc was trying to cup my face.

"I don't know!" Linc shouted hysterically. "She saw my car and just started screaming!"

"Your *car*?" Demetri repeated, his voice calmer as my screams turned into silent sobs against his chest. "What car? You have a truck."

"What?" Linc's voice was hoarse from yelling my name. "I brought my car up because she's scared of trucks. It's right there."

Demetri tensed then swore violently just as Wes met at his side.

"Take her to Jay's." Demetri got up, and suddenly I was being lifted into muscled arms and carried away. Tears blurred my vision. I opened my mouth to speak, to say something like, *"I'm okay, just freaked out that Lincoln has the same car,"* but the words died on my lips.

Because my brain was firing faster than my words.

And it had already put two and two together.

Linc had been there the night I lost my voice.

He was the one who had triggered it in the first place.

"How's that for irony?" I heard Demetri curse again and then fighting, like people were throwing punches.

The key to my voice had also been my curse.

"Shh," Wes whispered in a calming voice. "It's going to be okay, Dani. I promise."

But it wasn't.

It was so far from being okay.

CHAPTER THIRTY-EIGHT

Lincoln

THEY WOULDN'T LET ME SEE HER. Demetri had been in and out of her bedroom for hours. They even let marshmallow man in, or at least he was able to peek his head through the door while I stared helplessly at the doorknob, willing it to twist, praying she would walk out to me — better yet, run into my arms and let me hold her.

Damn it. I was trapped in the living room, driving myself insane with worry. Wes, Gabe, Saylor, and Kiersten left with Alec and Nat, meaning just Demetri, Lyss, and the rest of us remained at Jay's house.

I pressed my fingers to my temples while I tried to eavesdrop on the conversation Pris was having with Dani's therapist.

It all seemed so wrong.

To be talking about her like she'd died, when she was in the other room freaking breathing! She was eighteen! And they were treating her—

Like she was broken.

It wasn't the way I would treat her.

Guilt stabbed me in the chest, even though I knew in theory it wasn't my fault. I'd started a car, and it had scared her. End of story.

But at least the secret to the tattoo on the back of her leg was solved. Apparently it was too brief for me to actually put two and two together, but the minute Demetri explained everything, I knew. It also allowed him to get at least two punches in before Alec pulled him off me.

I touched my bleeding lip and winced as the stinging continued.

"Okay, thank you." Pris tossed her cell phone onto the counter. "Her therapist says that she should be fine. We just have to be more careful with her known triggers."

"Bullshit." I jumped out of my seat. "The last thing she needs is for her entire family to treat her like she's an invalid! So she freaked out. It sucks. Believe me, I feel like shit about it, but using kid gloves with her isn't going to make everything better! It enables the issue!"

"It's a serious issue!" Jay shouted. My ears began to ring.

Zane cleared his throat. All eyes turned to him. "I'm with Linc."

"Thank God, at least one of you is thinking clearly."

"Zane has known her for exactly two weeks!" Demetri's voice was even louder than Jay's. "And Linc has known her for what? Four?"

"Let me talk to her," I pleaded.

"No!" Pris blocked my way to Dani's door. "You could make her worse. She could never speak again. I just got her back." Tears filled her eyes. "I just got my sister back."

Did they miss my role in that? Seriously?

Sighing, I looked to Jaymeson for help, but he was staring at the floor. Alyssa was the one to step forward; she'd been quiet the whole time.

"Dem…" She looked back at her husband. "… I'd like to think I know a few things about trauma, and Linc's right. She's never going to get over it until she faces it, accepts it. So we protect her now. What happens when she sees another car like Linc's? What if we make it worse by making her afraid of her triggers? We have to do our best, and our best isn't protecting her, by enabling. It's letting her go."

"No." Tears tumbled down Pris's face as she shook her head violently.

Jaymeson hung his head. We were at a standstill. Nobody made a move.

Pris was still blocking the door.

And desperation was already kicking in.

And I remembered the day on the beach when I'd chased Dani, when I told her I'd keep chasing her until I captured her, until she was mine.

So I pulled out my phone and started typing vigorously, praying her phone was with her in her room, praying my words, for once, would be enough.

Linc: *I'm sorry.*

I moved to the farthest part of the room, trying to stealthily type so that nobody saw. Jaymeson was holding Pris while she cried. Alyssa and Demetri were arguing over what to do, and Zane's eyes were trained on my hand. He nodded his head once then very carefully blocked my body with his by lazily leaning against the kitchen counter.

Dani: *Me too.*

Cursing to myself, I typed again.

Linc: *You let me in before. Let me in again. Please.*
Dani: *I'm embarrassed.*

I rolled my eyes.

Linc: *Because you freaked out? Everyone freaks out. Shit, I was afraid of the dark until I was fifteen because my mom used to tease me that some crazy man was going to steal me away. She made me afraid of Santa, Dani. What kind of monster makes you hate Christmas?*

Dani: *That's horrible!*

Linc: *We all have issues, but the really great thing about family? We stick together. And I know that because my grandparents never gave up on us, even when I was a punk teen trying to rebel and get high at the neighbors, Grandpa swatted my ass and told me to get good grades. Family sticks together. You have an incredible one.*

I waited for an answer, but my phone remained silent. After several minutes, it became clear she didn't plan to answer.

I sighed then sent another text, one that might have been harsh, but harsh seemed to be what she needed.

Linc: *Your parents are dead.*
Dani: *I know.*
Linc: *They aren't coming back.*

A few seconds went by, and then my alert went off.

Dani: *I know.*

Linc: *Life is scary as hell, but I'd rather believe you were spared for a reason, maybe so that on your eighteenth birthday you could make a stupid, spoiled, Hollywood actor give up his heart and fall in love. Selfishly, I'd like to think, that maybe, just maybe, there's a bright side, and that's us.*

She didn't text back.

Shit. I shoved my phone into my jeans and faced the wall. I banged my head slowly against it as I fought to keep my emotions in check. Ramming my body through the door wasn't going to help anyone, except, it would make me feel a hell of a lot better.

The room fell silent.

Hell, they'd found out I was texting. Slowly, I turned and nearly fell on my knees as Dani stood before me, her face red and blotchy with tears.

She opened her mouth, and I could tell she was struggling with speaking. Pris made a move toward us, but Jay held her back.

Dani closed her eyes.

"No, sweetheart," I whispered, "keep them open. Look at me. It's only us."

Tears spilled onto her cheeks. Nodding slowly, she opened her mouth. "I'd..." Her voice was hoarse, gravelly. "... I'd like to think that too."

My knees shook, but I gripped her by the shoulders and pulled her against my chest as I kissed her head. "It's a miracle you're alive, Dani. You're my miracle. Maybe it is selfish to think that after living in a loveless family, I'd finally be rewarded with a better one — with you. But I guess in my messed up mind, that's how the world works."

Her tears were hot against my shirt. "I love you."

Demetri and Jay turned away, ushering the girls out toward the balcony and shutting the door, which was exactly what needed to happen. It was too raw, and I didn't want them witnessing any more.

Zane stared us down then silently walked over to his room and shut the door behind him.

"Dani," I whispered into her hair, "look at me."

She lifted her head, her blue eyes swollen, cheeks puffy.

"I love you too."

"Are you s-sure?"

I burst out laughing. "Pretty. Damn. Sure." My mouth met hers in a whisper of a kiss before I pulled her against me again; hugging her so tight it was hard to breathe, hard to speak.

"I'm sorry." Her voice was muffled against my chest. "I'm sorry I freaked out. I had no idea, it was you, and I was so angry at first, and I blamed you, and I'm sorry." She hiccupped. "But it wasn't your fault. It wasn't even mine or my parents'." Her eyes cleared. "It's life."

I nodded. "It's life, Dani."

"Life… means I leave what's behind me behind me."

"Can't drive a car in reverse," I agreed.

"Can't drive a car period. It's why Jay got me an SUV," she joked.

Laughing, I kissed her nose. "I'll keep that in mind."

CHAPTER THIRTY-NINE

Dani

Three months later

IT WAS HARD. I ALWAYS HATED movies that ended with *"And they lived happily ever after,"* because that was never how the real world worked. Going through hell didn't automatically give you a free pass to happyland. But having Linc by my side? It made it better, easier, because I finally had someone who understood and accepted me.

"No way!" a girl shrieked next to me. "I think that's Lincoln Greene!"

The friend started fanning herself. "Seriously, tell me he isn't the hottest thing you've ever seen?"

"I heard he's basically engaged to some local girl back in Oregon. Damn, there must be something in the water over there. Did you know AD2 both got married to local girls too?"

"Well." The girl with dark hair rubbed her hands together. "That's settled. I'm moving to Oregon!"

They busted up with laughter until Linc grabbed our coffees and made his way in our direction. Then, absolute silence.

He handed me my coffee, brushed a soft kiss across my forehead, and whispered, "You ready?"

"Sure." A satisfied smile crossed my face as the three girls dropped their jaws in unison and watched me walk out the door with his hand on my hip, shoved into the back pocket of my jeans.

Eat your heart out, ladies. He's all mine.

"So..." Lincoln threw on his aviators and gave me that perfect movie-star grin that had my heart thumping loudly against my chest. "... where to?"

"Well..." I tapped my chin. "... we have to meet Zane for dinner, so we only have a few hours. I say Disneyland."

Linc gave me a thumbs down.

"Put on a hat!" I laughed. "Please?"

"Oh, what? What was that?" He handed me his coffee then dug two tickets out of his pocket. To Disneyland.

"LINC!" I shouted.

"Pris said your parents always promised to take you and never could, so I'm yours and Mickey's for the day. Demetri, Lyss, Alec, and Nat are meeting us along with baby Ella. It's her first trip, too."

"Aw, we can get matching ears."

"Great." Lincoln chuckled, but his excitement matched mine, I could tell.

"Thanks..." I swallowed the lump in my throat. "... for doing this on the anniversary of their death."

"Baby..." Linc took his coffee from my hand and kissed me on the cheek. "... I will always be here for you. Always."

I stared hard into his grey eyes. "I know."

"Good." He brought my hand to his lips. "Now let's go get this over with so I can take you back to my house. We only have three weeks before we need to go back to Seaside to re-shoot the last two scenes that your drama king of a brother-in-law is convinced will look better if we just used a different camera angle."

"Genius, you mean?" I arched my eyebrows.

Linc refused to admit it, but this movie had so much buzz that people were even saying it might gain a few Academy Award nominations for the soundtrack alone, not to mention Best Director for Jaymeson, which was pretty amazing for someone so young.

We walked hand in hand back to his car.

And it felt better, not easier. I still struggled in crowds and with strangers. The last interview Linc had done had me looking like a lunatic because I couldn't even answer yes or no questions, but he hadn't cared and, oddly enough, neither had the reporter.

Life, I was starting to figure out, was never going to be easy. There would be hard days, and there would be great days, but the most important thing to remember was that I was given those days.

And my parents weren't.

So my new goal was to live them to the fullest, and thank God, I'd had them in the first place.

EPILOGUE

Zane

"Hey, you're famous, right?"

"Nope," I lied then steered my way out of the grocery store line, brown paper bag in hand, my vision blurring already from the extreme concentration it took to walk into a stupid public place by myself.

By the time I reached my Range Rover, I was already sweating.

My hands shook as I tried to hit unlock on the key fob. I struggled, missing it with my thumb at least three times before my lights blinked and the car opened.

I secured the package in the passenger's seat and put on my seatbelt, then drove across town to the beach house.

Everyone was asleep, or I would have begged, maybe even bribed someone to come to the store with me. I always made a joke out of it. *"Come with me so I don't get sexually harassed."*

When really.

It was fear.

It was always fear.

277

The door to the house was unlocked. I turned the knob and walked inside, then softly closed the door behind me, making my way into the large gourmet kitchen so I could put my stash in the pantry.

I was almost home free when the kitchen light flickered on.

Linc was sitting at the table, a glass of scotch in front of him, a bottle next to the glass, and an empty glass in front of that.

"So..." He scooted the full glass toward me. "... I think we need to talk."

I rolled my eyes, shaking off the fear from being in public and presenting myself with my usual armor. "One kiss, Linc. To prove a point. Get over it, better yet, get over her, and when I say over I mean in bed, then call me later and say thank you."

"Thank you," Linc said quickly. "But not what I'm talking about."

I frowned. "Then, I have no idea what we need to discuss."

"You're one of her best friends. She worries about you. Therefore, I worry about you. She doesn't sleep... I don't sleep, so sit your ass down and tell me why you're really here."

"Because God hasn't taken me home yet?" I offered sarcastically. "How much of that scotch have you drunk? Be honest."

"Zane."

"Get laid, call me in the morning, things will look... up."

"Zane."

I nearly growled as I turned and gripped the counter hard with my fingertips. "What?"

"Why are you here?"

Loaded question. And I would lie. I would continue to lie as long as Jaymeson allowed it. "Because. I find the sea breeze positively... exhilarating."

"Truth?"

"Yup." I choked on the lie more because I actually liked him.

"I'll believe it when I see you actually visit the ocean."

Caught. I stared at him dumbly. "I visit."

"By yourself?"

My entire body seized.

"That's what I thought." He knocked on the counter. "Night, Zane. You know where to find me if you need me."

"My best friend's bedroom?"

Linc's body tensed. "Don't make me punch you. Again."

He walked away.

Which was good, because had he stayed any longer, he'd have seen the sweat pooling around my temples, the tremors that wracked my body, and the twitching hand. With a curse, I stomped back into the pantry, grabbed an entire bag of marshmallows, and dug in.

ABOUT THE AUTHOR

RACHEL VAN DYKEN is the *New York Times, Wall Street Journal,* and *USA Today* bestselling author of regency and contemporary romances. When she's not writing you can find her drinking coffee at Starbucks and plotting her next book while watching "The Bachelor".

She keeps her home in Idaho with her husband, adorable son, and two snoring boxers. She loves to hear from readers.

You can connect with her on Facebook at facebook.com/rachelvandyken or join her fan group *Rachel's New Rockin Readers*. Her website is www.rachelvandykenauthor.com.

ALSO BY RACHEL VAN DYKEN

The Bet Series
The Bet (Forever Romance)
The Wager (Forever Romance)
The Dare

Eagle Elite
Elite (Forever Romance)
Elect (Forever Romance)
Entice
Elicit
Enforce
Ember
Elude

Seaside Series
Tear
Pull
Shatter
Forever
Fall
Strung
Eternal

Wallflower Trilogy
Waltzing with the Wallflower
Beguiling Bridget
Taming Wilde

London Fairy Tales
Upon a Midnight Dream
Whispered Music
The Wolf's Pursuit
When Ash Falls

www.rachelvandykenauthor.com

Made in the USA
Charleston, SC
18 December 2015